Institutionalized

Published by Bad Dog Press
302 Northgate Mall Dr, Suite 1413
Hixson, TN 37343-9998

Cover art by Tim Warner
Book design by J.T. Langhorne
Edited by C. Rose

ISBN: 978-0-998062433

To victims of abuse at the hands of the church, may you know that you aren't alone, may God grant you strength and peace, and may you never lose faith in humanity. This book is for you.

"The great religions are the ships,
Poets the life boats.
Every sane person I know
Has jumped overboard."
— Hafiz

Institutionalized

By J.T. Langhorne

omega

I F YOU DOUSE THE PEWS with gasoline and flick a Marlboro Red into the puddle in front of the pulpit, a church will light up like a bright, flaming Nile Delta. Jesse Baker did exactly that after his mind went Judas Iscariot on his ass.

He stood in the center aisle, arms outstretched, looking at the ceiling like a cult leader basking in the power he's claimed. Calmness rained on him instead of the water that should have been pouring from the disabled sprinkler system.

Flames danced with smoke that rose to the rafters and gathered like a storm cloud about to strike lightning on the head of a scorner. Some might say the Almighty cusses after He fires off a bolt of electricity. The rumbling boom can shake the doors of a church or scare children out of their beds, inspiring them to climb in the sack between Mommy and Daddy, ruining any chance at marital intimacy.

When people get angry, they usually cuss before they swing. God doesn't. He throws a heavyweight haymaker, and something somewhere takes the full force of His wrath.

In one of the first stories of men, God got so pissed at humans that He brought thunder and shocked the earth and rained down more water from the sky than people had ever considered possible. The deluge continued until every mountain was underwater. Every person and animal, save a few of each species, drowned. The unluckiest, unicorns and dinosaurs and saber-toothed tigers and wooly mammoths,$^{\Omega}$ didn't make the cut. The few people who survived wrote a book that claimed God felt bad about drowning His creation and gave a colorful peace offering that looked like the happiest frown you've ever seen—His promise to never do it again. We still get that frown after it rains.

Many years later, people wrote in the same book that God will get pissed enough to break His promise. And when He does, it won't be lightning and water. It will be pestilence and fire and war.

It's an interesting idea that an all-powerful, all-knowing, creative keeper of the universe felt guilt. How did the survivors know that? Did God tell them? Or did they make it all up?

After the apocalyptic flood, it was also written that the survivors got hammered and had incestuous sex with each other. Maybe that had to happen for humanity to continue. It wouldn't have been the first time brothers and sisters made babies to keep it all going.

Maybe they felt guilty about that and wanted God to feel bad too.

$^{\Omega}$ Scientists claim these animals went extinct millions of years ago because a meteor hit the earth. Most Evangelical pastors claim it was because of the great flood from the book of Genesis.

Maybe they wanted to believe their creator was just like them.

Maybe they *knew* nothing. But that didn't stop them from telling a story. People need to know things, or at least pretend, so we tell stories.

But maybe they *did* know things, and God actually talked to folks back in the day. Either way, people formed a narrative. And maybe we need our narratives. And by giving our Gods human qualities, we can cope with our miniscule place in this world.

Our story says we were made in His image. But, hypothetically, if that's not the case, and the story is backward as our reflection in a funhouse mirror, we lose nothing. We're insignificant. God's indifferent. We live. We die. And the world spins. Even if this were the truth, we might keep our stories because they would strengthen us, assuring that we're loved by the One powerful enough to worship. We'd tell others. Because, after all, who wouldn't want to believe that?

We'd become powerful because we own the rights to the story. We might even force it on everyone because we *know* God's perfect will for their lives. It might bless our soul to showcase our enlightenment. Our natural urges might grab for power. We could become gods ourselves, realizing our authority to tweak the story and claim superiority over people, races, and even nations. The masses would rejoice in the beauty of our words. And we would relish our image. The ruler of Tyre.[Ω] We would transcribe it in every language, creating thousands of translations until we've perfected it. Then we could give it to our kids, and

---

[Ω] Ezekiel 28

they'd give it to their kids, who'd give to their kids, who might tweak it for the changing times before they give it to their kids, and on and on and on... Hypothetically, of course.

It's hard to admit that it's easy to believe but impossible to *know*.

Jesse surveyed the burning landscape of his old church, like a modern-day Abednego who stood unburned inside the fiery furnace. Here, a man could become a god and preach his understanding to thousands, convincing his flock that he *knows* the ways of the invisible, holy, sovereign God.

Religion can be fascinating in the same way insanity is fascinating. The logical mind struggles make sense of the odd or supernatural. And in most cases, the insane do not realize they're insane.

The duality of religious hope is fascinating too. To thinkers, hope can be like Heller's *Catch-22*, and what some women say about men, and some men say about women. Can't live with. Can't live without. Fucked if you have it. Fucked if you don't.

Modern intellectuals might get sad or bored because stats and facts curb creativity. Storytellers might be blindly happy because they aren't bound by facts to tell their tales. Hope artists can be good listeners who are often relieved when someone tells them where to find a thing that could not be. Some poor souls who punt hope go mad. Others are put through so much fire and pain, they *grow* mad. And the poorest of souls are hard-wired for madness. But despite our differences, we come into the world doing the best we can with the personality we're born with. Then somewhere along the way, we learn how to fuck it up.

Short-circuit brain is served cold with deep-fried heart—not the blood-pumping muscle, the proverbial heart, the one where a person can sense God. People have always desired to establish and maintain this connection. When it is severed in this life, it can be too much for some to handle. It's possible that if the connection is severed in the afterlife, one could stay mad forever. There may be nothing worse than losing your mind, and separation from God may just be the most barbaric form of madness—that eternal fire the storytellers spoke of, hell. Insanity.

And that is where we find Jesse, the mad usher of a congregation of flames. He heard the music playing in his head. Jeff Buckley wailed. He smiled and hummed along. Blood dripped off his beard. It wasn't his.

chapter: 1

The Life and Times of Jesse "Take-All-Comers" Baker
By Jesse Baker
December 7, 1996

MAYBE I SHOULD BE A PAINTER and capture our sophomore essence like a grunge Norman Rockwell. LL Bean on our backs and Doc Martens stomping on the rough carpet in the halls. Inconsequential chatter bounces off our lockers as we slam them shut, one after the other. My regular crew is Deric Harris and Joe Dixon from my class, and Jamal Charles, who's a senior. We call ourselves—*The 4-Pack*.

"Are we kickin' it after the game tonight or what?" Deric said, tossing books into his locker.

Time froze as I had a fleshed-out thought. That's how my brain works. Time in my head doesn't flow like time in the real world. When I go inside, everything stops, and I can talk to myself for hours up there. Is that normal?

Doesn't matter. But I'll tell you this, if we lose tonight, I sure as shit won't be hanging out. Fuck that.

We ain't losing. I haven't sinned much this week, didn't even beat my meat.

I have an emotionally polarized relationship with my meat.

Then I thought God might make us lose because I thought the word *fuck*. Is that dumb? Surely, God don't care about our basketball game. He's gotta have bigger fish to fry. But just in case, I asked Him to forgive me for thinking the f-word.

Then Jennie turned the corner. She half-smiled when our eyes met. Her friends talked dramatically around her, and she pretended to listen but kept looking at me. I scanned her body. She wore a flannel shirt and a long denim skirt. There wasn't much to see, but I know it's glorious beneath her modest school attire. So my imagination filled in the blanks, and I have a vivid imagination and a photographic memory. As she walked by, she broke from her clique and whispered in my ear,

"Under the stairwell after next period."

I smiled. She cliqued back up without missing a step. I looked at Deric. He was staring at her ass. I punched him in the arm.

"Dayum. It's a compliment, bitch." He rubbed his right shoulder. Then whispered, "I wanna fuck some shit up tonight after sitting through this Fat Bastard parade."

The IFB conference. The acronym IFB stands for *Independent Fundamental baptist*, but Deric dubbed it—the *International Fat Bastard* conference. And the name stuck.

Independent Fundamental baptist preachers roll deep into our home church every December. They break out their best double-breasted suits, and many travel hundreds of miles to agree with each other on everything from the inspired, infallible Word of God to the ungodliness of women wearing pants. I find it odd that most of them are fat bastards.

Most days I wish I was a bastard.[Ω]

These pastors hoot and holler and amen like they're at a Garth Brooks concert. Maybe it's a southern thing. The more animated a preacher gets on stage, the more they all go ape shit. What's weird is they beat on their Bibles the same way apes beat on their chests while they shout their *amens*. Like they're trying to display their dominance. Or like the Bible did something to piss them off, but they sure seem to love those Bibles. It's confusing. Or maybe it's natural that people beat on things they love sometimes.

Oh, that takes me back...

[Ω] A bastard is a child that is born without a dad, wait that's wrong. That's a messiah. A bastard is a child born to a woman that a daddy rents and rolls out on.

chapter: 2

The Life and Times of Jesse "Take-All-Comers" Baker
By Jesse Baker
December 8, 1996

MY DAD'S NAME IS CHARLES. Everyone calls him Chuck. I think I'm gonna call him Chuck from now on too. I'll still call him Dad to his face, because if I don't, he'll probably kick my ass. But in this story, he's just Chuck.

Lemme tell you a little something about Chuck. He's a mean motherfucker. When it comes to parenting, he's the *my way or the highway* type. Scratch that, he's the *my way or my belt* type. I'm sure I'll cross a few people in my life, but I still do everything in my power to not cross Chuck. These days, he doesn't seem to care about anything. He's tired all the time, but that's not how it used to be.

When I was a young kid, it seemed as if his goal in life was to make me tough. Until I was 11-years-old, I got the belt when I crossed him. I like to remember I took it like a champ, but maybe I took it like a punk ass bitch. Jury's still out on that one.

I bet his dad used to beat the shit outta him, and he probably hated him for it, but he got hard. He told me that his dad was a mean drunk. Maybe that's why Chuck never touched the sauce. He's never needed any help to be mean.

He didn't wanna be like his dad, so he found Jesus, as if Jesus was lost or something. Or got kidnapped, and they put out an Amber Alert. Or like Jesus was some magical Easter egg. I bet, in his mind, Jesus keeps him from being a degenerate.

A degenerate can't trust himself. He needs someone to tell him how to act. He needs an articulated life plan, true north on paper, a life coach, a God to obey.

Maybe we're all degenerates to some extent. The Bible says so.[Ω]

It's obvious Chuck thinks his hardness is his biggest strength and the best quality he could pass on to me. Maybe his hardness saved his life in Korea or something.

After Chuck "found" Jesus, he heard in church that he shouldn't spare the rod or he'd spoil the child. So he made damn sure it wasn't spared, but his actions were always justified by God. It's right there in the Good Book, for the good of the child.[Ω]

But I wasn't as familiar with justifications back then as I am now. I just thought the rod was part of every kid's life. I looked up to Chuck. Pleasing him was my mission. But Chuck rarely let me know if he was pleased, so I always wanted more.

Chuck never explicitly told me about the importance of being hard. He just had his ways of

---

[Ω] Romans 3:23
[Ω] Proverbs 13:24

molding me. We lived in a little house in Upton Park. Still do. It's the section of town that most people consider the hood. The section where most suburban folks in cars look straight ahead and avoid eye contact with anyone walking by. Our house is two blocks north of the housing projects and sits on a corner across the street from the Upton Park Rec Center.

It happened six years ago. I was ten, but I remember it like it was last week. It was the last time I've gotten my ass kicked, but Chuck probably thinks it's the day I got soft because he's an asshole.

One way he thought up to mold my toughness was a makeshift boxing ring in the backyard. Chuck was an avid boxing fan. He learned how to fight in the army and wanted me to take up the sport. But there were no boxing gyms in our mid-sized Southern city, so he took matters into his own hands.

The ring was three ropes wrapped around three posts and a tree. Every Saturday was fight day. Chuck had two pairs of boxing gloves, a pair for me and a pair for any kid who walked by and accepted the challenge. I'd shadow box in the middle of the ring. When boys walked by, he'd talk shit to them until one got pissed enough to put on the gloves and fight. At first, it was boys I played ball with at the Upton Park Rec Center who'd jump in the ring.

I was small, so I got my ass kicked a lot on those first Saturdays, but Chuck would always be there to give me some pointers after each fight.

After telling my opponent to go home, he'd climb in the ring and pick me up off the dusty grass. I'd stumble to my feet, and he'd teach me how to stick and move, bob and weave, and tell me all sorts of shit that sounded like those adult voices on Charlie Brown's Thanksgiving Special in my ringing ears. Chuck wouldn't pull any punches either, knocking my head back with jabs and straight shots, and occasionally putting me right back down in the grass. He always seemed a little angry when I lost a backyard brawl, so he peppered his training with vicarious rage. I learned fairly quickly that if I lost a fight, my ass would be kicked twice. Fear drove me. I had a choice—kill or be killed.

I think Chuck's technical advice was weak, but he sure didn't think so. He thought he was the obscure Lou Duva—the best boxing mind the world had never heard of.

I feel like I learned from getting knocked around. How to take a punch. How to dodge a punch. How to dodge a flurry. How to counter. I didn't learn these techniques from Chuck. I learned from getting my ass beat over and over. The pain that lingered in my skull and my survival instinct taught me how to fight.

It's simple really—just don't get hit. If you get hit, don't go down. If you go down, don't stay down. And always come up swinging.

I bet Chuck fantasized about telling our story to people when I made it to the top, the story of how he made me into a world champ. He'd tell about our inner-city backyard boxing ring. Maybe ESPN would do a documentary on me, and they'd call me Jesse "Take-All-Comers" Baker.

The kids I had to fight kept getting bigger and bigger because the kids my size wouldn't fight anymore. They'd gotten savvy to Chuck's game, and I was getting better and kicking their asses. Nobody likes to get their ass kicked, and rarely will someone voluntarily get it kicked twice by the same person in the same situation.

I never talked to my boys about it when we hung out at the Rec Center, but they knew if I lost, Chuck would kick my ass again. They used to look back at me as they walked away. And sometimes, I'd see their blurry figures lingering behind the huge oak tree on the corner. I'm not saying they enjoyed watching me take more punishment. They just couldn't look away.

But soon enough, it got to the point where I never lost. I never stayed down. People learn pretty quickly that you don't want to fight a desperate sumbitch.

If we were out there for an hour without a challenger, Chuck would get bored and make me fight him. Of course, he always won. He was a grown-ass man. Mom would have lemonade and a bag of frozen peas for my swollen face when I came in from the Saturday fights. She also had butterfly bandages for the occasional cut over the eye.

I don't think she liked it. She always looked like she was on the verge of crying when I came inside, but I don't remember her saying anything about it to Chuck. From what I've seen, good Christian wives keep their mouths fucking shut. At least that's how it goes down in my house. She don't question her man. Submission, of course, is a prerequisite for being a godly woman. I learned that in Bible class.[Ω]

As I got better, Saturday fight day started to lose its luster. By the end of the summer, I just trained and sparred with Chuck every Saturday. There weren't any more comers. Until Jamal.

[Ω] Ephesians 5:22, 23

Jamal Charles was 12-years-old and new to the neighborhood. He was tall for his age and built like Riddick "Big Daddy" Bowe. He had a long reach, thick legs, a big butt, undefined fat looking arms, and a belly that didn't quite hang out over his waistline but was the same width as his shoulders. It's safe to say he never missed a meal. He didn't know me, and he didn't know about the Saturday Fights at the Baker house when he walked by that day. His new friends, who also happened to be my buddies, forgot to tell him not to pay any mind to the crazy, shit-talking old man on the back porch.

"Look, Jesse. A new challenger. He looks soft. Whaddaya think?"

I kept my head down and shadow boxed.

"Who's soft?" Jamal shot back.

"Who you think?"

Jamal laughed, thinking he was joking. My other buddies picked up the pace, looking at each step they took down the sidewalk and failing miserably to get Jamal to move along.

"You look like the teddy bear I won at Six Flags on them dollar-a-toss games. I bet Jesse here can take ya. You big kids are always soft."

"That white boy?"

"Yeah that white boy, what are you stupid too?"

I didn't even weigh a hundred pounds, and Jamal had at least sixty on me. Disregarding the obvious body language of his friends, Jamal didn't hesitate and climbed through the ropes and put on the gloves. The new kid had something to prove.

"We'll see bout that old man."

I danced around the ring, pissing my trunks but projecting irrational confidence. I couldn't let Chuck see my fear. Even more, I couldn't let Jamal see it.

We danced around each other for a minute. I stuck and moved, but never moved Jamal. When my glove slapped his face, he smiled like he wanted me to know he didn't feel it. He toyed with me like he didn't want to hurt me, but I knew what he didn't—this could never end without pain.

I got desperate and hit him square in the forbidden speed bag. He doubled over, and I threw all of my sub-hundred-pound weight into a vicious overhand right across his head, sending him to one knee. I stepped back.

Chuck let out a loud "Yeah, boy! Finish him!" from his box seat on the back porch.

I came back with a left hook. Jamal put up his strong right arm and blocked my punch. His arm didn't budge. It felt like punching a tetherball pole. His eyes met mine, and the rage in his glare gives me pause to this day. Then he threw a Mortal Kombat-style uppercut that lifted my feet off the ground and sent me flying back first into the matted short grass.

I popped up of course, but everything was out of focus. That didn't stop me from swinging. I thought of what Mick said to *Rocky* and tried to hit the one in the middle, blindly firing big shots that whiffed or barely grazed his shoulders.

Then Jamal threw one hard, straight shot that sent me to my back again.

I got up slower this time, crawling to the ropes. From one knee, I grabbed the flimsy middle rope by the tree to pull myself up. The knot slid down, and I fell again, scratching my face on the bark. I finally got on my feet and ran right back into him, throwing all my learned technique out the window, hoping against all odds I could land one Hail Mary shot. Jamal pushed me, and I stumbled backward. It was a long awkward stumble because my legs felt like jelly. It felt like a trip to *The Twilight Zone*, like the one Trevor Berbick took when he fought Mike Tyson.

When I gathered my bearings, I wiped a mixture of dirt, sweat, and tears from my eyes. When my glove touched my nose, it hurt like hell. I was sure it was broken, but I danced again. I guess Jamal felt bad for me and figured I wasn't stopping until he put me out cold. He'd proven what he set out to prove and took off the gloves as my ring dance slowed to a stop. I was relieved.

He dropped his gloves and turned to exit the ring. Right after he climbed through the ropes, my old man came flying across the ring like a 250-pound gorilla, going through the ropes like they weren't even there, and hit Jamal with a cross-body block that sent him flying 8 feet across the yard.

"The fight ain't over!" Chuck shouted.

The other kids, who'd stopped to watch when the fight began, stood stunned on the sidewalk as Chuck stood over Jamal, who was on one knee. Then he threw a downward punch that left Jamal on his belly, face down in the grass.

Chuck mumbled under his breath, "Never walk away from a fight."

I stood ready in the center of the ring as my father climbed through the ropes and strutted toward me. Those were the longest five seconds of my life to that point. Scary slow-mo like the guys in the movies who leave disaster in their wake and never look back at explosions. Those guys seem cool on the big screen, but a guy like that walking toward you in real life... Shit.

I knew what was coming and put my gloves up. Chuck threw a right hook around my gloves. His fist was heavy, like he was squeezing a roll of nickels. It connected clean on my left temple and knocked me the fuck out.

That was the last Saturday Fight Day, and Chuck went away for a couple months.

chapter: 3

The Life and Times of Jesse "Take-All-Comers" Baker
By Jesse Baker
December 9, 1996

B ACK AT THE *INTERNATIONAL Fat Bastard* conference again today, the pastors in the audience are still shouting positive words that don't match their tone of voice. It's hilarious. They always try to one-up each other like the more elaborate the *amen* gesture, the more spiritual they are. It seems people who are used to being the center of attention make really shitty, distracting audience members. I'm the casual observer today, the people watcher. I brought my journal. This should be a great way to kill time.

A pastor in the congregation just made sure all eyes were on him. He just randomly stood up during the preaching and yelled so loud his face turned red and veins popped out of his neck and temples. His words didn't match his angry tone either. "Praise you Lord, Praise you Lord. Praise... you!"

The inflection in his voice sounded like what you might hear right before a brouhaha between two rowdy and riled up dudes ensues. Just replace the word *Praise* with *Fuck*, and *Lord* with a man's name.

And you wouldn't believe the shit that has been spewing out of these pastor's mouths from the pulpit today...

Ω

The angry shouts quieted, and Pastor Luke Scott brought his voice down to a whisper. "We are dirty, dull pieces of metal, but God will mold us into a polished sword if we let Him."

Most of the preachers here are masters of effective tone changes while they bring the Word.

He pulled a fencing sword from the pulpit and presented it to the crowd. Then he turned sideways, showing his profile. His right hand held the sword under the hilt right in front of his belt buckle as he pointed the blade upward in front of his face. Dr. Scott slowly put his head back as he closed his eyes. Then he opened his mouth wide and let his voice flow in orgasmic tones while his left hand beat off the blade with a handkerchief. The motion seemed so familiar to him.

"Ah, Ah, Ah, Ah," he moaned, sporting his best cumface while he jacked the weapon.

Then, in an instant, he switched voices. It's a ploy pastors use to create a dialogue between them and someone else, or even God himself. This time, Scott conversed with the Almighty to make his point.

"Shut up, son, I can handle it. I know what I'm doing," Scott replied in a calm, dietic voice while still whacking away with his left hand.

His voice turned nut-busting as the jacking motion sped up.

"Oh, it hurts, I'm so tired. Oh God, please don't make me do it. I can't. I can't. Oh!! Oh!!! Oh!!!! Oh!!! Oh!! Oh! Oh." His voice descended from climax.

He slowed the jacking to easy, smooth strokes and continued his schizophrenic conversation.

"Ah. You love me so much, don't you?"

"Yes," a calm god-Scott responded.

"Oh God, thank you for what you're making me."

"You're welcome." He continued to polish the shaft.[Ω] This guy can't be serious. I don't trust a preacher with two first names.

What sucks about going to a school run by an Independent Fundamental baptist church is we have to sit through conferences like this three times per school year. We also have school chapel every other day, Sunday school, Sunday morning service, Sunday night service, Wednesday night prayer meeting, and Monday night soul-winning. Every... Fucking... Week.

And there's the death rate calculator. Oh yeah, I love the death rate calculator. It's a giant digital clock on the wall of the auditorium that just counts away. They hang it up there for the conferences. Each number represents a person who has died. The point is for the congregation to get convicted by how many people die and go to hell every minute. In theory, you're supposed to respond to that conviction by going out to win souls, but I think it's become a novelty, and an entertaining novelty at that.

[Ω] I polish my shaft three times a week and feel like a sinner every time.

The calculator ticks on as we watch preachers yell at each other for three hours before noon and then two hours at night. Every student at the Upton Park Christian School is forced to sit through the entire clown show.

I guess the death rate calculator has lost its convicting power somewhere along the line.

So did the tracts. Stacks on stacks of Gospel tracts sit in a clear display case in the lobby, waiting for a hungry soul-winner to pick up. They are about fifteen pages long and rectangle-shaped like the coupon books we sold in kindergarten for a fundraiser. Each tract has a unique story and reads like a mini graphic novel. Most of them are scary as hell, literally, because they end with some poor guy getting thrown into the lake of fire for all eternity. It's usually the protagonist in the comic. It's the oldest trick in the institutional religion handbook. Scare the hell out of 'em. If the tract is scary enough, we can just pray another silent insurance policy prayer, and we'll feel safe again from the wrath of God... for the moment.

We don't take the tracts out to win souls. We read them for their entertainment value. It helps combat the insufferable boredom that ticks on with the calculator for what seems like an eternity. We hit the tract dispenser and grab one of each to pass around with our classmates. We're like junkies passing joints in a crack house.

Even though we didn't think it was possible, the boredom is becoming more palpable. We've read all the comics and need a fresh form of entertainment, so the calculator has become a game to us this year. When it's 100 or so deaths away from reaching a milestone number like 777777 or 500000, there will be students across our whole row quietly hitting their fists on their knees, drumming to the beat of souls passing to the afterlife. As I write about what we do, I realize we might be morbidly apathetic. I mean, an entire row of kids just pounding away, anticipating a death significant enough for a response. Not of sadness. But of elation. Damn.

When the milestone hits, we have a silent celebration with big smiles connecting one side of the pew to the other. A sinister twenty-five-foot grin. I guess this could be considered by some as sociopathic, or at the least, degenerate behavior, but we're numb and don't think of what we are actually celebrating. We're just bored.

A new Fat Ass just got a turn on stage.

"Some may ask, Can God make a rock that is so big that He cannot move it?"

My head fucking hurts.

"Well folks the answer is yes, and when he creates it, He'll move it."

The fact that they answer the questions for you is a microcosm of their methods.

Next man up... "Way-ell... doctors are prescribin' the red pills and the green pills and the blue pills... but what we need today my brothers is the gos-pill... can I get an amen?"

Amen!

I'm a big fan of rhetorical affirmatives. Always have been.

I can't talk to anyone about this stuff. I don't know who's safe to talk to. So I'm writing my confusion. Since I've been defining things in the most literal senses, I've been dissecting the words I hear. I've realized that taking every word of the Bible literally might be a dangerous game to play. If you really did, you might find yourself in jail within a week. But the preachers say we should obey the Word because it's literal, inspired by God,Ω and infallible.

Since I've gotten into writing, I've also become a big fan of irony, symbolism, and metaphor. And the Bible is covered in it. Even Jesus spoke in parables. Can we really have it both ways? It's a paradox.Ω

Here's my attempt at metaphor. Food comes from the preacher's spoon. You eat up and don't ask questions.

Ω

The fucking session tonight was a damn chore. For more reasons than boredom. It went like this...

Amens carried across the auditorium and bounced off the walls. They landed in my numb ears while I stared a hole through the stage. Someone in the choir behind the preacher just picked his nose and rubbed it between his fingers for two minutes. Then he looked left, then right, and brought his fingers to his lips and started chewing.

The lady with the huge hair two seats to the booger eater's right looked straight ahead. Someone

---

Ω The phrase they use is God-breathed. Like... God literally told the writers the exact words to write.
Ω A paradox is something that seems like a contradiction, but may prove to be true all the same. It's also those expensive grunge boots half our school wears.

shoulda told her this ain't 1986. Her glossy eyes slowly closed. Her head bobbed forward, then jerked back slightly. She repeated the process over and over until she looked wide awake because her last head bob was so violent, she'll probably have to go to the chiropractor to treat mild whiplash.

When I'm not indulging in the church entertainment, my people-watching is showing me maybe it's not just me who's bored. When I'm not people-watching, my mind wanders. This is a dangerous game for a sixteen-year-old sitting in church.

I'd been roaming around the daydream world since the choir lady's last head bang. Then I noticed I had a serious problem growing in my pleated khakis.

No, not now. We'll have to stand soon. Why? Channel your inner Frank Drebin and think about baseball. Double plays, liners down the line, chin music and angry glares, Nolan Ryan headlocks, sunflower seeds... Fuck. Why is it getting bigger? I hate fucking baseball.

For reasons unknown to me, I get a lot of boners in church. It's frustrating.

There's an Independent Fundamental baptist College under the umbrella of my church, too. And my biggest fear is that a college chick in a pew around me will catch a glimpse of one of these poorly timed, unexpected tents I pitch in my pants.

The preacher asked the congregation to stand so he could "lead us to the throne of grace." What the fuck is that?

"Jesus, we come before you today asking for..."
Dammit.

I started sweating. I stood a full second after everyone else did, keeping my head down. I did a quick survey of the chicks in the surrounding pews to make sure their eyes were closed and wouldn't see the last-minute adjustments I made to my crotch. I tucked it in my waistband and pulled out my tucked-in shirt a little more, so it would hang over my belt.

Please God. Don't let it be a mass invitation.$^{\Omega}$

Stuff like:

"If you love God and are committed to serving him, come forward."

Or...

"If you want to be the best you can for God, come forward and pray with us."

Or...

"If you believe in Jesus and are not ashamed. Come to the front with us so we can pray for our nation."

Implied–If you're lost, carnal, completely apathetic, or an Atheist, by all means, stay in your seat so everyone can look at you.

You can't win against a mass invitation, like when Deric, my dick of a friend once asked me, "Jesse, did you enjoy having anal sex with your Uncle Sal? It's a yes or no question."

So if you stay in your seat you're pretty much flipping God a bony bird. I don't always see the glares of my fellow congregationalists when I don't go forward at altar calls, but I can feel the heat of righteous judgement every time. These days, I just go. It's less work.

$^{\Omega}$ Mass Invitations were calls to action where a preacher could put on an unbreakable full-court press. The jist—walk to the front as a statement of faith, or you hate God.

In church nobody wants to feel like a scorner. So most everyone goes forward during the mass invitations, even if they didn't hear a word the preacher said because their thoughts ran crazy throughout the service. Bored thoughts run at random like that. The end of a thought connects to another thought that connects to another thought, that connects to another thought that isn't even in the same topical hemisphere as thought number one.

I had only one thought during this prayer. And the topic of said thought was precisely 5.75 inches long and tucked under my belt. I know this because I've measured it with a ruler.

"In Jesus' precious name, Amen."

I figured the preacher must have forgotten he was talking to Jesus at the beginning of the prayer. I hate when they do that.

"Keep your heads bowed and eyes closed. Today you will get the opportunity to demonstrate your commitment to Christ."

I'm fucked.

"You get to give yourself to his will. It's not my will, Lord, but thy will. We've brought out offering plates at the front of each aisle."

I peeked. The deacons rolled out offering plates designed not to swallow 10% of a man's income, but an entire man. They were each four feet in diameter. Nearly thirty in all, placed side by side in front of the platform. The production value was impressive. Someone had put significant money and time into this stunt that would let the preacher tell all his friends that his last message had a 90% response rate.

"If you're ready to surrender your will to the Lord, come kneel in one of these offering plates. If you have surrendered and you're committed to staying the course, come kneel before God and pray a short prayer for his guidance. If you've lost your way, and want to renew your commitment to Christ, come. If you aren't saved and don't wanna go to hell for all eternity, come give your life to Christ. He's the only way."

Yep, that had just about everyone covered.

"Offer yourself, your will. Commit to God's will for your life. Place your entire being in the offering plate. Please come now."

The choir sang, *"Just as I am without one plea, but that thy blood was shed for me..."*

Everyone, and I mean *everyone,* filed out of the pews and made long lines in the aisles. Dread blanketed me like a white sheet on a corpse. You know how hard it is to walk normal with a hard gongus tucked in your waistband, and you gotta keep it there?

But it was the walk back that worried me. When I kneeled in the plate, that thing was sure to pop out of place. 5.75 inches wasn't near long enough to keep it from giving me the slip. Then what? Was I gonna stand like a batter in the on-deck circle adjusting my cup, unaware that fans are getting uncomfortable with how long my hand's been on my unit? Or would I just walk back? The tent pitcher, hoping no one looked down.

I know good Christians hate immodesty. Cleavage peeking through a low neckline. Tight pants that place a healthy cock bulge, camel toe, or bulbous ass on display. Short shorts or skirts that barely cover ass cheek smiles. A sexy outward appearance brings hyper-fundy[Ω] judgement faster than you can say *hot damn*. So how would the fundies feel about my bowsprit? And what if the line stopped when I wasn't paying attention, and I accidentally stabbed someone in the butt with it?

When it was my turn to climb in the big offering plate, I half kneeled, bending the knee but keeping it a foot off the ground. I kept my back straight and leaned forward at the waist with careful precision. I held the awkward pose for a five-second prayer and went back to my seat, cock still tucked in. A win's a win.

When I sat in my pew, I prayed. It was a prayer I'm familiar with because I pray it almost every week, silently asking forgiveness for my boner. I don't know why I ask. I don't know why they pop up at the most random times. I do know I shouldn't be toting hard-ons in church.

[Ω] A hyper-fundy is an extremely legalistic fundamentalist Christian.

chapter: 4

Reflections
By Nick Jackson

THERE IS A WORLD where truth is absolute and the Word is infallible and the secrets of the universe are known to laymen. It's a place where white is right and black is the road to eternal suffering and the rest of the color spectrum has disappeared. It's a world where Jesus paid it all, and all to Him we owe. Sin left a red stain, but He bleached that shit.

Roughly 93.8% of humanity knows nothing about this world. Approximately 6.2% does, and they can mostly be found scattered in clusters across the Midwestern and Southern United States. I've spent most of my life in this world, and I'm good at making up stats on the spot.

Hello. My name is Nick Jackson and I'm a recovering fundamentalist. I was born to a God-fearing, flag-waving, church-going Midwestern couple in Toledo, Ohio. My first memory was accepting Jesus Christ as my personal savior and being baptized. I was four-years-old. By eight, I had memorized the

"Romans Road" and was poised to become a solid soul-winner. By twelve, thanks to the Godly examples of my parents, the righteous tutelage of my teachers and pastors, and inspiration from legends of the faith like Patch the Pirate and Bibleman, I had all the answers. My life was easy.

Mom was a homemaker by profession. All moms were at our church. She always said I'd be a preacher, and they put me on the path. It was one I was more than happy to be walking. In elementary school, I competed in OACS (Ohio Association of Christian Schools) competitions against kids from other schools in events like scripture memory, preacher boy contest, Bible sword drill, choir, Bible testing, and relay race. I racked up awards. My dresser drawer was lined with trophies with golden Bibles on top. Colorful ribbons for first and second and third and fourth and fifth place hung from them. There was even a medal or two. The shrine to my Biblical genius made Mom and Dad proud.

At OACS competitions, people from every school knew my name. If you wanted to win an event, you had to go through me–the prized horse of Calvary Baptist School. After winning state events, I'd travel to Nationals at Miles-Franklin College and compete against kids from schools like mine from all over the country.

Many fine, upstanding Christian schools were originally named using the location/denomination technique—Stateline Christian, Hammond Baptist, Upton Park Christian, etc.

Other schools employed a significantly less original technique—the Biblical technique. This meant they shared their names with other schools in the United States—like the 22 different Berean Christians, 31 Bethels, 112 Temples, and 379 Graces.

Whatever name they went by, they competed for second place because I was the Michael Jordan of my age group in the National Association of Christian Schools competitions.

The only exceptions to my Jordan-esque domination were the relay races. Being on the pastor's path, I was fat and slow. Athletics weren't really a thing for me. Mom said I was husky. I thought that was a kind of dog. I guess it's a kind of kid too, but you don't have to be fit to preach the gospel or win a sword drill. You just have to be fast with your lips and fingers.

Whose idea was it to have relay races, anyway? It seemed like a useless skill. The only time we were told to run was from temptation, and I was exceptional at that. Girls weren't allowed to run in the races, come to think of it, they weren't allowed to be in the Preacher Boy competition or pray out loud either, but they got to compete in events for girls like the cooking competition and help-meet quizzing. For the 93.8% of you who aren't in the know, *help-meet* is a term for a Godly wife who has been put in this world for one reason–to help meet the needs of her husband.

It was probably a good thing the girls didn't get to run because the mechanics of running in an ankle-length skirt or dress would have been challenging. It was hard enough for us boys running in our shirts and ties and pants and wingtip shoes.

The reason we ran in our church clothes was explained to us after one of my friends asked our youth pastor why we couldn't wear athletic shorts and shoes.

He told us it was so the girls wouldn't be tempted because "You know how the devil is." So we ran, putting pit stains in our white shirts and scuffing our shoes, but the girls weren't tempted. The armor of Christ prevailed.

For some reason, the 4x100 relay was a big deal. It was the Christian School version of the Kentucky Derby. Ironic. We weren't supposed to be like "the world." Our church hated the Kentucky Derby. The congregation wouldn't watch the event. We endorsed nothing associated with sins like gambling.

We didn't go to the movies either. The Devil's Hollywood never saw a dime from the Calvary Baptist membership.[Ω]

My preacher called our little derby the "Wingtip One-Hundred." It was technically a four-hundred, but "Wingtip Four-Hundred" didn't sound as catchy, and preachers like mine have a knack for what sounds good coming off their lips and what doesn't. The kids from all the schools lined up in an empty parking lot to run. One of the youth pastors actually fired a real gun into the air, and we were off. It was the most exciting two minutes in sports. We weren't very fast.

However, we *did* have basketball teams where we competed against other schools that wore uniforms with sleeves and sweatpants. The girls' basketball teams wore culottes and short-sleeved uniform tops, and our cheerleaders wore skirts that covered their knees and long-sleeved tops. We were never very good at basketball, and I was the worst player on the team, but excellence in sports wasn't a big deal at our

---

[Ω] Except for the time our church rented out an entire theater to watch *The Passion of the Christ*.

school. We were concerned with more spiritual things. Sucking was a badge of Godly honor.

On Halloween, nobody wore costumes. We didn't put candy in baskets. We passed out tracts and won souls. On Easter, we didn't hunt for eggs. We went to church all day and most of us performed in the passion play during our evening service. On Independence Day week, we celebrated America at church because it's the greatest country in the world and the only one that really knows how to do freedom. On Christmas, we read the Christmas story from the Book of Luke before we opened presents. We never got presents from Santa because we learned he wasn't real before we could speak in full sentences. We didn't have school on President's Day and got a week off for Thanksgiving, but always had great attendance on Dr. Martin Luther King's birthday.

There was one thing that bugged me about my path to the pulpit. Most of the evangelists and preachers that spoke in our small church had riveting testimonies of how Jesus had saved them from their alcoholism or drug addiction or whoredom.

My testimony sucked because there wasn't enough depravity. The only thing I was redeemed from was the occasional fatigue induced temper tantrums of a toddler. I was born bad, but not bad enough to move masses to tears with my story. I considered working on a better testimony, but then they would have kicked me out of school and labeled me a rebellious backslider at church, so I thought maybe later.

It's all about the timing of your sin. If you lived a life of sin in another time and place and found redemption in Jesus, you were a hero of the faith–an inspiring story that collected a chorus of *amens* when you told it. If you fell into sin after you were saved and already in church, you were carnal. Having been saved at four, I was in a pickle. My preaching was destined to be expository instead of inspiring, but I wanted to breathe fire and brimstone.

In my first semester of college at Miles-Franklin in the fall of 2011, I met Dr. Luke Scott. I learned that even a pastor's son raised in the Word his entire life could inspire as long as he brought the heat with righteous passion and used the proper vocal inflections.

The world thinks Frank Black and Kurt Cobain and Billy Corgan started the Quiet-Loud-Quiet technique with their music, but it was actually Billy Sunday. And his spirit dwelled in Dr. Scott. I learned it wasn't boring to be a lifelong Christian. You just had to know when to yell.

I took extensive notes in my classes and on Dr. Scott's oratory tactics during his sermons and took it to the streets to hone my craft. I was a college freshman on fire for God. I wanted to graduate as soon as I could and get my masters and my doctorate in Theology so I could have my own church sooner rather than later. That summer, I stayed on campus and took extra classes and dedicated my free time to street preaching and winning souls. I made a cross from two 2x4s and found an old pallet to craft into a 3-foot tall platform of proclamation. On Tuesday, Thursday, and Saturday nights I drove 45 minutes north to take God to Chicago, just like Jonah took God to Nineveh.

My first street sermon was on the corner of Diversey and Clark. I stood on my box with my cross propped up against the wall behind me and brought the Word for forty-five straight minutes, preaching directly to men that walked by and over the pedestrian women, just like Dr. Scott. Then the Chicago police made me leave, but my spirit would not be moved, and I carried my gear to the corner of 53rd and Harper.

On Tuesday of my second week, after three sweaty days of straining my vocal cords only to be taunted by the passing crowd, a man pushing a cart finally approached me and asked about Jesus. When I gave him the gospel and asked him if he wanted to be saved, he looked at me and said, "Whaddoo I got to lose." That was good enough. He repeated the sinner's prayer after me. Then we hugged, and he left. My white short-sleeved dress shirt smelled like BO until I took it to the dry cleaner that weekend, but I was on a spiritual high. I saved a soul.

On Tuesday of my sixth week, a haggard, dirty woman with more welts on her face than teeth in her mouth approached me and asked, "Whatchu got?" After witnessing to her, she said the prayer with me too. Then she asked for ten bucks and got mad when I lied and said I had no money. "I thought you preachers were supposed to help us out," she said as she walked away rolling a beat-up suitcase behind her. "Some preacher you is." Hey, she said the prayer though. That made two. I'd take it.

On the hot July Thursday of my sixth week of preaching, I felt weary in well-doing. My cross was heavier than I remembered, and my box more awkward. I had only saved two people. Everyone else despised me, cursed at me, and made jokes. But I took solace that I was being persecuted for His name's sake. Until this one guy.

He was older, clean cut and sharply dressed, and had a calm disposition in his voice. He had these eyes that pierced mine when he looked into them. He stopped beside my box pulpit and watched me preach. I preached as hard as I could for thirty minutes, spitting and sweating on the concrete below. He never took his eyes off me. Then I saw a police car approaching up the block. I had been getting better at beating the authorities to the punch and leaving before they asked. Sometimes it was twenty minutes, but never more than thirty-five, and if I ever saw a blue and white squad car, it was time to pack it in.

I got down and started to ask him if he had accepted Christ as his personal savior, but he stopped me right as I opened my mouth.

"Hold on, son. Can I ask you a question?" he said.

"Yes, sir."

"Is it possible there's more to all this than the manual?"

"But sir, the Bible says...

"I know what the Bible says, son. Just think about it. Okay?"

I nodded my head. An officer walked toward me. The man held out his hand and said in the kindest tone, "Think, my friend."

I shook his hand and took up my cross and headed to the alley where I had illegally parked my car. The officer yelled at me, "Next time I see you on this corner, I'ma cite you for public disturbance."

I was running out of corners, and I would never see the old man again, but his words loitered in my brain like a chain smoker in a Walmart parking lot, and sleep didn't come easy the next three nights.

My world was rocked the next Tuesday when Faith Baptist Church and Miles-Franklin fired Dr. Luke Scott. He had committed a sin in his life, and that sin caused him to forfeit his right to be the Pastor. The rumor mill was running wild, as do rumor mills in Christian institutions. Dr. Scott had allegedly had sex with a 15-year-old girl in his office. I didn't believe it at first, but because of undeniable evidence like text messages, he eventually confessed. In September, he was charged in a U.S. District Court with child molestation and statutory rape.

Dr. Scott wasn't the first, but after his arrest, many more stories came out and crushed the reputations of pastors all over the country like Red Sea waters devouring Egyptian soldiers who chased Moses and his refugees. According to news outlets, these stories had a common denominator—Faith Baptist Church and its abhorrent offspring, Miles-Franklin Baptist College.

It was the last day of July 2012. And the first day of my unshackled life.

chapter: 5

The Life and Times of Jesse "Take-All-Comers" Baker
By Jesse Baker
December 13, 1996

S O, MR. HAYNES TOLD ME I should start writing. My shrink said the same thing after Chuck kicked my ass when I was a little kid. She said since I wouldn't talk to her, maybe I should write about my feelings. I tried but lost interest after a few months. I still have the journal though. I felt nostalgic the other day and flipped through it. It sucked.

This English teacher I got this year though, Mr. Haynes, he's different. The stuff we read is actually interesting. The characters aren't perfect. In fact, most of them are shitty sometimes, but their words make me laugh. Most of the books even have cuss words in them. I hope he doesn't get fired for that. My favorite is *Breakfast of Champions* by Kurt Vonnegut. Mr. Haynes didn't assign that one. He had us read *Slaughterhouse-Five*, which is about a bombing in Dresden and shenanigans with aliens from a place called Tralfamador or some shit. It was pretty good. Dark as hell.

But the way the guy writes... I needed more. So last week, I went to a used bookstore and picked up *Breakfast*. I finished it in less than a week. KV, not to be confused with KJV,[Ω] defines something that everyone would know as a common thing, but in the simplest, silliest definition possible. It almost gives said *thing* a new meaning altogether. You see things you think you know with new eyes. I'm gonna do that for the rest of my life. I know I'm only 16, but sometimes I think I know a lot. I imagine I don't. But maybe if I start defining things like KV, I'll be able to see things the way they really are, or at least, differently.

Mr. Haynes told me I should start writing fiction. He called it a proclivity. I had to look that up. It means an inclination, predisposition, or penchant for something. I had to look those words up too. They meant proclivity.

So I'm gonna take Mr. Hayne's advice and write a story. My story. KV writes about himself all the time. Why can't I? This will be my life in my words that move cinematically. When I write, I can see it in my head like a movie, accompanied by the soundtrack of my choice and narrated by Morgan Freeman's soothing voice with the perfect rasp and objective insight of a voyeuristic sage. Sometimes I hear the soundtrack in my head when I'm walking around in my day-to-day. I pretend I'm being watched by millions, setting box office records.

Here I go, justified and stripped. My truth. "Bleeding all over the page" as Mr. Haynes would say. Offering my body, my life, and my soul to literary science. The Life and Times of Jesse "Take All Comers" Baker. All I've ever wanted is to be a star. This could be my chance. I'm takin' it.

[Ω] The Holy Bible. 1611 King James Version.

chapter: 6

Reflections
By Nick Jackson

FOUR YEARS AGO, I was blind, but now I see. Let me clarify—it's still fuzzy, but I see better than I did. In my blindness, I spoke as a child and was irrationally confident about my place in the world and eternity. It's amazing how quickly your confidence can be shaken. What has seemed like only weeks later, I find myself here, sitting in an empty circle of metal folding chairs in an old warehouse across the street from a mega-church in Chattanooga, a church that was burned to the ground a decade ago but rose from the ashes only to become one of the biggest religious institutions in the Southern United States, a church led by a man with an influence over his congregation that could only occur if he possessed the poetic swagger of Luke Scott and convincing power of Billy Graham.

I'm waiting for my new friends to come and pour their hearts out in the circle. Here, there's no judgement and no advice. We are men and women wandering the earth and trying to make sense of it all. We can't remember much we said as children, but we remember vividly what was said to us. Some days, we miss our old spiritual confidence and wish we could be those kids again, but we can't.

We are Agnostics Anonymous, and together we cope with the unknown. I started this group when I moved down here to get away from my upper Midwest roots and study journalism at the University of Tennessee at Chattanooga.

Everyone back at home and most of the Kool-Aid drinkers who are still buried in their Miles-Franklin pastoral studies just went on with their normal church lives after Dr. Scott went to prison. They simply closed their eyes and blamed Satan because "You know how the Devil is." I can't do it. My pastor didn't believe in shit. I want to believe, but it's hard. And it's harder not to judge a God by His people. And these days, I wonder if I even want to follow a God whose spokesman fucks underage girls.

I can't seem to get out of my head lately. Guess I took the old man's advice. If Jesus and God are real, and I want so badly to believe They are, surely, They must be disgusted with the people who claim to be Theirs and the institutions formed in Their names. There must be another way, and I guess I'll have to find it on my own.

Just like magazines, newspapers, and local T.V. pulled back the curtain on Faith Baptist Church and Miles-Franklin, I'd like to write a novel about growing up as an Independent Fundamental Baptist. A novel that sheds light on the confusion that comes with stepping out of the institutionalized religious box. The things I had once adamantly believed "beyond the shadow of a doubt" make little sense now when I gaze at them with free thinking eyes, and I don't know exactly what to do about that.

Some days, I imagine God and Jesus watching us, and the Son asking the Father a question they both know the answer to. "How could they have gotten it so wrong?" I guess it would be more of an observation than a question.

Maybe Humanity even amazes the Almighty with our species-long quest to make ourselves more important than we are.

But as I've already mentioned, my life has been a bore, like someone who waxes existential as I have done in the four paragraphs above. If I'm going to write my novel, I'll need actual stories. This support group I've started accomplishes two needs I have right now. I get to vent my spiritual abuse, and I get stories. As they say in Leviticus, I get to "kill two homosexuals with one stone." That's not a direct translation, but it's something to that effect. I guess it's a good thing we've never had the balls to take the Bible's words literally. We just pretend and condescend, and nobody gets hurt, right?

I started a Facebook group and posted an ad in the classifieds of the Chattanooga Times Free Press, and there wasn't an empty seat in the circle at our inaugural meeting last Tuesday. Looks like I'm not the only one around here who needs to vent.

chapter: 7

The Life and Times of Jesse "Take-All-Comers" Baker
By Jesse Baker
December 24, 1996

WHEN I WAS YOUNG, Chuck made me get up early to read the Bible for one hour every morning. It wasn't a search for truth, it was like homework. I plowed through it out of obligation. The Bible has always been a foreign language to me. People don't talk like that. I would read chapters at a time and couldn't tell you anything about them. I don't speak German, French, Chinese, or any other language besides American. King James's Bible, the only acceptable version in my world, wasn't written in American, and it definitely wasn't written in the Southern Ghetto American we speak.

Jamal and I got close in the months after the last Saturday fight day. We shared something special—the wrath of Chuck's fist. We've never talked about the incident, but he's become like my big brother.

After Chuck went away, I got my first taste of real freedom, a life without fear. I threw myself into it every day and, for a long time, didn't read a word that old king named James had copied onto his thin pages. I'm not gonna lie—I've had a hard time accepting the Word at face value these days. It seems so easy for others, but since I've become such a literal guy, it doesn't make as much sense as it did when I was six.

Six–that's when I got saved and baptized. It's a good age to make the most consequential decision of your life. Sometimes I wish I could go back and be that boy who accepted everything and didn't ask questions. Life was so much easier when everyone did your thinking for you, and you could just play with your He-Man action figures, and the most difficult thing about life was figuring out how to scam your way out of eating all your green beans. But things change, and life gets strange and confusing, and Chuck threw away all my He-Man toys when I was eight because Skeletor was demonic and He-Man obviously dabbled in the occult. We couldn't have that filth in our house, and I would NOT be impressed upon by the world and its agenda. Maybe that's when I became somewhat of a contrarian. I don't know, but I was pissed. Still am.

Mom's always there for me though. It's like she knows Chuck's the bad cop, so she's the good cop. She displays her affection and holds nothing back. Chuck probably hates that, but she seems to enjoy her job. I think she's a great Mom.

"That's enough. You're gonna make him soft." Chuck always says. She just smiles at me every time.

I love my mother and find comfort in her words, but her words can't quite fill the void that Chuck leaves with things unsaid. I guess I love him in some primal fucked up way, but I hate him too.

Is the psyche of every teenager cloaked in duality,$^\Omega$ or is it just me?

But I did miss the old guy while he was away. Part of me even missed Saturday Fight Days and the angry, piercing shots his salty voice fired across my bow. I guess bad attention from Chuck is better than no attention at all.

I mean, can it be that hard to say something nice to your kid? I'm obedient, for the most part. I don't get in trouble ·at school, very often. I'm smart, at least I make good grades. I'm tough. Listen to me whinging$^\Omega$ I guess I crave attention from him. Well, the stars might align one day, but I'm not gonna hold my breath.

Whatever.

Mom's love is free. Of course, it's appreciated, but I don't think people crave free shit. We like it, but it usually means as much as the number on the price tag. It's a nice thing, but you can take it or leave it. Most likely, you'll do both. You'll take it... for granted... before you leave it to collect dust in some forgotten corner of your house.

I remember when Chuck came back home. It was six years ago today. Christmas Eve. I was happy to see him and maybe felt a slight sense of guilt for his temporary incarceration, like I shoulda fought better

---

$^\Omega$ Duality is the quality of being dual. It might be my new favorite word. Dual means two parts. It sounds the same as the word *duel,* which is a fight to the death with weapons, or a sporting event where two masked athletes try to stab each other with Dr. Luke Scott's symbolic cock.

$^\Omega$ Another good word I've collected. Heard it on a movie. Some British guy said, "Stop ya whinging." At first, I thought he said, "Stop Yah-Weh," which would mean—stop God. Then I looked up the word. *Whinging* sounds so much cooler than whining.

against Jamal and none of this woulda happened. When Chuck walked in the door, he opened his arms for a hug. I couldn't help myself, I ran to him and jumped in. He didn't *say* he was sorry, but his face did. That's as good as it ever gets with Chuck, so I'd take it. It was the first time in years I'd gotten any affection from him. The old man held me for five seconds. I sobbed. I wanted it to last forever, but there was no way it could. It was the shortest five seconds of my life but felt like an eternity of love from Mom.

"That's enough. Pull it together, son. Let's be men here," he said as he reached into his little plastic bag and pulled out a gift for me—a shiny new King James Bible.

chapter: 8

The Life and Times of Jesse "Take-All-Comers" Baker
By Jesse Baker
January 24, 1997

IT'S MISSIONARY CONFERENCE at church, which means another mission to save our never-dying souls or inspire us to try to save everyone else.

Have I ever mentioned most of the guys that try to save my soul are morbidly obese?

Well, their version of the Bible doesn't allow them to fill their bodies with the chemicals that get your average adult working Joseph through the absurdity of his day-to-day life. So they make up for it by stuffing obscene amounts of food down their throats.

Evangelical Substance Therapy.

Today—Another mission. Another Fat Ass. Another scare tactic that'll probably work. Because, hell, what've I got to lose? It's just another free insurance policy. And you should know, I have no intention of going to hell, so I'm very familiar with the phrase *just in case.*

If the redemptive part of the Bible is true, there's absolutely no way I, Jesse Reginald Baker, will go to hell. How could I? I've been saved 78 times. That's 78 policies. The preacher preaches hellfire and brimstone—I get scared and take a dump in my pants—I get saved. Wash—Rinse—Repeat. But I'll never forget my first time when I was 6-years-old and went to a Bible camp at some shitty campsite.

$$\Omega$$

Counselor Matt gathered all the kids around a bonfire on the last night of camp.

"Everyone remembers Timmy, right?" He held up a ventriloquist dummy we affectionately knew as Timmy. Timmy was fucking hilarious. He had jokes on jokes. We all loved Timmy.

"Timmy, I think it's time we had a talk." Counselor Matt said.

"Okay. Sounds good. What do you want to talk about?" Matt had sick ventriloquist game. When Timmy talked, his lips didn't even twitch.

"Timmy, do you believe in God?"

"I don't know, Matt. I just don't really see the need."

"Timmy, don't you know that God created you and He loves you? His Son Jesus died on the cross for your sins so you don't have to go to hell when you die."

"Yeah, I know. But I'm gonna live a long time. I'll get saved later. Right now, all I just wanna tell jokes and hang out with these wonderful kids."

Looking back, Timmy mighta been a pedophile.

"But Timmy, you never know when your time will be up."

"It'll all be okay, Matt. Don't you worry 'bout me. I'm young."

Right about that time, Counselor Matt pretended to stumble and lose control of Timmy, tossing him onto the fire. He started screaming in his Timmy voice.

"I'm on fire! Somebody help! It burns! Please help! Kids help me!"

I wanted to jump into the fire and grab Timmy with complete disregard for my own body, but I just sat there in shock and cried. Some kids cried so hard that no sound came out. Mouths wide open. Eyes squinted. It's the most agonizing of children's cries. The silent cry. It's always followed by a blood-curdling horror movie scream when their breath catches up with their desire to let it all out.

Counselor Matt stopped Timmy's screams and stood over us as we sobbed and watched the plastic of Timmy's face shrink into itself as it melted in the fire.

"Children, I know we all loved Timmy. He was our friend. He had a chance to get saved, but he thought he had all the time in the world. Kids, you never know when it's your time. Now Timmy is dead and in hell. Burning just like that," Matt said as he pointed to the charred dummy melting away in the fire. "Forever."

Counselor Matt knew his audience as well as anyone ever has. Timmy was the ultimate carrot, and the conversion rate was off the charts.

We all got saved.

Ω

So I'm sitting here at the Missionary Conference. My right ass cheek fell asleep when I drifted off mid-sermon into another series of interconnected daydreams. The pins are sticking all over my leg.

The death rate calculator is back on the wall. It's counting again, and I still don't care.

The last Fat Ass at the pulpit was a little different. His name was Randy, and he had a strange power over his audience, like our emotions were his favorite toy. He was funny then serious, logical then bat-shit crazy. He took us on a roller coaster ride that has invoked laughter, thought, terror, and tears. I gotta admit—he was good at his job and could probably make the Apostle Paul doubt his salvation. Near the end of his sermon, he told a story of a dream he had.

"About a month ago, I had a dream. I saw my brother, Billy. He stood in a hotel lobby and walked to the elevator. He saw me watching him and called out to me."

"Randy, come with me."

"Where are you going, Billy?"

The schizo-sermons always stick to my face like the parasite on the movie *Alien*.

"I don't really know. But I'm scared. Will you stay with me?"

"Yes, Billy, I'll never leave you alone."

Occasionally, Evangelist Randy would break out of his schizo-conversation mode to become the narrator of the story. I took notes. Surely this guy's storytelling methods could help me write my best-seller.

"The buttons on the elevator had no numbers. Only one had a letter. The lowest button. The letter *H*. We didn't know which one to press. After a few seconds, there was a ding, and the *H* button lit up on its own, and the elevator started moving. It was going down.

"Billy looked at me. I can't put into words the fear I saw in his eyes. My ears popped. It was going down fast. Each light that flashed brought us closer to our destination—the *H* floor."

"It's getting hot in here. You feel that, Randy?"

"I do."

"The silence slowly became faint screams. The screams got louder with each flash of a new button. There was pain and agony in the screams, and it was getting hotter. I heard a blazing sound. Oh, it was so hot. Like we were in an oven."

"Are we going to hell, Randy? Am I dead?"

"I couldn't say a word. Paralyzed by dread, I put my head down, and my tears mixed with the sweat dripping off my forehead."

"Randy. You knew! Why didn't you tell me?" Brother Randy screamed in his alternate voice. *"How could you let this happen, Randy? I thought you loved me. I'm your brother."*

"Billy, I'm so sorry. I wanted to, but then you were gone. It happened so fast. I'm sorry. I'm so sorry." Brother Randy blubbered through his spit and sobs.

"I'll never forgive you for this. You could've done something."

The people in the congregation started looking at each other. I wondered if they felt like I did. *Is this for real? Is he going insane?*

Brother Randy took the schizo-method to the next level, a level I thought unattainable by a sane man. His conversation with his dead brother felt more real than anything I'd ever heard, like his brother was speaking from the grave through him, like he was possessed or something.

Brother Randy continued.

"The heat had gone from oven to furnace. Billy's skin boiled, and smoke rose from it. But I wasn't burned. The screams from outside pierced the walls of the elevator and became deafening. Then I screamed as loud as I could to block out the agony that rang in my head." Brother Randy fell to his knees and put his hands over his ears to block out the imaginary weeping and gnashing of teeth. Then he yelled loud. Uncomfortably loud.

Then he brought his voice down. "The *H* bell rang. Me and Billy leaned against the back of the elevator, clutching the rails," he said, shaking while acting out every movement he described. "When the door opened, the fire burst through consuming my baby brother."

"MAKE IT STOP RANDY! HELP ME!"

"BILLY! NO-HO-HO-HO!" His voice decrescendoed back down to a whimper. "His skin charred black, and I reached into the flame and didn't feel a thing. It had no effect on my skin. He was burning alive, and I couldn't help him. Then, a long pair of charred arms reached out of the flames and grabbed my brother. I grabbed his burned hand, trying to pull him back in. I c-c-can't hold my ground. My feet are sliding toward the door as his hand is slowly being pulled away from me. I have him by his ashy fingers.

Right before I lose my grip, he looks right into my eyes and says,"

"Randy, why didn't you tell me about Jesus?"

"And he disappeared into the flames."

"His screams wake me up every time." He said as he openly wept. "It was so visceral. So real. You see, Billy died in a car crash fifteen years ago. Not a day that goes by that I don't think about him. I miss him so much. I found Jesus before my brother died. I didn't tell him. And now he'll burn forever, and I live with the guilt every day."

The Associate Pastor of the church got saved *again* during the mass invitation that followed Brother Randy's sermon, and I picked up another policy for myself. #79.

chapter: 9

The Life and Times of Jesse "Take-All-Comers" Baker
By Jesse Baker
January 25, 1997

One thing I'm figuring out—you gotta do stuff you hate to do stuff you love. Church conferences and basketball. I've written plenty about church. Feel like that's been pretty good therapy, but today, I wanna write about the other half of the duality that is my life—the half I love.

All of us in *The 4-Pack* love sports, but basketball is the chosen one partly because Jamal grew to 6'7", and his baby fat turned into lean muscle. And he's got freakishly long arms, insane hops, and a motor that never stops. Shit... I should be a poet.

Also, it's our favorite because our tiny church school in the middle of the hood has one of the best basketball coaches in the state. His name is Tom Watts. He built his program from the ground up by instilling a strong foundation of fundamentals into grade schoolers and developing them into well-oiled basketball soul-killing machines. I know this because I was one of those grade schoolers who became a killer on the hardwood.

Coach Watts can inspire the uninspirable. We love playing for him, and all the grade schoolers dream of the day they will don the scarlet and gray and take the stage in the Den for their beloved Wolves.

We used to hoop in the Upton Park Rec Center every day during the summers. We were rats. Nobody could keep us outta the gym. I would stay late into the night if they'd let me. I did anything and everything to delay going home to Chuck and Mom. It's not that they were loud or violent. They just walked around each other in the house like they didn't speak the same language. A nod of recognition. Occasional smiles. Then go on about your business. The fewest possible words are ever exchanged between them. Maybe their marriage is *soul-killing* too. Whatever it is, they're an extreme case of concise communication.

The gym became my new comfort zone. An escape from a world that told me what to do, how to be, how to dress, what to think, and who to listen to. I love everything about the gym at the Rec. The smell of sweat and hardwood, the flicker of the old light on its last leg in the corner, the echo of a ball bouncing and the squeak of a sneaker, the north goal that was a half-inch low and let me entertain my dunking dream last year.

It's always hot in there. I even love the heat.

The Upton Park Rec never had air conditioning, so we rarely wore shirts. I loved the perma-sweat that made my skin shine, and how it helped me slide out of any opponent's attempt to grab me.

And the tiny sweat circles that peppered the ball when I did my shooting workouts. And the brown dirt stains on the tips of my fingers after shooting hundreds of shots on a given day. The court is my home.

A home isn't a place you lay your head. It's where your problems go to rest, even if only for a few moments.

I'd be much humbler if I wasn't so damn good at basketball. My plan is to be the best that ever walked the halls of Upton Park Christian School.

Chuck raised me to never show weakness, not even the slightest chink[Ω] in my armor, and I won't. I know I'm cocky and stubborn, and I guess that's why me and Coach butted heads early last year. But we're good now.

I could tell right away Coach Watts was the Alpha dog in our locker room, but I had to challenge him. I probably would've started last year if I didn't do that, but I'm learning. Coach Watts seems to like me. I mean, how could he not? I'm 175 pounds of skill, motor, and unadulterated badassery, if I may say so myself. But if I'm gonna be the best I can be, I need to be coached. He's made that perfectly clear, and I have no choice but to believe him. He controls the playing time.

I'll tell you about our confrontation last year. One day during preseason practice, Coach taught us the fine art of shot selection. I believed I could do anything, and of course, most rules don't apply to me.

[Ω] A chink is a dent or a weak spot. It's also a racial slur for an Asian person. I'm one-quarter chink and I don't mind the term that much. Mixed raced people are more evolved. Jokes on the haters.

As the Christian school con artist, I've built a savvy habit of working the system to get away with things. I always know how much I can get away with, and what to say if I break off more than I can chew. But that shit don't fly with Coach though. He's a different cat.

After the short monologue from Watts, I pulled a step-back fadeaway three-point shot over the outstretched hands of two closing defenders. Coach blew the whistle.

"Jesse. What did I just say?"

I stared at him.

"That wasn't a rhetorical question, son."

"Don't settle for tough shots. Get an easy one," I answered.

"Just making sure you heard me."

"I heard you."

"Oh. Okay. Then you chose to ignore it?"

"Yes, sir."

Mixing respect with disrespect has been an effective strategy against weak authority figures at school. And it lets me put my duality (which I've grown fond of) on display. But Coach didn't appreciate that. Like I said, he's a different breed.

"Okay. Go run 5 sprints, down and back."

I hustled to the side and sprinted every line. My last sprint was faster than the first. Watts wasn't getting the satisfaction of thinking he could cause me physical discomfort. I had to make sure he knew I was too hard for that.

After my last sprint, I stood on the sideline for a few trips waiting for Watts to put me back in the scrimmage. When he did, I dribbled down the floor in my team's first offensive possession and fired a pull-up three from ten feet behind the line. Watts blew the whistle before it swished through the net. Everyone stood silent, waiting for him to explode.

When he glared at me, I immediately ran toward the sideline again and started sprinting, not waiting for him to chew me out. Coach wasn't smiling, but I found our battle of the wills funny.

"Just keep running till I stop you," he shouted across the gym. Fifteen minutes later, I was still running, and it was significantly less funny.

Practice continued for 45 minutes. Coach Watts kept his back to me most of the time. I ran as hard as my body would let me. Coach blew the whistle and called my teammates into a huddle. I kept running. The players gathered around him. I kept running. I'm pretty sure he forgot about me.

"That's enough, Jesse."

Finally.

I slowed to a stop. Sweat soaked every square inch of my jersey and shorts—a shade darker and clinging to my torso and thighs. My face, neck, arms, and shoulders were covered in a slippery glaze. Sweat dripped from my nose and chin and stung my eyes, salty and uncomfortable.

I gave him the ol' *Is that all you got* look. I wonder if he knew what my look meant. I still wonder if the competitive beast in him liked it. He started his post-practice speech as I jogged to the huddle and stood at his right hand.

"On this basketball team, I'm the chief. The Alpha wolf in this pack. You'll get that straight or you won't play here. That's up to you. Am I clear, Jesse?" He turned and looked right at me.

"Yes, sir," I said.

"Good. Bring it in. 1-2-3..."

"WOLVES."

"DO WHAT?" Jamal yelled.

"EAT." The team shouted together.

In the locker room, I went into the una-shower to ring the sweat out of my jersey. It was the same una-shower that we used in middle school when we played for Coach Bill Henson. Coach Henson was also a counselor for the church youth group and an all-around weird guy. He always walked in on us taking showers and gave us pep talks. Usually, his eyes were down. Each talk concluded with a slap on the naked ass of whoever was showering closest to the entry. After a week of these post-practice shenanigans, we'd race to the spots near to the back of the mildewed showers. After two weeks, none of us showered in there again. I don't think the una-shower has seen a naked body in years.

Sweat poured out of my mesh jersey with each twisting squeeze, letting out a loud splash on the tile. By the looks of it, one woulda thought I'd jumped into a pool with it on.

Jamal walked in.

"B. You know I got nothin' but love for you, right?"

"Yeah, man.

"Don't fuck with coach. He don't play, and he knows what's up. He'll make us real."

"Whatever man."

"Just believe me. It ain't worth it. I tried too for a minute, but I'm tellin' you, listen to the man. He knows."

"I gotchu." I said, ending the conversation.

That wasn't the last time I bucked against Coach, but he eventually earned my respect. He'll never waiver in what he believes, and I realized quickly that this wasn't a battle I was gonna win. Since I couldn't beat him, I joined him. Of course, it didn't happen all at once, but I can see now that Coach really cares about us. He pours his soul into us, and I believe he has our best interests in mind. So we let him coach us as hard as he wants. He's the boss and a damn good one in my book.

The Upton Park Rec Center, my old comfort zone, was replaced by the Den last year. The Den is within walking distance from my house too. And Coach Watts always gives a key to the captains so they can get in work whenever they want. Jamal has been a captain since his junior year, so me, Joe, and Deric get to hold the key too as long as we don't abuse the privilege, and we'd never do that.

I guess Coach Watts is the only man who's actually gained my respect outside of Chuck, but I didn't give it because he shot me out of his shlong. He earned it. I feel like he genuinely loves me, and he isn't afraid to show it. He cried in the locker room after we lost in the tournament last year, and the seniors cried like babies and hugged him for a long time. I've never seen anything like it. How can tough guys cry like that? They were so upset because it was over. Coach gave them what Chuck has never given me—a real father that cared. They were no longer his player, and that broke them up inside.

Even though it's not always sunshine and rainbows with Coach, and he rips me up one side and down the other sometimes, I want what those guys had. That feeling so strong that it broke the strongest kids I know—the ones I've looked up to as far back as I can remember. Maybe a lot of kids have two dads—the dad we're given, and the Dad we choose.

Regardless of whether you agree with Chuck's extreme parenting methods when I was a kid, or think them necessary, you can't argue the results from an athletic standpoint. I'm always the toughest player on the court, but now I have the best of both worlds—toughness instilled by my father and empowerment from my coach.

We're poised for a good showing this year. Right now, we're 15-1. With Jamal, our All-State senior, and my talented sophomore class who have completely bought into Coach Watts, the sky is the limit.

chapter: 10

DON RIZZO SAW THE AD in the classifieds. He didn't usually read the meetings section, but something had caught his eye as he was turning the page, and now he had to go back and find it. He scanned down the column through the Grief groups, Alcoholics Anonymous, Narcotics Anonymous. He swore he'd seen it—Living with Disease, Food Addicts Anonymous, Sex Addicts Anonymous—and there it was—Agnostics Anonymous.

The print underneath the bold title read, *You don't have to be alone. Together, we can cope with the unknown.* The meeting was at 7:00 p.m. in an abandoned warehouse across the street from his old stomping grounds, the Upton Park Baptist Church. That was in an hour. He fumbled through a pile of dirty clothes on the floor and grabbed a polo. He put it to his face, breathed deep and decided it would do. Then he couldn't find his shoes.

His apartment looked like a Goodwill storeroom. There were still stacked boxes and dirty clothes everywhere. He had a two-piece living room—one chair sitting in front of a 50-inch rolling box LCD TV. The chair looked like a god. Well, at least an idol built for god—like the golden image of Nebuchadnezzar. It was worshipped by empty beverage containers and empty little buckets with dry sesame sauce on the inside from his last Chinese takeout. There were eight empty cans of Diet Coke, twelve beer bottles, four cans of Red Bull, and a bottle of Crown Royal on its last legs. They looked up to their Lazy-Boy lord in wonder and hope that it could help them overcome their hollow existence.

Don had always struggled with the self-sustaining side of bachelor life. You know, like laundry and home décor and eating. During their twenty years of marriage, Susan did absolutely everything around the house.

These days, they were estranged, and Don had been traveling a lot. He hadn't spent more than two consecutive nights in his apartment ever since he became the C.F.O. of Banksy's Auto Parts two years ago. He had fast-tracked his way to the top of the company since the day he was promoted to Southeast Regional Manager in the fall of 1998. Back when his daughter Jennie was a senior in high school. That's when his job put him on the road, and it all started.

Wait.

That's not exactly true. It started before that. On a night he could never forget. It was the night a middle-aged man began to suspect his reality and wonder if the centerpiece of his ordinary life was, in fact, a cosmic joke at his expense.

Twenty years later, his suspicions had been confirmed. The events of his life had crushed his never-dying soul. If his compartmentalized lives were residences, his professional life was like the showcase place for a season finale of MTV Cribs, but his personal life was the white trash tribulation trailer. He worked tirelessly to occupy his mind during the day and spent his hard-earned money on Adderall and alcohol and takeout and prostitutes at night. He didn't try anymore and hadn't for a long time.

He pulled into the parking lot at 7:02. Since he'd become the boss, being fashionably late was kind of his thing. It was a power play. Why? Because he could, that's why. He smoked a cigarette, then walked into the warehouse at 7:07. A guy named Jeff was telling the group about his grievances with being raised a Catholic.

"It's like... we can do whatever we want, ya know?" Jeff said. "No matter what crazy shit you pull, you got your *get outta jail free* card. Just climb in the tall box and tell a dude in robe what a dick you are, and you're good to go. Well... as long as you don't have an abortion or kill yourself."

Everyone seated in the circle laughed. Don thought, *Catholic angst is the first world problem of spiritual meltdowns... as long as it doesn't involve a priest with wandering hands.* He kept the thought to himself and sat down in the only empty chair next to a middle-aged man in a suit that he knew from his Upton Park Baptist days. A mid-20s looking kid, that he also recognized from church, sat directly across from him. He couldn't put a name to the kid's face.

"Hey, Joel. Didn't expect to see you here," Don said to the man in the suit.

"We all have our reasons. Good to see ya, Don. You look well."

Don raised his eyebrows with a one-breath chuckle. He was aware that he'd aged more than thirty years since he'd last seen Joel seventeen years ago.

Catholic Jeff went on for a while, and Don checked out to gather his thoughts for his turn to talk. Based on where he sat, he was due to go after the woman beside him, who would speak after Jeff wrapped up airing his beefs with the Vatican, the Pope, communion, half the saints, and those god-damn priests.

"Thanks for sharing, Jeff," Nick said. Nobody clapped. There were a few *mmm's* though.

"Lucy, do you want to share?" Nick asked as Don tried to remember the name of the scruffy kid across from him. The kid wore a fake leather jacket, a Rolling Stones T-shirt, a pair of carpenter jeans, and dirty Chuck Taylors. Don thought the kid looked sad, tired, and possibly high on something. The kid glanced at Don and perked up like he recognized him too. Don looked away.

Lucy was an attractive woman in her mid-30s. The kid across from them kept looking at Don—more like looking through him. He had those crazy eyes. There was a 99% chance he was high. The 1% in question only exists because one should be very careful about speaking in absolutes.

"Okay. Hi. Um. My name is Lucy, and I used to be a Christian. I might still be. I don't know." Everyone chuckled. "Um. I grew up in the Cornerstone Baptist Church in Jacksonville, Florida."

Don knew a little something about Cornerstone Baptist because their pastors always came to the IFB conferences at UPBC. It was another huge church. They seemed like good guys. They all did.

"Wow, where do I start... Well... I guess I'll get right to it. When I was a kid in school, they taught us that sex is something sacred, only for marriage, and we should wait. I believed that. I still do, kind of. I don't know. I guess this is why I'm here. I've needed to talk to someone for a long time." Her voice got shaky and her eyes glossier with each sentence.

"It's okay, Lucy. It's why we all here. We need a safe place to unload this stuff that builds up inside us," Nick said.

"Okay," she said with a sniffle. Joel pulled a blue satin folded handkerchief from the chest pocket of his double-breasted suit, walked across the circle, and handed it to her. "Thank you," she said as she wiped her nose. Don hoped Joel hadn't used it recently. Don had a dumpster fire of an apartment, and the shirt on his back hadn't been washed in three wears, but he couldn't do used handkerchiefs. Every man has to draw the line somewhere. Lucy didn't seem to mind though. Maybe she lived by a different code, but more likely, she was too nervous to think about it. Judging by the tremors in her voice and her affinity for the word *um*, that was surely the case. Public speaking wasn't a thing for her like fashionable tardiness and musty clothes were for Don.

She sniffled again and blew her nose. It was a cute little blow, not the obnoxious head-turning honk that the satin cloth was used to. "Sorry, um, I knew it was wrong, but I couldn't help it. I mean... Y'all should have seen him. His name was Brian, and he was the quarterback of the football team. I was a cheerleader. I wasn't the most popular girl in school, but I wasn't unpopular either. I had a thing for him since we were in middle school. We talked some here and there, and I always tried to be clever, and he laughed at my jokes but never laughed hard. More like a courtesy laugh. I'd feel so stupid.

"Brian was always the crush I couldn't quite shake. I always thought he was out of my league, but then one day it happened. It was the third day of school our senior year. I said something that made my friends laugh. He was at his locker, a few down from mine. I heard him laugh too." She snickered and blushed. "He was eavesdropping. My friends walked off because the bell was about to ring, but I took my time, hoping he'd walk me to our Algebra 2 class. He did. Before we walked in, he asked if I wanted to catch a movie that Saturday.

"We had a great time on that date. He kissed me and asked me out again the next Saturday. I said yes again. I thought we might be official soon. The school power couple.

"We went to the shortest movie playing on our second date—some stupid romantic comedy. I can't even remember what it was. I was too into him to care much about it, and I was distracted when he put his arm around me ten minutes in."

She smiled almost as if she was re-living the moment—a time when she thought, even at her young age, true love was a legitimate possibility. A time when innocence kissed naivety. A time before her bubble burst, sprinkling tiny drops on a sidewalk to be trampled on without anyone knowing—or caring—that they were once there.

"We smiled at each other when he reached down and held my hand. Everything I'd wanted since middle school was happening. The movie ended around nine, and he asked me when I had to be home. I told him my mom said ten. He told me he had an idea and drove to an empty park behind a fire station that had a really dark parking lot. I knew he wanted some. I wasn't sure what *some* meant exactly, but I was okay with being there—excited, actually. I'd give him some. I mean, I wanted some, too. It's not like it was all him. I knew we both had pledged to stay pure until marriage and felt safe enough. What's wrong with a little foolin' around? I was serious about that pledge to save myself for the man I married. Him… not so much.

"It got crazy in the car and felt like the real thing—like I would know at 17, right? He told me he'd had feelings for me for a long time. It was fun, but he kept making moves for more until it got uncomfortable. Then he said he wanted to go all the way and wanted me to be his first.

"I said no. He told me there was something different about me than other girls. I said no, but he kept on—how it would be just between us, and that he wanted me to be his girlfriend. He even said he could see us getting married."

Everyone in the circle chuckled and Jeff rolled his eyes and said, "Of course he could."

"I know, I know, but seriously y'all, I liked what he was saying. So I caved in. We did it. Right there in that parking lot. We were only there about twenty minutes—twelve minutes of making out, six minutes of him begging, 25 seconds of sex, and a minute and a half of putting clothes back on. Totally worth it."

"He walked me to the door and kissed me before I went inside. I felt guilty, but after all the things he said to me, I figured we were a couple now. And honestly, I didn't even care if I had to have sex with him to be his girlfriend. I wanted that more than anything." She dropped her head and wiped her nose again.

Don thought about some punk putting moves like that on his daughter Jennie. It made him angry, but he quickly banished the thought. He always ran as fast as he could from any thoughts of her. He had his reasons.

Lucy continued, "We got back to school on Monday, and he was kinda stand-offish. It was weird. He was like a different person. He hung out with his normal group, and I hung out with mine. I waited for him to go out of his way a little bit. Like... ask if we could go out again... or eat lunch together... something. But he didn't say a word to me all week. I was a stupid girl. Then on Friday, I was at my locker by myself, and he walked by and asked if I wanted to go out again. I said, 'Why, so you can have sex with me again? You've ignored me all week.' He told me he was confused and didn't know what he wanted, so I told him to figure it out, and then we could talk. He never figured it out.

"Long story short, I got pregnant. 25 seconds. 25 goddamn seconds. Just my luck." She shook her head and looked at Nick. "The way I saw it, I had two choices—get a secret abortion or get kicked out of our

Christian school and ostracized by the church. The only thing worse than pre-marital sex at my school was murder. And abortion is murder, so I guess I was having a baby." She shuffled through her purse and pulled out a picture.

"This is her," she handed it to Jeff, who took a gander and passed it to Nick. "I don't regret it. That's my 14-year-old baby girl."

"She's beautiful," Nick said.

"I know... I hope she's smarter than I was."

She began to cry.

"The whole ordeal was hell. I didn't know what to do. I told Brian. *He* actually started crying." She snickered through the tears and sniffs. Don laughed loudly. A little too loudly. Everyone looked at him with disgust. This was his first meeting, and he didn't know the unwritten rules about laughing etiquette. He also lacked what the old folks call—*couth*. "Sorry," he said.

She continued. "Sonofabitch begged me not to tell anyone he was the father. He was all like—'I got offers to play college football and if I get kicked out of school and can't play this year, I'll probably lose them.' I was like—'What about me? What about the baby and being a dad?' He promised we could tell everyone before the baby came, and he'd support me and be a dad. And for some stupid reason, I kept his secret.

"I didn't tell a soul, not even my parents. I said I'd tell them when school was over. They were so mad. They made me confess to the school and take my punishment before I started showing. They told me I had committed a terrible sin against God and my future husband and needed to repent in front of the church."

"Jesus," Jeff said.

"They grounded me for the rest of the year which isn't that big a deal to a pregnant teenager that just got kicked out of school. It was the humiliation at church that almost killed me. I went forward with my parents during the invitation the night after I told them, and the preacher told the whole church that I came forward to ask God and the church to forgive me of my immorality. I felt like such a slut," she said with a disgusted look on her face. "Then he said that a baby is a gift from God, and that God works all things together for good. Then he asked the church if they would help us raise this child. A lot of members amen'd. Then he put his hand on my belly and prayed for the baby. It was so awkward... and embarrassing."

Nick cringed.

"They still kicked me out of school though," she said through a nervous chuckle. "Forgiveness only goes so far, ya know."

"Hmmph. Standard," Don said.

Joel shot him some side eye.

"Ha, I know right," Lucy replied. "How's this for standard—the preacher...it was Brian's dad." She couldn't decide between crying and laughing, so she did both.

The circle maintained their silence and let her cry for a full minute. By the end of the minute, her pain had swallowed every hint of laughter.

"I'm sorry. I've never told anyone that story before."

"It's okay," Nick said. "It helps to get it out."

She couldn't continue. Jeff put his hand between her shoulder blades and rubbed slowly. He wore torment on his face, empathizing but also visualizing a priest outing the darkest secret he spilled in confession at mass in front of everyone he knew.

"Thank you for sharing, Lucy," Nick said.

She nodded and wiped her eyes again.

Nick looked at the kid sitting across from Don Rizzo.

"Bobby, this is your third meeting. Is today the day?"

For a split-second, Don was relieved he wouldn't have to talk yet. Then he remembered—*Bobby Corban.* The face now had a name.

Bobby shook his head no.

"That's fine. When you're ready," Nick said. Then he turned to the fresh face on the other side of the circle, "How about you, Don?"

chapter: 11

The Life and Times of Jesse "Take-All-Comers" Baker
By Jesse Baker
March 15, 1997

S O LAST WEEK, we reached our goals and became the talk of the town by winning a state championship in front of over 6,000 basketball junkies from all over the state. I scored 25 points in the championship game and was named Most Valuable Player of the tournament. A steel star had been forged in the ring, sharpened in the Rec, shined in the den, and emerged victorious in battle under the bright lights of the big stage. I've arrived.

The world seems to be revolving around me. Mr. Haynes once said you have to give your protagonist some flaws or people won't relate to him. So I guess a little self-deprecation is the order of the day.

I heard the word *narcissism* in class last week. I looked it up.

Dammit.

Well. There it is. I know, but listen. Even though I have a general disdain for authority, don't trust most people, am pretty much consumed with myself, and hard as a tombstone cross, I think I'm, all-in-all, a good kid. I figure my biggest flaw, the one that leads me to believe I am the center of the universe, doesn't make me any different from most kids, right?

Whatever. I just am who I am. I'm not a bad kid. I choke down what the preachers and teachers feed me with their sacred spoons, but I am aware that I've been finding ways to compartmentalize it all. Shit... maybe I *am* a bad kid.

I know the scriptures. But the word *why* rarely crossed my mind until high school. How could it? The truth has been spelled out for me. If I ever asked the question, the answer was always the same.

"Why?

Because the Bible says so. That's why."

So I've stopped asking. This has to be completely normal for us Independent Fundamental baptist kids. Thinking is actually discouraged from the pulpit. Our pastors even preach against philosophy, or any other search for truth that isn't found in your shiny leather-bound KJV with your name written on the bottom right corner in perfect cursive gold. These days, I file away the food from their sacred spoons in my sub-conscience next to countless memory verses from years of Bible class.

I can quote a verse for any situation. Occasionally these verses form a dark thunderhead that soaks me in showers of guilt. But I don't know if this is my guilt. It's like guilt that's superimposed over a Polaroid of the real me. I'm supposed to be the white wall where people can project their movies. Now I feel like a black sheep. I used to be that easy target—an impressionable adolescent mind. The images that played on me when

I was a wall never felt like my true colors. But now I see they can be useful to me. They can be the mask I hide behind when the time calls for it.

I realize the need for that mask in my world. That's why I'm learning to compartmentalize so well. I heard that word the other day.

"He had the ability to compartmentalize his life." I love that sentence. I can relate.

Don't get me wrong, I'm not some tortured soul. I'm just a scripturally educated kid who says the right words and does the right things at the right times. Despite my narcissistic tendencies, everyone seems to love me. At least it feels that way. Maybe they talk behind my back. I don't care. Well, maybe I would, but ignorance is bliss, right? I'd rather not know.

Maybe my star-athlete status makes me popular by default. I hope it's my personality, but should I really care what it is? Even the teachers I give a hard time to can find a smile for me when I walk by. The guidance counselor told me my magnetic smile is like a weapon. It can light up a room, or a hallway, or a person, and I can use it for good or bad. Kindness or manipulation. That's deep man. Maybe I do a little of both. I don't know, but I do know I ain't stingy with the smiles—just like Chuck wasn't stingy with his belt before he went to jail.

Ω

When Chuck came back home, he was different. He never hurt me again. Mom sold all his belts in a yard sale while he was gone. He wears suspenders to church now. The suspenders that overweight dudes wear that make their pants and shirt form a perfect circle with a line splitting the arc right in the middle of their belly. Like their belly and pelvis area are one round flesh. Like the equator. It's the suspenders that *just say no* to dunlap[Ω].

Chuck works in the maintenance department of the church and wears coveralls to work. If he wears regular pants or jeans, he's beltless now. Which makes him a fashionable old man around our neighborhood because he's the only middle-aged white dude bustin' a sag.

Maybe it was Chuck's decision. Maybe he couldn't trust himself with belts anymore. Maybe Mom sold them all because she'd grown to hate belts just like me. I don't wear belts either. Never will.

But Chuck's still Chuck. Still mean as ever, but only with his words. Or with silence. Never with the belt. Maybe he felt bad about beating on me. Maybe he knows he went too far.

Maybe he didn't want to risk losing everything and going back again.

Maybe it's because he was on the other side of abuse when he was trapped behind that shiny silver fence with a razor wire crown. And being an asshole of a father meant his asshole would never be the same again. I'd like to think that.

[Ω] Dunlap is a condition where the belly of a fat ass done lapped over his belt. It's also a tiny town in the sticks of Tennessee.

chapter: 12

The Life and Times of Jesse "Take-All-Comers" Baker
By Jesse Baker
September 9, 1997

S O WE'RE JUNIORS NOW, and I gotta tell ya—girls are on my mind way more than I think is healthy. I'm uncertain of the source, but it may or may not have something to do with this new NetScape Navigator on the computer my parents put in my room last March.

The Upton Park baptist Church and Christian School have an interesting take on relations with the opposite sex. I guess it's not that interesting since it seems like the rest of the Fundamental baptist movement holds the same views. The moral stance our church has on sex, like all their other moral high grounds, is based on the words that King James transcribed all those years ago. Words that attempt to repress the most incendiary of natural adolescent urges. The urge that seems to rewind itself every fifteen minutes of my day. The urge to get off.

"But I say unto you, that whosoever looketh on a woman to lust after her hath committed adultery with her already

in his heart. If thy right eye offend thee, pluck it out, and cast it from thee: for it is profitable for thee that one of thy members should perish, and not that thy whole body should be cast into hell." Matthew 5:28,29 KJV

I ain't about to pluck out an eye and don't know anyone who is. It's just words on a page.

King James didn't use the dirty words that saunter around in my head this year. If he did, I wonder if those words would've been as taboo as they are today.

So I did some research on the internet. It's so cool. You can look up anything from naked celebrities to the origin of swears. I've had this thing almost six months, and I'm surprised it's taken me this long to look up where cuss words come from.

Fuck can be traced back to the 1500s. The earliest uses of *fuck* meant hitting or striking something, not sticking your penis in it. According to an article[Ω] I read, the first examples of the word were found within names. Names like Willard James Fuckever, Ricky Mindfuck, and Hank Fuckabeggar. Maybe these guys just did a lot of fucking, so people made a word from their names that could be defined by their notorious actions. Their reputation in a verb. Their being in a breath.

Like *munsoned*.

Or like my word, *whinge*. There was a guy in the 1400s named Donald Whinger. He was a bitch, and pretty outspoken about it.

Shit originated as a matter of fact, not a swear. It was the term farmers used for what cows shot out of their asses when they had the trots. Which may be

---

[Ω] I choose to believe in the accuracy of the things I read on the internet if they fit my narrative.

where the term *bullshit* comes from. The word musta stuck and eventually became used for all fecal matter. And since everyone knows how unpleasant fecal matter can be, *shit* became a word for anything that fucking sucks.

Makes me wonder how much right and wrong is determined by our cultural comfort zones. Is it wrong to say because people hate shit? Or hate fucking?

Or maybe they hate that they secretly love shit? Or wish they could do more uninhibited fucking?

I love shit. It's not even a secret. Shitting has never not been funny in school. In fifth grade, our teacher Ms. Carson tripped over Deric's backpack that was illegally parked between the rows. She fell backwards, feet straight in the air. We saw her granny panties. We all laughed, but Deric laughed a little too hard. So hard he shit himself a little and had to go home, but not before he took a visit to the principal's office to be spanked on that shitty ass of his for disrespect.

Nowadays, if I'm pissing in a urinal, and someone sitting on one of the johns$^{\Omega}$ beside me bellows an airy, beefy fart that echoes in the toilet bowl, I laugh every time. They usually follow up with a grunt or a soft-spoken *sorry*. I laugh harder and shake off my Billy Joe Shaver really fast and get outta there before they open their door and see me. It sucks when I don't shake it thoroughly.

If I drop a log worthy of recognition in a john, I don't flush it. I call in all my boys to witness the

---

$^{\Omega}$ A john is a porcelain contraption that people can sit on and piss and shit into. It was also a furry man's name who ate bugs and told people in the Middle East about God coming to kick it with them. It's also a person who rents another person for sex because they don't or can't get enough fucking.

spectacular feat. Fat and round and longer than the water could keep down. The guys laugh and say, "Ah, Nasty." They know exactly what they're coming in to look at, but they have to see it, even though they might gag. They hate and love the sight. It's the shit. I guess both ends of the emotional spectrum are addicting, but who woulda thought? A massive little shit could bring a young man so much joy. You can even find duality stuck like a kernel of corn in *shit*.

I also have grown to love cussin'. I've gotten over the guilt I used to feel about it, but I don't swear out loud in public. Never. Not even on the basketball court. No one's allowed to swear in our Christian environment. Not even damn, ass, or piss. Which is ironic since those words are in the Good Book. I know this because I keep the thin ribbon attached to my KJV in Samuel's first book, where folks be pissin' on walls. The ribbon also shares time with Solomon.

Solomon was a silver spoon kid that made it rain and always sang songs about tits and ass. It could be argued that he was the world's first rapper. Money and hoes. Or mammon and harlots.

Did you know that 72,206 plus 7,879 equals BOOBS? I do, and I told all my boys.

I guess I've learned how to compartmentalize my cussin' too—there's a time and a place for anything under the sun, but not in the church house. So we cuss a lot when it's just us guys. But since we don't have much experience, sometimes the combos we throw at each other don't quite fit.

"That's bullfuck."

Apparently, the thing in question is bovine gay sex.

"Are you serious? Or just shittin' with me?"

I am serious. And high school boys do like to take team dumps in side-by-side stalls for whatever reason—so the answer to both questions is yes.

Jamal has more experience with foul-mouthery though. He's heard a fair amount of cussin' at home. So naturally, his game is more on point. And he always laughs at how shitty I am at swearing. Which pisses me the shit off.

I often fantasize about the day I could walk into school and start cussin' the place up. My other recent fantasies bring us back to King James.

King James used words like 'lie with', 'commit adultery', 'lust of the flesh', and 'immorality'. Most of the words about sex in his Bible had negative connotations. Even the word 'lie.' I think I have a hard time breaking the word away from the first definition I heard as a kid.

"*Thou shalt not bear false witness.* Children, this means you should never lie."

I never used to wonder why sex is wrong. It was just wrong. If an adult asked me about it, I'd repeat what we've been told. Or quote a verse. But that's never kept me from doing what feels natural. Thinking about it all the damn time. But the more I think about it. The guiltier I feel. It's like my conscience is always at war with my nature.

Lately, we've been taught a little more about sex, but nothing specific. Nothing about where it fits into our lives. That would be so helpful, but no. We only get info about sex through the eyes of married adults. Because that's the ONLY place where it's acceptable. Not only acceptable, but holy.

I first learned about sex the easy way. The way most boys of my generation did. School had just started and our fifth-grade teacher Ms. Carson had to take one of our sickly classmates to the nurse's office because he'd hurled all over the floor. It would be a five-minute trip to take him, then find the janitor to come throw some orange sawdust on the sour classroom carpet.

She gave the rest of us a Bible chapter to read for our devotional time. Joe and I opened our Bibles flat on our desks and stared blankly at the pages while Deric leaned down beside his desk and shuffled around in his bag. We always sat in the back corner, and Deric had his back to the rest of the class during his dig.

"You guys aren't gonna believe this."

"Believe what?" Joe asked.

"What I found in the trunk of my dad's car yesterday."

We stared at him with eager anticipation to see what he'd pull out of his two-strapped treasure chest.

When he rose, he showed us his trapper keeper. It was closed, and he held it up in front of his chest, his back still to the rest of the class who had their faces buried in their Bibles.

"Check it out, dudes."

He slowly opened the trapper keeper so that only the two of us could see it. My eyes got big as silver dollars. There she was. I didn't know who she was, but she was right there on the page in all of her bare naked, voluptuous glory. I hadn't seen a pair of tits since Mom was throwing them in my face for 10 meals a day, but I didn't remember that. The image lay spread across two pages of the inside of a Playboy magazine. Her eyes invited us to examine every inch of her curvaceous beauty. My mini cock was at full attention in a matter of seconds, and my hairless balls tightened as they worked to produce some sort of concoction in there.

"Put that away, Deric. You're gonna get busted," Joe said.

I said nothing. Eyes and mouth open. Stunned by the magic this single image had on my body. I hoped Deric would never close the trapper keeper. Actually, I hoped he'd let me take it home.

In the shower that night, the image was still stuck in my head, and my Wang Chung was hard as a rock. I learned later that it's better to use lubricant and a clean sock to solve that problem. But that was the first time I jacked off.[Ω] I used soap and water. Burnt the shit outta my pee-hole. But whatever.

It was the best feeling I'd felt in my entire life. My unit and my brain could rest. The most natural relief known to man. I've been doing it ever since and perfecting my technique. Unfortunately for me, guilt always follows the euphoria.

Ω

I learned about the act of real sex the hard way, like the unfortunate kids of my generation did.

[Ω] Can also be called whacking off, jerking off, beating off, beating your meat, choking the chicken, spanking the monkey, flogging Jimmy, handling the bar, polishing your shaft, or masturbating if you wanna be technical about it.

A year after Deric had showed us the magazine, my curious hormones had persuaded me to discover more about the female form. I watched movies from Mom and Chuck's DVD collection in a desperate search for the ever-elusive sex scene. I also devoured the new Playboys that Deric would bring from his dad's secret stash. Guilt still followed my busted shower nuts, but my prick always trumped my conscience in the quest to relieve my beanbag.

Looking back, I feel like Mom and Chuck have always scheduled their sex life around Chuck's nuts. Mom's like any good Christian wife, right? So she has to fulfill his needs. Her body is not her own. That was supposed to be part of the Biblical deal—one flesh and all that. The way they avoided each other in our tiny home made me never consider them having sex when I was little. Maybe it was because I rarely saw them kiss. Maybe it was denial. Likely, it was because I didn't even know what sex was.

But I remember now. It was like clockwork once a week. I'd be half asleep on a Saturday night and hear what sounded like a builder hammering nails. I never thought about it, and it was like a sleep metronome that was the rhythm to a dream I was having. Always the same pace. Boom... boom... boom... boom...

One night after Christmas, I was wide awake when I shoulda been sleeping. I'd just gotten a new video game—*Mike Tyson's PUNCHOUT!* I was so competitive that I couldn't sleep until I put Iron Mike on the virtual canvas. I was pounding Mike with body shots when I heard my sleep metronome.

I pressed pause. I imagined the pictures musta kept falling off the walls in my mom and dad's room.

So stupid. Kids think weird shit when they don't know what's going on because they *are* stupid. Maybe Chuck was always having to nail the frames back on the wall, hammering meticulously with patient precision so they would stay up this time. Of course, I wasn't going just because I wanted to be helpful. That's what I told myself. Nothing would have been able to pry me away from that game, except for curiosity. One question—*What's all that racket?* I got up, walked down the hall and cracked opened the door to their room, prepared to offer my help.

Chuck didn't need any help. And I can't unsee what I saw that night. Chuck's bare ass staring right at me. Slightly wrinkling with each clinched thrusting motion. Mom was on her elbows and knees in front of him with her head in a pillow making muffled moans. I could only see the outsides of her ass making waves as he jack-hammered away. I slowly closed the door and tiptoed back to my room. I pressed start on my controller and got back to battle with Mike.

I finally put one and one together. Even though I didn't know what to do with them before this scarring night, I'd seen fuck holes in the magazines, and I'd seen my rock-hard Dong Juan when I was jacking it in the shower. Now I knew. Turns out there was no metronome, and my father wasn't nailing the wall, he was nailing my mom. I felt like I was gonna gag. Little Mac hit the canvas. And it bothers me that to this day I sometimes get chubby at the thought of it.

A few weeks later, Chuck tried to tell me about penises and vaginas. He stumbled around about sex for about five minutes, only mentioning missionary position. I sat there embarrassed and wanted to ask what the fuck him drilling Mom from behind was all about, but I held my tongue, and, after my awkwardly forced sex-ed lesson, Chuck said, "All right. You got anything you wanna ask me?"

"Nope. Got it, Dad."

"Good. I'm glad we had this talk."

After that, I tried to make sure I was at a friend's house if I thought it was gonna be Chuck's servicing night. It was usually a Saturday.

Ω

Sexual repression isn't a tactic only used on the youth in the Independent Fundamental baptist Church. I'm noticing it's for everyone, but no one more than gays. Gay people are so ostracized in our religion that they can't tell anyone who they really are. They try to hide it, but like most things, the truth eventually comes out. I'm not sure what makes a dude attracted to guys, but if it's anything like how I feel about girls, then it *can't* be a choice. I mean, damn, I feel sorry for them. At least God gave me an option if I wanna get some—I can get married. He didn't seem to leave any outs for these poor bastards. It seems to me you like who you like. But according to our preacher, "The Old Testament has made it very clear that God doesn't like queers."

Gay people get treated like shit around here. But it seems like I'm the only one who thinks it's a bad thing. Someone peeks out of the closet. The church slams the door on their fingers. If it's a kid who's gay, they get sent to this healing camp like it's some kind of illness. If it's an adult gay guy, they make him[Ω] ask for forgiveness from the church for being gay and promise to change—mic'd up on stage in front of the entire congregation. I've only seen it happen twice, but those services were so uncomfortable. I'm sure it was hell for them.

Of course, that only happens if the gay in question wants to change bad enough to stick around. The gays that want to stay gay, something stranger happens. They fall off the face of the earth, never to be seen around here again. Exiled.

A common idea preached from our pulpit is that gay people become child molesters and sexual deviants. Really? That doesn't add up to me. If all our gay people go away or find a cure for their "illness", why the fuck do we still have so many pederasts around here?

I think they got it wrong. Seems more likely to me that sexual repression turns people into pederasts? Because the more they tell me how bad I am for having immoral thoughts and desires, the more I have immoral thoughts and desires. In fifth grade, my teacher told us to not think about a pink elephant. Of course, you know the rest of that story. Now we're teens, and they tell us not to think about pink vaginas.

Catholic priests are celibate, right? I wonder how that's working out?

Of course, I should, as Mr. Haynes would say, "challenge my worldview." So here goes—could it be the other end of the sexual self-control spectrum

---

[Ω] I've never seen this happen to a girl. It's like lesbians don't exist in our church. It's the gay guys that really piss off the preachers around here. I wonder why that is?

fucking up our brains? This Focus on the Family dude, Dr. James Dobson, spoke at our church one time and said Ted Bundy claimed he became a killer because of dirty magazines. If that's true, we all might be fucked because this Netscape thing is crazy, man. Anyway, Ted Bundy was a trustworthy guy who gave sound advice, right? Well, Dr. Dobson sure thought so.[Ω]

Maybe church people look a lot of porn. Maybe church people never look at porn. I don't know. But I do know this—in this church—moderation is not a positive way of life. It can never be present in a black and white society. White's gotta flow. Black's gotta go.[Ω] But I'll tell you what *is* ever-present around here—motherfucking perverts. Well... us kids would be safe if they *only* wanted to fuck our mothers, but unfortunately, they don't. We've been fair game for a long time. And our church has never addressed this uncomfortable fact.

We've had more than a handful of deviants preach at our church before they were indicted for sex crimes. And more than our fair share of creepers in high places. Last year, the rumor was a male worship leader had a secret relationship with a boy in my class. The worship leader took a job at a new church. The boy's family moved away.

Three different bus church bus pastors have preyed on the neighborhood kids since I've been in school here. And then there's our middle school basketball coach Bill Henson—don't even get me started

---

[Ω] I guess I'm not the only one who cites questionable sources if it serves my narrative.

[Ω] Yes, I'm aware of the irony of this sentence combination whilst talking about a church that has over 2,000 members and only two black families.

on that motherfucking piece of inbred shit. I know there's way more of these deranged fucks. Don't ask me how I know. I just know.

If exposed, our local deviants disappear like they never existed too. Their actions are swept under a top-secret rug,[Ω] and church goes about business as usual. Don't mind the kids who've been abused. It's over now, and we'll be all right. Maybe it's always been this way—generations of former fondled kids fondling kids who grow up to fondle kids.

There are situations where the only victims are the families who are blindsided by a preacher's secret life. Maybe their pain coulda been avoided if the guy coulda just been himself from the jump. One story I recently heard was kinda sad, but funny at the same time. There was this missionary to an Indian reservation in New Mexico. He wore a headdress and sang the same song to us every year at Missions Conference...

"Swing In... to the saddle Christian cowboys."
"Start riding and start riding hard."
"To the canyon of sin."
"For the souls of lost men."
"Bring in the strays for the Lord."

Well, he was arrested for lewd acts and public indecency when the gay sex orgy he was swinging his dick in got busted by the cops at an elementary school playground in the middle of the night. I bet his wife was pissed, and his son probably didn't have a very good time at school on the reservation the next day.

[Ω] But church members are terrible at keeping secrets. Or maybe they're generous with information. Yeah... that sounds better.

chapter: 13

H I, MY NAME IS DON RIZZO. I got saved when I was 25-years-old. We had a two-year-old daughter named Jennie, and I wasn't being an exemplary husband and father at the time. I won't get into that too much, but alcohol wasn't helping."

"Word," Bobby said.

"Then Susan dragged me to that church across the street one Sunday," Don said as he pointed to the building with the digital sign that read:

Upton Park Baptist Church
That Old Time Religion
For the 21st Century

Don turned to the man in the suit and asked, "Joel, I've been outta the loop. Dr. Germaine still preaching, there?"

"Yes, he's a great man. A real legend of the faith."

"Oh, he's a legend all right." Don scoffed, then he continued, "That legend of the faith over there preached a powerful sermon the morning I visited. I went in skeptical but a little desperate too, and halfway through the message, he had me eating from the palm of his hand." Don shook his head, embarrassed. "Susan said she'd leave me if I didn't stop drinking. I didn't want that to happen, but didn't think I could do it on my own. That morning, I felt like Jesus was the answer. You know, that feeling you get in there.

"I didn't have any better ideas, so I got saved, and it actually worked. I quit drinking. Dr. Germaine led me to the Lord when I went to the alter, and after that morning, he was my mentor, always there for me if I needed anything or just wanted to talk. A few years later, I became a deacon.

"Me and Susan were doing better than we ever had. Jennie grew up in the Christian School and a few years after that, Dr. Germaine made me the head deacon. His secretary Linda called us *The Dons*. I guess ya'll can get the idea that me and the boss were close.

"But when Jennie was starting her senior year in high school, everything went to hell. It was a rainy Wednesday night in September. Susan and I drove separate to the service because I came straight from work. I also had to stay and lock up after church. By this time, Germaine had given me an office down the hall from his. He preached another great sermon, and I turned off the lights, locked the building, got in my car, and drove halfway home when I remembered I'd left my wallet in the office. I had to turn around because I had an early flight to Nashville the next morning.

"When I walked in the church offices, I heard something fall off the desk in the back toward Germaine's office. No one was ever there at night, and my first thought was we were being robbed. But we always put the offering money in a safe in the basement, and

Linda deposited it in the bank on Monday mornings. If it was a robbery, the burglars were uninformed, unless they were trying to steal a bunch of Gideon Bibles or Germaine's mahogany desk. Unlikely. Then I thought it might be the school pranksters. They'd been active that year. More likely, and they were about to get busted.

"I walked down the hall to Germaine's office and the noises got louder with each step. There was a rhythm to it. I knew before I heard her moan. The Gideon Bibles weren't in play, but the mahogany desk sure was."

"Oh shit," Bobby said with a giggle, his fist covering his mouth. Joel shot him a glare that might have slowed the roll of someone who gave a fuck.

Don Rizzo turned his head slowly and made eye contact with Joel. "Yes, my friend. Our legend of the faith, the great Donald Germaine, had our secretary Linda Maples bent over the desk. Her right hand was on his King James Bible, and he was workin' her hard. That's your pastor."

Lucy and Bobby chuckled. Catholic Jeff, riveted, said, "Go on..."

Everyone laughed, but Joel did not. "You lie."

"Lemme tell you a few things, Joel. I pay for sex almost every week. I'm a chain-smoking drug addict and a drunk. I walked out on my family, my life is a wreck, and perhaps I'm the most miserable person in U.S. history, but there is one thing that I am not, sir, and that is a liar," Don said.

"Okay, let him finish, Joel." Nick said.

"That's it. I'm finished. I just walked out." Don looked at his shoes and then back at Joel. "He was my hero too, you know."

chapter: 14

The Life and Times of Jesse "Take-All-Comers" Baker
By Jesse Baker
December 13, 1998

I'LL ADMIT IT—by the beginning of this year, my senior year at Upton Park Christian School, my ears have become more spiritually tone deaf with every passing sermon. I always go to the services—not my choice, but I rarely hear a thing. I just sit there staring off into space, counting down the minutes until I can get the fuck out. It's worse than it's ever been. Excess can lead to familiarity. Then you gotta raise the stakes or quit, and I'm ready to be done.

But last week, they raised the stakes. I sat in a familiar pew. A familiar tune played. Familiar voices sang a familiar song, but the feeling in the air that night wasn't as familiar. I heard some of the funniest jokes, most thought provoking sentences, and heartbreaking stories ever uttered from the UPBC platform. The guy who'd just graced the stage was, much like "Elevator to Hell" Randy from sophomore year, a grand master of the Evangelical Arts. He could touch every emotion inside thirty minutes with his perfectly timed delivery that loosened you up, then cheap-shotted you square in the feels. And everyone in the auditorium seemed to feel it. When he was done, he just sat down, and the singers made their way under the lights with tears in their convicted eyes. Their pre-existing emotion made the sounds that entered my tone-deaf ears surprisingly powerful. Maybe even cover artists can produce a knock-off masterpiece when a little pain is a string on their Les Paul.

Despite it being a song someone else wrote, they owned every second of it. They were the lyrics. They were the melody. Well, at least one of them was. Her name was *actually* Melody, but she sang harmony and killed it, and I felt a piercing through my guarded, apathetic psyche. I didn't go forward, but I kinda wanted to change. I wanted to avoid sin, do good, be kind, and serve God. So in my seat, covered by the emotion of the night, I rededicated my life to Christ.

I don't know exactly what that means. It's just the phrase that we Christians use so we can let people know we've re-Christianized ourselves. Kinda like renewing your vows in a marriage, but Christ is the groom and you are the bride.

If I'm being honest, I've never felt comfortable with that analogy. But last week I was moved. Moved enough to become a two-millennium-old man's wife. Again.

My decision lasted a few days. And I'm noticing the short life span of decisions triggered by emotional manipulation. I guess I'm back to my old ways. Just being. Compartmentalizing and all that. It is what it is.

Church is so funny now. The closer we get to the college kids age, the better seats we have for the show. We get a great view of the morally polarized population of our older sibling higher Ed institution. It's a whole new level of people-watching. We've come up with a system to form hypotheses[Ω] as to what sexual base each couple is standing on. It's become our new game—arguing about random couples' probable sex lives.

Here's what we've come up with in our observations so far:

The Sneaky Hand Holders. Technique: Girl crosses leg away from boy. Boy puts opposite arm across back of pew. Both boy and girl slightly lean away from each other. Both drop closest hand in the space between each other's hips. Fingers interlock. Occasional back hand brush of girl's lower butt by boy. Girl repositions and makes sure boy knows he's stepped out of bounds. Physical Max Verdict—French kissing and occasional light petting over clothed breast. Extremely rare dry humping.

The Front Row Gappers. Technique: Couple maintains a one-arm gap. If gap is compromised for any reason resulting in physical contact, probable jerky movement occurs, followed by an optical scold.

[Ω] Hypotheses are educated guesses. We're getting an amazing education around here, so we're good at hypothesizing.

Usually happens when boy or girl is an RA[Ω] Physical Max Verdict for girl—holding hands at skate night. Physical Max Verdict for boy—oral and/or anal sex, but not with a female.

The Jacket Bandits of the Chilly Auditorium. Technique: Must occur when confidence in being seated for a long time is high. Girl tells boy she's cold. Boy sheds jacket and puts it over girl's waist and legs like a blanket. Boy's inside hand sneaks under jacket and does finger exercises to strengthen the joints. In the rarer cases that this move is flipped, there are some requirements—jacket must be big enough to be shared. Unzip only. Tissues on hand. Couple must have row to themselves behind everyone. It's not a common play, but if you're sitting in the back few rows and a brave couple is behind you, there's a chance you'll see the subtle rhythmic rising of the jacket. Just don't stare, or the fun stops. And nobody likes a cock blocker. Physical Max Verdict—oral both ways. Absolutely NOT fucking.

The Pinky Touchers. Technique: Boy holds hymnal in front of girl so they can both see the words and sing. Inside arms hang down with hands close to each other. Girl rubs back of pinky up and down boy's pinky until eye contact is made. When eye contact is made, they are saying something without saying it, and it's very

---

[Ω] *Resident Assistant* in the college dorms. Motherfuckers rat out their peers and give them penalties called demerits for the most stupid ass, petty shit. They love to put their piety on display. There has to be word or phrase for this. I can't think of one. ***Editor's note—Virtue signaling is the phrase Jesse was looking for. One of the greatest philosophers of all time used to hate that shit. What was his name? Oh yeah, Jesus.

serious. This micro-technique is known as optical intercourse. Stakes are high enough to be extra careful in public. Physical Max Verdict—definitely fucking.

Ω

The music is getting funnier too. Maybe we're just at the age where we catch sexual innuendo in everything. Listen, if I'm not supposed to laugh at sexual stuff and potty humor, just kill me now.

A girl went on stage last Wednesday night and sang this new contemporary Christian song. Deric thinks she's so hot. She's alright, I guess. Not really my type.

She sang about getting on her knees. Deric looked up from his procrastinated accounting homework and raised one eyebrow. He was as locked in as I've ever seen him in church. I bit my lip. He breathed from his mouth. Then she sang the last line about how there was power when she was on her knees.

The music stopped. Amen's rang. No clapping. No one claps except the preachers at the IFB conference. Deric shouted, "HAYMAN."[Ω] I've never heard him say that in church. Never. Then he leaned toward me and whispered out of the side of his mouth, "I'm gonna find out just how much power?"

I did that laugh thing where it sounds like you're choking. An old lady turned around and shushed me like an angry librarian. I pretended to have been coughing, and she seemed to lighten up about it.

Ω

[Ω] HAY-man— the Bible Belt way of saying *amen*. Must be shouted.

We're trying to take the Wolves back to the state championship. We've become small town celebrities since we won it all in '97. Coach Watts has motivated us to reach our potential on the court, and we've been beating the shit outta people.

Every game on the road, we're like rock stars on tour. Cheerleaders for the opposing teams fearlessly walk up to us and hand little slips of folded paper with their phone numbers inside while we were going through the pre-game layup lines. I stick my folded flirtations in my sock and flash them my patented smile. I've hollered at a few of them. What? Me and Jennie were on a break.

Every home game might as well be homecoming. Even though our school is small, the gym's always packed with church members, alumni, and random basketball fans from the area. Most Friday nights, the fire marshal has to come close the doors.

I'd like to think I don't allow my small pond star status to change me, though. I'm obsessed with basketball. I don't drink, smoke, party, or fuck. Not because my KJV says it's immoral, but because I don't want to fuck up my game or get kicked outta school. You don't have to do much to get kicked outta school here. Two years ago, someone ratted out a senior baseball player named Bobby Corban when they saw him smoking a cigarette at the local go-kart track. He copped to it, and they kicked him out. He had to change schools in January and couldn't play baseball his senior year for one fucking cigarette.

If someone finds out you're having sex, you're gone. No questions asked. I think it'd be a hard thing to prove. I'd make them show me the footage. But people get convicted and confess shit around here at an astonishing rate, but confessions don't keep you from getting the boot from school. It's crazy, man. I don't get why anyone would rat themselves out, but I'm tellin' you it happens every year. Guilt's a helluva thing.

Me personally, I ain't havin' sex because I'm terrified I might knock someone up, but that doesn't keep me from taking a few bites from the fruits of my stardom.

I like to tip-toe close to the lines in the evangelical sand when it comes to girls. The girls seem to love us, and of course, we have an obligation to love them back. If I've ever been cavalier with the hearts of the fairer sex, let me go on the record and say I'm sorry, and I don't mean to be. I'm just young and having a good time.

Ω

The Purity Chapel was a day that an evangelist came to school and told us about the dangers of sex before marriage. He never talked about safe sex because, according to him, no sex outside of marriage is safe, and people still get STDs or get pregnant when using condoms. "Abstinence is the only safe way," he said. This guy pressured all of us into making a commitment to abstinence by going to the front and getting our *purity ring*. This ring is a commitment that states we will save our virginity for the person we marry.

Implied—if a guy didn't go get himself a ring, he's a pervert who has no respect for women. And he's fucking around on his future wife. If a girl didn't go get a ring, it's plain and simple—she's a whore.

I'm sure the ring falls off a lot of fingers at some point in pre-married lives. My vivid imagination sees it bouncing off the ground to the smacking of a wavy ass. Virgins have incredible imaginations. But a dirty ring on the ground might be okay. As long as you keep it to yourself no matter what. Never forget you could always rededicate your life to Christ. The Christian re-set button has to exist for a reason.

But questions I ask myself are:

If I pressed reset, would I be any less of a whore to the spiritual giants at the Upton Park baptist Church and School? Meh.

And...

Is it worth gambling with the consequences? Not yet.

How can you know what it's worth if you've never experienced it? Someday I'll know. I do know this—when I get married, we'll have sex at least three times a day. I'm marrying someone pure who's down with making up for lost volume. I don't care whether we live in a house, apartment, duplex, or a damn tipi—we gonna fuck that place up, down, and side-ways. And upside-down.

Ironically, my sex life exists in the same place Jesus said I'm supposed to pray—in secret, in the closet. Not literally in a closet.[Ω] You know what I mean. I wonder how much Jesus thought about girls when He was my age. I wonder what He was like. I wonder why nobody knows what the hell He was up to.

[Ω] Well, Jennie did tug my Rikki-Tikki-Tavvi in the janitor's closet that one time.

Anyway, my secret life is gonna come one step short of home base. I guess I'm still the projector's white wall in some ways.

Don't ask questions, just enjoy the black and white grainy film.

But there's a slight catch that works to my advantage when it comes to sex—a dick inside a pussy seems to be the only black to me. And it's obvious that I'm not alone in feeling this way.

Pre-marital Intercourse = Black.
Marital Intercourse = White.
Anything but Intercourse = OK since nobody talks about it.

We conveniently interpret silence.

So yeah, I guess I've become the lick'em but not stick'em guy. I mean, I'll stick'em. It just depends on what your definition of stick'em is. The long and thick[Ω] of it is—I won't stick 'em in the pussy. Just in the mouth or fist whenever I get the chance.

I guess there was a lot of pure fun with the roster of girls at school. For me, it all started with French kissing. My first was Jennie in the 7th grade. Oh, man, I'm all about her. She's my regular girl. We're an item on and off every couple months or so, and I'm most comfortable with her.

We've rounded the bases together through the years, usually under that stairwell or in my car. Make outs, dry humps, hand action which recently became mouth action, which I gotta say, is amazing. Dry

---

[Ω] Okay, it's not very long, and its thickness and the word mediocre share the same definition according to Webster.

humping though, I don't get it. It seems like dry humping is the go-to move for Christian girls who won't go all the way. Of course, I'll take it, but man it can be uncomfortable especially if you have a zipper down there. And your night is pretty much finished if you blow your load in your pants. Jennie loves her some dry humping. If I feel like that's gonna be the move du jour, it's a dress down day. Two layers of basketball shorts. No zippers. Because she's gonna rub that thing raw, and I'm spewing loads for sure. Technique—remove top layer of shorts and throw them in backseat. Enjoy the ride. Replace loaded shorts and boxers with fresh shorts commando post game.

But hey, we still wear our rings so it's all good. When we're on, we're as monogamous as high school couples get, but high school relationships can be a fickle thing. Such is young love.

Then out of nowhere, we're off. She always ends it, and I always get mad, at least until the other girls at school go on the offensive. But it's understood I won't be fucking anyone. Maybe that makes them feel safe. Maybe they like the idea that we can fool around without our purity rings falling off our fingers. Maybe that's part of my appeal.

I'm always kind to them and try to be gentle with their feelings. They seem to like that too. I tell them, "Me and Jennie just broke up. I don't think I'm ready for a relationship." My wording might give them hope, but they usually respond with the standard high school girl defense mechanism. It's a tried-and-true quote that semi-protects their heart but also might give them a chance to reel me in if they can put it on me good enough.

"Who said I wanted a boyfriend? I just wanna have some fun."

In for the kiss. Out with the tits. I mean—boobs. Jennie hates the word tits.

I love boobs. Ever since I saw that Playboy centerfold in fifth grade, I wanna see them all. Indiscriminately. Maybe that's why me and Jennie are on and off so much. I don't discriminate, and at times, I feel high school monogamy is boob discrimination. And somehow, she can feel that I feel that.

But when Jennie has had her fill of hearing about who I hooked up with, she takes me back. She has a strange power over me. I guess it's that love-hate relationship I've always had with comfort. I know I've mentioned my duality a few times, but did I mention the fickality of teenage love?

Oh yeah. I did. Well, fuck you for judging.

Last year, I started branching out to the layup line girls from other schools during me and Jennie's breaks. These girls are much more aggressive than the girls at my school. Many times, tops are off before I can put it in park. They're always shocked when I tell 'em I won't fuck 'em. A few have even laughed at me. But that doesn't keep them from trying. They go deep into the playbook—the *no panty* play, the *get buck naked without warning* play, and the *look what I found in my purse* play.

So I guess you could say I compartmentalize sex too. The squeaky clean, purity ring wielding super virgin. But in my secret world, I'm the Foreman of Foreplay. The Boob Collector. The Badass Mother-everything-but-Fucker.

But I genuinely like them all. I think. I genuinely like most people. So it's not like I'm just taking advantage all the time. At least that's what I tell myself. Justification is kind of my thing now. What am I supposed to do? They're just always there, freely offering. Do kids turn down free candy at Halloween? Does anyone turn down free shit?

Sometimes I feel like I'm being used, a trophy on their dresser in their room they can tell all their friends about, a 5.8-inch golden plastic shlong with a name plate engraved Jesse "Take All Comers" Baker.

I've only gained .05 inches since freshman year. I think I've been cheated.

chapter: 15

Ruminations
By Nick Jackson

THE MEETINGS ARE GOING WELL, I guess. We're venting for sure, and it's nice to know I'm not alone in feeling disenfranchised with my ex-religion. I guess I should have known, with a church and school as big as Upton Park, some people that come to the meetings would know each other, but I feel like Don, Bobby, and Joel have a deeper connection than just being acquaintances. It's not what they say, it's the subtext in the air. It's the way they look at each other. Like they have played a meaningful role in each other's lives, and they have a secret that they aren't ready to get out in the open yet.

I've heard things about that church across the street burning down ten years ago. People around here talk about it like it's a new urban legend. I don't know what is true and what is rumor, but I imagine these guys have the inside scoop. I bet they knew that crazy guy who did it, and I'm hoping that it'll eventually come out in the circle.

There's something off about this guy who wears the suit to the meetings—Joel. I don't think he's an agnostic at all. I know what a guy who is knee deep in the Independent Fundamental Baptist movement looks like—I know what that double-breasted suit means. I know how he talks, how he looks at people with that condescending eye, how he listens without listening, even how he smells—Old Spice deodorant and Brut aftershave. I don't think he's here to vent, or even to listen. I think he has schemes. If I had to guess, he's here to save our souls. I swear he even looks like our old college dean at Miles-Franklin. Now there was a guy with schemes...

Ω

In the spring of 2012, toward the end of the second semester of Nick's first year of college, he sat in chapel with twenty of his most pious peers. They were applying to become resident assistants and listening to their college dean—who would be their boss if they got the job—elaborate on the responsibility they would have to walk uprightly, enforce the rules, lead by example in the dorms, and how to snitch effectively.

"Welcome future leaders of Miles-Franklin Christian College. What a mighty God we serve! As most of you know I'm Pastor Roberts—the associate pastor at the church and the dean of students at this great university. This is my 15th year at Miles-Franklin and my third year sitting at the right hand of Dr. Luke Scott, and I consider it, not only one of the great honors of my life, but a great responsibility to edify you—our students—in the Word of the Lord. Just like it's my responsibility to lead you down the narrow path, if you receive the honor of being chosen as one of our resident assistants, it will be your responsibility to lead your fellow students.

"There are a few job requirements that aren't on your application. First, you must have a strong devotional life. Since graduating with my doctorate degree from the Bob Rice Seminary twenty years ago, I've woken up the same way every day. I take my coffee black and sit in my swivel chair in my home office with my Bible and this month's edition of Our Daily Bread. I read, I pray and I think about how I can help my students stay away from the temptations of the world and grow closer to Jesus Christ. I can't tell you how important your quiet time with the Lord is. If you don't make your walk with the Lord a habit, you'll be more likely to stray into sin.

"Second, you must live your life above reproach. I think that's tougher than it's ever been. Things sure have changed since I was in college. To me, it wasn't that hard to live a life committed to Christ—separate from the world. What the world had to offer back then didn't seem nearly as toxic as the carnal missiles bombarding you today. Take secular music for example—we had Michael Jackson, Queen, and Lynyrd Skynyrd. Now though. Dadgum. It's gotten worse. It's clear in God's Word that you live in the world but must not be of the world. If the music you're listening to, or the movie or T.V. show you're watching, or even the video game you're playing doesn't glorify the Lord, it is of the world. If it's of the world, you can't take a chance or the world will make its imprint on your never-dying soul.

"Twenty years ago, when I was a resident assistant at Bob Rice, the lyrical content of the CDs we found in those dorms made me shake my head. One day, I found a full case of music in a room on my hall. I confiscated it and turned him in. I don't know how you can claim to be a Christian and listen to that filth. Each CD was placed in the sleeve in front of little covers with lyrics inside. I pulled a few of the covers out and read the words. If it wasn't pornographic or vulgar, it was violent.

"I grabbed one that caught my eye. It was the famous picture of the monk who lit himself on fire in the streets of Vietnam. The band was called Rage Against the Machine. I read the lyrics for the first two songs. I could sense the hatred for authority when I got to the end of the second song where author said, 'F-you, I won't do what you tell me.' He seemed adamant about it since he repeated it sixteen times! I couldn't believe this was the type of thing my brothers in Christ were listening to. And if you think that's bad, the garbage out there today is even worse. Students, I implore you, guard your hearts.

"When I was in college, I was always proud of my fellow resident assistants. We had a hard job and were committed to upholding Christ-likeness in our dorms. We held Bible Studies and prayer groups after curfew with our student peers. And even though we were students ourselves, we earned the job of assisting our Student Development staff in upholding the standards of our college. Largely because of our example and discipleship, many of our students were born again[Ω] during my three years of college. That still blesses my soul.

"Lastly, you must stand on the front lines with our school leadership to evangelize our community. This means working in the bus ministry, teaching a Sunday school class, or working as a leader in the church youth group. We have special events with service opportunities too. A highlight of my year every year is our Judgement House production on Halloween. I don't know if any of you have seen it, but it's a haunted house that'll get you saved. On Halloween, the world has Freddy Krueger and Jason Voorhees. We have Jesus. We win. Amen?"

As customary, this queued the audience to serenade the dean with a chorus of *amens* to affirm him.

"This event is a blast, and I really look forward to it. It's one of our most successful soul-winning events. If you aren't familiar with how it goes, this will get you excited. There's a unique story every year, but it always ends the same. We always have two pivotal characters: A troubled teen who smokes and drinks and is probably wearing a rock music t-shirt..."

Queue audience condescending chuckle.

"He lives fast and puts off getting saved or rejects Christ completely. The other either repents of his ways and changes his life. The tricky part is coming up with a new scenario where both will die. It could be a robbery, a car accident, or anything. We need students for this year's production. So if you can write a script, act out a part, or assist in production in any way, it will help your chances of being picked to be an R.A.

[Ω] A more confusing way of saying *they got saved.*

"Last year I wanted to show the dangers of being consumed by the secular world. I wanted the lost soul to get shot in a night club, but I couldn't figure out how to get the saved boy in a situation where he would get killed too. Why would he be at the nightclub when he lives a holy life? Then one of the students helping with the script had a brilliant idea—he backslides.[Ω] We could have the saved boy succumb to peer pressure. We could set the stage beforehand so the audience knew our Christian boy was saved, but his worldly friend was not. It worked perfectly. God's grace on display for all. Once saved always saved. And we had a record number for salvations at Judgement House last fall.

"The judgement seat scenes are my favorite part. They're always the most visceral. Honestly, it scares me every time, and I've never doubted my salvation for one second. When our student who plays the role of God at the judgement seat stands and shouts, 'Depart from me ye cursed into everlasting fire prepared for the devil and his angels!' Oh man. I can't imagine being lost and not getting saved right there. Amen?

Then you walk into hell. We always have it set up perfectly. You walk across a bridge in a room of smoke and heaters and flashes of fire. The talented actor playing Satan is in the top corner, laughing and welcoming his new lost soul to an eternity of torture. As you get to the top of the bridge, demons bulldoze their way through to the line and throw the teenage lost soul into the lake of fire. All you can see is dozens of

---

[Ω] Christian regression, so to speak. The art of sliding back into a life of sin.

hands reaching up through to smoke to grab him and pull him in.

"After the hell scene you walk into another room. It's white from top to bottom. All our actors are wearing white robes and smiling. Our Jesus sits on a tall chair, and the song 'I Can Only Imagine' plays on the speakers. Our saved actor walks in, Jesus opens his arms and the boy runs to him. They embrace and the boy sobs as our Jesus holds his head to his chest.$^{\Omega}$

"After the heaven scene, you walk into the counseling room. This is where I come in. I give them a three-minute recap of what they'd just seen and explain the path to salvation. We always have the most well trained, hungry soul-winning students in that room prepared to lead people to Christ. I'll ask, 'Is there anyone here who doesn't know for sure if they are going to heaven when they die?' When the hands go up, our counselors go to work. Each one leading a lost soul into the counseling booths we have set up. That's where some of you will serve, and that's where the magic happens.

"Now if that doesn't light your fire, your wood's wet. I started Judgement House at Bob Rice, and this fall's event will be our sixth production here. As you can see, I'm excited about it. Auditions are next week, and if you want to help, we'll make sure each of you gets the best potential role for your skill set. We're going to set a new salvation record this year. Many people will know beyond the shadow of a doubt they'll be going to heaven. Amen?"

$^{\Omega}$ It was important that the actor portraying Jesus was tall, and the one playing the saved boy was significantly shorter. Subtleties like that made the production more effective.

Ω

Self-anointed mouthpieces of God have an uncanny ability to frame opinions as indisputable facts.

When I think about the lengths we took to manipulate people into getting saved, it makes me physically ill. I'm serious, I get diarrhea for like two days every time. I didn't see it for what it was when I lived in it. I thought I was doing the Lord's work but now, I know exactly what I was doing—scaring folks saved to keep butts in the pews and cash in the plates. It isn't about helping people. It's about converting them. And keeping them inside those walls.

The things you tell yourself... If my intuition is correct, Joel Inglewood is probably telling himself an elaborate story about his attendance at our meetings...

"This year I feel the call from the Lord to get out in the world and win the souls that lukewarm Christians would say are unwinnable. I ran across this Facebook group the other day. Agnostics Anonymous of Chattanooga. I'll go see what it's all about. I'll observe for a few weeks and pick my spots. Might even talk to a few over coffee and donuts and build rapport. Surely, I can get some of them to Judgement House in October. I'll wear my best suit to the meetings. They will know that I am not of the world. There will be something different about me, and they will know I care where they spend eternity, which will make them more likely to open their hearts."

chapter: 16

The Life and Times of Jesse "Take-All-Comers" Baker
By Jesse Baker
January 14, 1999

We have a ritual after Friday night wins—post game poker night. We go to Joe's house and play with a few friends from school. The Dixon family has been doing well financially and moved out of Upton Park and into the suburbs. Their house is big and has a den downstairs that doubles as Joe's game room. As often as his parents allow, we kick it over there, and they almost always allow. Joe's dad figures it's better we hang out at their place rather than out getting into Lord knows what.

While other high school kids party and get their underage drink on, we sit around the table telling jokes and raking in pots. The pots weren't money at first, since we never had any. We played with hard candy for poker chips. Specifically... Runts.

Bananas—$25
Strawberries—$10
Apples—$5
Limes—$1

There are two reasons that poker is the game of choice when we hang out.

First, we love to compete, and poker is the best form of competition possible that allows you to rest your body. It's mano y mano. A psychological battle instead of a physical one. And heavy competition is our type of fun.

Second, poker and any other form of gambling is taboo at our church and school. Toe that line, baby.

In time, the competition got fiercer. The Runts held more value than money. They represented pride. We started studying the nuances of the game. I bought a book called *Super System* by poker legend Doyle "Texas Dolly" Brunson. It was thick—over 400 pages of ahead-of-its-time strategy from one of the all-time greats. It wasn't an easy read by any means, but I buried my face in it on bus rides and during study halls, trying to get the edge on my boys. Joe did the same thing, but with a different book—*Caro's Poker Tells*. Deric doesn't give enough fucks to read books, but that doesn't keep him from getting pissed off when he loses.

Most people don't know how to play poker. There's a difference between knowing the rules and having the skills to work the rules to your advantage. But everyone thinks they're good. I think me and Joe are figuring it out. I don't know if it's because we *are* good, or if everyone else just sucks donkey balls. But we could be destined for greatness. We've watched the movie Rounders dozens of times and can quote it in the most random situations. We have old tapes of the World Series of Poker exploits of Phil Hellmuth and Johnny Chan. I imagine myself on TV holding that winning hand one day—two cards behind a mountain of chips and bricks of cash I can barely see over.

In time, the Runts weren't enough. The stakes had to be raised to meet our increased experience and insatiable hunger for more. Always more. The Runts became pennies, nickels, dimes, and quarters which became denominational plastic poker chips from Walmart.

Now, what started as a game played with cards and candy, has become a top-secret, invite-only game played with premium hands and fancy clay casino chips that me and Joe bought online by pooling some of our recent winnings.

Every once in a while, Joe's mom comes down to check on us.

"That was a good game tonight, boys."

"Thank you, Mrs. Davis."

"Can I get ya'll some snacks or anything to drink?"

The eight of us smiled.

"Yeah, Mom. That'd be great."

"We have sweet tea and a few two liters, and I can make some chicken nachos. Joe, can you come up and grab the drinks, and some plates & cups?"

"Yes, ma'am."

"Bring Jesse, you'll need a few more hands."

We walked upstairs to the kitchen.

"Joseph, y'all don't play for real money, do you?"

Joe hated when she called him Joseph in front of us.

"Ugh. No, Mom,"

I kept my head down and my mouth shut.

"Good, cause you know your Uncle Billy..."

"I know. I know. You've told me about Uncle Billy like twenty times. I'm not Uncle Billy and we're just playing cards with chips."

"Okay. Well, y'all have fun, and I'll bring down the nachos when they're done."

We walked down the stairs with the drinks and red Solo cups. Before we entered the den, Joe turned back to me and said, "I think she knows, man. She can't prove it, but she knows. We gotta find a new place to play."

"If she can't prove it what does it matter?"

"Easy for you to say. You don't have to live here."

"Wanna trade?"

"Whatever. Listen, man. I can lie to a lot of people, but I don't like lying to my mom over and over."

"Quit being such a pussy. It ain't exactly lyin' if you ain't doin' nothing wrong. Sometimes you just gotta keep people from wiggin' out about stupid shit, ya know?"

"No, Jesse. I don't."

Joe obviously isn't as talented at justification as I am.

We walked back to the table, and Joe put the two liters on the felt.

"Who wants a brew?"

"That's not a brew..." Deric pulled a small bottle of Captain Morgan rum out of his backpack. "... but I can make it one."

Most everyone was in. I wasn't. Maybe after the season, I'll give it a shot.

Joe made sure all the money from everyone's $10 buy-in with unlimited re-buys was safely hidden away in his backpack at all times. Me and Joe always won, but we tried our best to ensure everyone in the game tasted some success and had a good time. College basketball games ran on the TV, and bellies were always stuffed with the goodies from Mrs. Davis. Deric spiked the beverages just enough to loosen everyone up, but not enough to get anyone hammered drunk. Me and Joe are the only ones that know this is a hustle. We play chess while everyone else plays checkers. And we always abide by one of the fundamental principles from our favorite movie, *Rounders*—"You can shear a sheep many times, but skin him only once."

There's never an empty seat around Joe's pool table.

chapter: 17

The Life and Times of Jesse "Take-All-Comers" Baker
By Jesse Baker
March 15, 1999

J AMAL'S STUDY SKILLS were right up there with Andre the Giant's ability to win beauty pageants. He didn't academically qualify for a 4-year school, so Junior College was his only option. But he's crushed souls on the court for the last two years. Division 1 Tennessee State University offered him a full ride for next year. I'm excited for him. Since he's been at college, he comes home whenever he has the time, occasionally taking in one of our games and gracing poker night at Joe's.

I doubt Chuck ever said sorry to Jamal for the Saturday Fight Day incident when we were kids. But the thing is, with Jamal, he didn't have to. Jamal's a natural on the floor, but his goodness comes even more natural. Sometimes, he makes me question the Bible's concept of the depravity of man. I know I've been questioning a lot of things, but he's a good dude man—I don't question that. He don't hold grudges and won't judge anyone. And if we ever bitch about someone judging us, he always says the same thing…

"Hey, to each his own, right?"

It's hard for me to say that. It's a great attitude to have, but I just can't say it with the grace he can. He lets everyone else be whoever they are and won't get worked up about things he can't control. He's his own dog, and nobody dictates his emotions.

And all this is coming from a good-looking, athletic guy who can't get a date at our school. I swear, at least ten different times, he's been rejected by ten different girls. He always told me before he was going to ask a girl out. I couldn't figure it out his problem with girls in our school until his most recent, and last, attempt. Last year, when he was a junior, he asked out Sarah Wilkes.

"Jesse, what you think about Sarah?"

"She's cool, you gonna ask her out?"

"Yeah. I think so."

Sarah's a pretty girl, one year younger than him. He asked her in the hall before our last class of the day. I asked Jamal about it at practice after school, "Did you ask her out?"

"Yeah. She said she couldn't."

"Really? I thought she liked you."

"She said she did, but her dad won't let her date black guys."

"What the fuck man. That pisses me off."

"It sucks. But she cried, B. She said she really wanted to, but her dad would kill me, then her."

"Fuck her man."

"Naw, she was honest. At least I know why the girls here won't go out with me now. And that my luck with the ladies will get much better when I get outta this backwards ass place."

"Still sucks, man. I'm sorry."

"Yeah. It does."

If anyone has ever been morally justified to be pissed, Jamal was in this situation. But he still found a way to see Sarah in a positive light and feel empathy for her. What her dad don't understand is the absolute best she could do is find someone who loves like Jamal. Prejudiced people don't know what they're missing man. And I imagine that "When we all get to heaven," it won't just be a "day of rejoicing that will be." It will be a day of saying over and over again, "Welp, I was way wrong about that, too."

I wonder if Chuck would be uncomfortable if I dated a black girl. I think he might be cool with it.

Sometimes, I think about Chuck and Jamal, and I'm aware that I might be a little jealous. Of course, I'd never say that out loud, but they seem to have a unique connection that transcends anything me and Chuck share.

Chuck always stands in the corner at our games. He's friendly to everyone in the community, but I suspect it's a cover. If I was him, I'd feel the heat of judging eyes in that gym. Church folk say they forgive, but they don't forget, and they love to talk about their memories. Surely Chuck feels it. What other reason could he have to stand in the corner every game to separate himself from the crowd?

I'm sure Chuck found himself pulling for Jamal in that corner—Jamal was easy to pull for. He probably even caught himself cheering for him a time or two. I never see him cheer for anyone—not even me. After good games, I'd often catch Jamal looking to Chuck's corner after we walked through the handshake line. Like a kid sneaking a peek for approval at someone they're trying to impress. His eyes would catch Chuck's. Chuck would nod. Slowly. Forehead dropping a few inches with his chin. Like Boba Fett giving props to a fellow bounty hunter in Jabba's palace. Jamal never nodded back, but he always looked at Chuck when he played well.

Maybe their bond is Chuck's guilt. Maybe Chuck respects the fact that his punch couldn't touch Jamal's soul. Maybe he respects that Jamal never plays the victim card and rises to his feet every time he goes down. I hope Chuck sees me like that too. I'll probably never know. I do know this—in so many ways, I'm no Jamal. He's the best of all of us.

The closest we've come to talking about the last Saturday Fight Day was when I was bitching about how much it pissed me off that Jennie never apologizes for shit.

Jamal looked me in the eye and said, "Ya know, the hardest thing to do is forgive someone who ain't ever gonna ask for it."

Jamal paused. I waited.

"But dammit B, if you do… you feel better. You can get on. Shit ain't on you no more."

And we left it at that, but I have a hard time letting go of stuff like Jamal does. I can't forgive without apologies, even if only for my own good. Maybe I'm a product of my environment. You gotta repent to get back in my good graces.

Ω

Last week was the State Championship game. Jamal was in the stands rooting for us. The game was a blur, but I remember the pre-game vividly.

I sat in a big wooden locker in the bowels of the Nashville Civic Center. Headphones on. The Prodigy. "Smack My Bitch Up" always gets me hype. My stomach was in knots. I don't remember being nervous for many games. But this one, the last game of my high school career, win or lose, was the culmination of everything I'd worked for. My obsession with basketball is a vital part of who I am. I love the crowds, my teammates, my coach, but most of all, I love each second of every game. The ride would be over that night. I closed my eyes. Time seemed to stop as I visualized the best moments of my career.

The work I'd put in to become one of the best players in the state.

The tears in the locker room after last year's state semi-final heartbreak. And all the tough losses that drove me to push harder.

The good and bad times with Coach.

My teammates—the high fives, the smiles, and the chest bumps during our celebrations after we made big plays in the Den.

Swinging my fist in celebration toward a standing, deafening capacity crowd after making a three-point shot in the final seconds of a close tournament game.

I saw Jamal grabbing me by the jersey my sophomore year and yelling, "We need you, it's your time B, you got this."

Going through warmups with one side of my face beat red because Deric would give me the full force of his open-handed palm before every game to pump me up. A little pain has always had a motivational effect on me.

As I relived my career, I heard a violent hacking coming from a stall in the bathroom.

"Damn, Joe. What's wrong with you?" Deric said.

Joe walked out of the stall, splashed some water from the sink on his face, then cupped his hand to his mouth, swished it around inside his cheeks, gargled, and spit.

"We all do our own thing," he said as he wiped the side of his mouth and sat in a locker next to me. "You dance like a fool and kick out the jams. Jesse sits there like a monk for a half hour, then gets slapped in the face and turns into a demon. I yack." Joe was right on the money.

"You're stupid, man," Deric said.

Jamal's words came out of Joe's mouth. "To each his own right?"

"Word," I said as Coach walked in and gave the most inspirational pre-game speech he'd ever given.

We exploded into cheers, then gathered around our coach in a huddle. 12 fists raised as one.

"In 20 minutes, you'll take the floor together one last time. Just know before you go out there…"

He paused.

"No matter what happens, I love coaching you guys."

"1-2-3…"

"WOLVES."

"DO WHAT?"

"EAT."

chapter: 18

IN APRIL 1999, she had a good idea of what was going on but didn't want to ask. Her mom cried all the time, but when Jennie walked into the kitchen in the mornings, Susan Rizzo shuffled around, got all perky, and tried to cook her breakfast like Jennie wouldn't notice her raccoon eyes.[Ω]

Susan was beautiful—Jennie knew this as a fact and was thankful for the genes she'd inherited. Her mom had never let her daughter see her unkempt like she had the last few months. Susan looked older because the story she was living deepened the lines on her face. She watched romantic movies and cried on the couch most nights after Jennie went to bed. Some days, Jennie considered asking, but she knew the truth was as frightening as it would be depressing. So she bit her tongue. And they played house. Just the two of them.

Four months before, they had promoted Don Rizzo to Southeast Regional Manager of Banksy's Auto Parts, and he started "working longer hours." After Christmas, things got strange. Don got strange. Don went out to get some strange. A lot.

[Ω] The sum of tears and mascara.

Don and Susan rarely spoke to each other in front of Jennie after that last merry Christmas in the Rizzo house. But some nights, when it was very late, they yelled things at each other downstairs—awful things. But Jennie never left her room. She'd put her headphones on and battle her tears. Some nights, household items were thrown down there. Most nights, her tears won. All nights, she felt lost.

The once commonplace Rizzo family dinners had gone extinct after Christmas. The delivery guy for Best China Restaurant knew all the shortcuts to the house.

On the last day of March, Jennie leaned into her bathroom mirror and opened her eyes wide while she used a tiny blue pair of tweezers to pluck her eyebrows. She put the tweezers on the sink, turned around at the waist, and got on her tip toes. She thought her butt was getting bigger, but was undecided on whether that was a good thing. Even though she'd just inhaled a box of fried rice, orange chicken, and two egg rolls by herself in her room, she settled on her backside looking just fine.

Then the yelling started again. She considered going down there and turning the tables by yelling and throwing shit herself. Then she thought if she went down there and contributed to the chaos, maybe her mom would spill the beans in a rage, and she'd find out why her dad wasn't home much, and why he quit going to church, and why he seemed to be quitting on them.

It was too much.

She went back to her room, slammed the door, put her headphones on and tried to fall asleep before the crying started again. Then the front door slammed, and Don drove away. This time, he didn't come back.

A week later, she hated him because she loved him more than anyone in the world. He vanished and wasn't answering her calls. He once played dolls with her. Then she grew out of playing with dolls, so they played outside together, and he even built her a tree house. When that got old, the family went on walks around the neighborhood and asked about each other's days. Until about four months ago, when the dolls had long since gone to Goodwill and the tree house had been condemned, he'd watch her favorite shows with her, even the lamer ones like *Dawson's Creek*. He knew all the character's dreams and desires as well as she did and didn't even make fun of James Van Der Beek when he cried. Truth be told—he hated that show but loved her.

She used to think, *I'll marry someone just like my Dad.*

"I'm his daughter for Chrissakes. What kind of man just leaves with no explanation? This is not him! What did you do?" she asked her mom.

"He'll be back. We'll get through this. It's nothing you need to worry about."

"But it is, Mom. Our family is falling apart?" Jennie started weeping. Her mom started weeping. They wept together.

When the sobs softened to sniffles, she asked, "Are ya'll getting divorced?"

"We're not getting divorced. Marriages are hard, and sometimes couples just have to get through stuff."

The same moment Susan said those words to her daughter, Don was in a hotel in Jacksonville, Florida, fucking a stranger he met in a bar.

Susan told Jennie they needed to trust Jesus, and he'd get them through the hard times. Jennie had always believed that, but was having a real hard time with it now.

Sometimes, you find out what people really believe when their life implodes as if it swallowed a live grenade.

Sometimes, you find out how crazy people *can be* when the emotion of the day trumps rationality. People ruled by the emotion of the day tend to hang out with some odd, odd thoughts.

Sometimes, people cling to hope until their knuckles turn white, and find strength somewhere, impossible as it seems, to keep holding on.

Sometimes, you find out that someone just doesn't give a fuck anymore.

Don stopped giving fucks.

Susan rivaled Sly with her ability to hang from cliffs.

Jennie wondered where Jesus was and asked Him every night and every morning, every lunch and every dinner, and randomly throughout the day to make her dad come back. The only answer she could hear was reality saying, *Tough shit, girl.*

Her Dad, the best person she knew, her hero, walked right out the front door with no goodbye or shred of hope that he might come back. His car was gone. The *his* piece of their *his and her* luggage was gone. Half his books were gone. His favorite suit—she snuck into their room and looked in their closet—gone too.

Susan still bought Diet Cokes at Bi-Lo every week, even though nobody in the house drank them but Don. A stack of 12-packs nearly reached the pantry ceiling.

Jennie would peek out her window twice an hour when she was in her room, but she stayed home less and less. Nobody wants to live in a sad house.

Jesse Baker made her feel better most of the time. It wasn't the comforting words he said—he wasn't great at comforting words, and he knew this, so he wouldn't try. It was the time he spent with her and the way he looked at her that was a welcome distraction. She had fun with him.

After a tussle with temporary insanity and self-loathing, she broke up with him on a Friday in early April. But he came over to her house the next day and insisted they hang out. He said he could never stay at home on Saturdays.

They went on a walk, then he took her to the movies, then they ate at Waffle House, then they made out on her back porch while listening to a CD of Dave Matthews playing a concert at Luther College. It was a lovely day. When she was with him, she could forget.

Jesse asked her to the Junior-Senior Formal Banquet in early May. It was the Christian school version of prom. There was no dancing, not even the kind of dancing that left room for Jesus. They just ate and took pictures and received a spiritual challenge from a special speaker.

Jennie put on her dress and tried to get pretty. Real pretty. She wanted to try harder than she normally did. Any human being on planet earth—straight, lesbian, gay, bi, asexual, pansexual, queer, non-denominational—could see her in no makeup and overalls and tell you she was a knockout. But that night, she went for shock value.

She hoped her Mom did something about those raccoon eyes before picture time. They were back when Susan served her breakfast that morning.

Susan answered the door when Jesse knocked. No raccoon eyes. She was beautiful. Deric once said, "If you wanna know what a girl is gonna look like in twenty-five years, look at her mom." Jesse never forgot this, and that day, he officially decided that Jennie was the "marrying" kind.

He waited patiently for her in the foyer while Susan scrambled for the camera. When Jennie's heel clicked on the first hardwood stair, Jesse looked up and watched her every step with a big smile plastered across his face.

chapter: 19

The Life and Times of Jesse "Take-All-Comers" Baker
By Jesse Baker
October 15, 1999

AFTER WINNING our second state championship in three years, high school basketball ended for the rest of *The 4-Pack*. It's time to move on.

Joe's going to the local community college to study business.

Deric didn't get to walk at graduation because he got kicked out of school the day before. We had finished our final exams and only had one more day left—senior dress-down day. It was a day where we'd pack all our shit and said our goodbyes. We got to wear T-shirts and sweat pants instead of the usual collared shirts and jeans. Deric took it a bit too literal. Can't tell Deric Harris he can dress down—jackass showed up in nothing but a jock strap and Jordan's. At least he still got his diploma. He just got a job working at a pawn shop and registered for a few classes at the community college. I'll be shocked if he goes to class.

The big surprise, to me, was that Jennie enrolled in Upton Park Christian College. I guess she probably just figured that college was the next natural step in her life, and UPCC was the most convenient option. And she got some special scholarship since her Dad used to be the head deacon at the church.

Jamal is poised to make his Division 1 debut.

I accepted a basketball scholarship at Calvin Newman—a Division 2 school a hundred miles up I-75. Close enough to stop in and check on Mom and Chuck and my old classmates from time to time. We all have all gone our separate ways, but we haven't gone far. And before my basketball season got underway, I went home for the weekend during fall break.

Jamal has been living the college lifestyle for last two years. He's still as serious about basketball as he ever was, but he parties his ass off on weekends. The rest of us, sans Jennie, have found our college freedom exhilarating too. No more rules. No more deans or pastors to answer to. No more guilt inducing chapels or church services. We never put any thought into it. It just happened naturally. We've all broken free of our conservative Christian chains and taken heed to Prince's advice. I mean, hell, it is, after all, 1999.

Joe has moved out of his parent's place and into a three-bedroom house at the foot of the mountain. It's off the road and solitary. The ultimate college party shack. He runs a poker game in the house three nights a week. He doesn't even take a rake.

He is the rake.[Ω]

The stakes are higher now. $200 buy-ins with un-limited re-buys. I couldn't wait to get into one of these games when I got back in town. Joe's housemate is an ex-Upton Park Christian Wolf too. His name is Bobby Corban. Yeah, the same guy that got kicked out for smoking. Bobby recently dropped out of college and works with Deric at the Pawn Shop. He just turned 21 and spends every dime he makes on alcohol and weed.

Joe planned our fall break reunion party last week. He knew everyone was ready to fucking party, so he took it upon himself to be the DJ for the first unified breakout from our repressed youth. He was pumped. His counter tops were covered with bottles of every liquor you can imagine.

I couldn't wait to get there. I'd been at practice all week as our team was getting ready for our home opener. Fortunately, we got the weekend off, so I sped down I-75 like the party was starting without me. When I pulled into the gravel driveway, I could hear that it had.

Master P was telling fools to bounce and asking them if they were about it. I love that song. I love Master P. And even though I don't know what *it* is I'm supposed to be about, I'm still about it. Honestly, I woulda loved any song that was rocking this house and will love it for the rest of my life.

[Ω] A rake is a stick with long teeth that closet pyromaniacs use in the fall to start fires in their front yards. Ever since the Timmy incident, I've become one of these closet pyros obsessed with fire. I got tons of party tricks. Burned the fuck out of my hand a few times. Anyway, a rake is also a piece of each pot in a poker game that the house takes for its time.

When I walked in the door. The new drinkers—the freshman—went ape shit and started hugging me. I've noticed alcohol elevates the impulse to hug. I don't like being hugged, but whatever.

The more experienced drinker in the house played it cooler. Jamal sat on the couch with a smile on his face and a beer in his hand. After the hugs, he stood.

"My boy Bakes."

"Haaarrrrhhh." I try to make my voice sound like the roar of a capacity crowd when I see him. It just feels like crowd noise is appropriate since he has that effect on the masses who pack the gyms to watch him compete. So why not in walkin' around life too?

Jamal wore mirror aviator sunglasses and curvy rows in his hair like Allen Iverson. I wore a tight vintage brown leather jacket and messed my hair up like Tyler Durden. I guess the world is projecting now. Pastor Joel would brick if he saw us.

Almost everyone was there. Deric, Jamal, Bobby, some other kids from high school, and even some layup line girls. But the most important person was missing—Jennie. I had looked forward to seeing her, but no dice. She didn't answer my calls. Fuck it. I was ready to get sloshed.

"Who's up for some shots?" Bobby shouted over the bass beats and conversations.

Without hesitation, we voiced our approval.

After a blurry night of hard drinking, I woke up wearing Jamal's sunglasses on the couch. My head felt like a medicine ball, and lack of depth perception caused me to trip over the bodies scattered across the floor. The living room looked like Jonestown the morning after. I'd never been that drunk.

I've found in my limited experience that I can't sleep late after drinking any amount of alcohol. I made my way to the kitchen and opened the fridge to grab a bottle of water. A cold sweat felt sticky on my body. I pulled out a fresh bottle, twisted the top, and started guzzling. When I brought the bottle down from my lips, water dripping down my chin, I looked at the clock on the microwave. 7:13. I felt queasy. I knew it was coming.

I threw up a little in my mouth as I ran for the door, not wanting anyone to think I was the pussy puking in the bathroom. Every one probably threw up that morning, but I had to try to be better. I made it outside to my car and sprayed the chunky gut smoothie trapped in my puffed-out cheeks. Projectile vomiting next to the driver's side door of my car. Spitting three or four times between every contraction. Shit hurt.

Deric, who had passed out in a pile of black trash bags by the road, rolled over and said, "Nasty, bruh. Fuckin' lightweight ass," he shifted around on the stinky bags and closed his eyes.

You shoulda seen my driver's side door with chunks and stomach acid and hot beer on it. I chuckled and spit again and thought of my college art class.

A truer portrait of a college freshman had never been painted, and there it was: Abstract art—a stage of life splattered across a metallic blue paint job.

chapter: 20

JENNIE'S FIRST SEMESTER of college was almost a wrap, and she didn't feel good about the things she had done. In fact, since her dad had left her mom and Jesse had left for college, she hadn't felt good about much of anything. But she never felt more alone than she did in the dorms of Upton Park Christian College.

Even though she lived in the city and could have easily commuted to school, she chose to stay in those dorms because there was a cloud of sadness permanently hovering over the Rizzo house. Jennie couldn't take it anymore. She moved on a Friday in late August. Her assigned roommate's name was Rebekah. She wanted to be called Becky.

Becky was from a small Christian School in Macon, Georgia called Tabernacle Baptist. There were a baker's dozen graduating seniors in her class. She had never kissed a boy, been to a movie theater, drank a wine cooler, or worn pants.

During the first month of school, Jennie introduced Becky to the world. They would go out around 9:30 at night, pick up some wine coolers and American Spirit cigarettes, and sit on the rocks by the

Tennessee River, drinking, smoking, and listening to Jennie's boombox. She introduced Becky to Dave Matthews, Keith Sweat, Matchbox Twenty, Jewel, and Alanis Morissette—all the most accessible, radio-friendly albums in her CD case.

Becky seemed nervous the first time they went to the riverfront, and Jennie was a little concerned Becky might rat her out to an RA. But every time a hip-hop beat hit Becky's ears, or she coughed as if the Spirit was a blunt, or swished the sweetness of Seagram's strawberry around in her mouth before she swallowed it, this naïve girl from middle Georgia felt on fire and loved every second. She felt dangerous.[Ω]

At UPCC, you'd find yourself in big trouble if an RA was made aware of this sort of tomfoolery. Smaller offenses would get you demerits, and if you racked up enough, you could get campus'ed. That meant you weren't allowed off campus, for any reason, for an allotted period of time based on the nature of your offense, like a prison sentence for a Christian college student.

For the young women, the smaller offenses were things like wearing a skirt that was too short, being ten minutes late for curfew, or being caught with a

---

[Ω] There are tiers of extremity when it comes to fundamental Baptists. Some (like Upton Park's Christian high school) are conveniently pragmatic about things like sports, so they played against mostly public schools. This meant the kids wouldn't be as sheltered because they had a few public school friends. Then there were the cult-like schools. Most of their students never met a kid from a public school. Their church leadership took great lengths to ensure that their children were neither in the world, nor of the world. Becky's family attended the latter, so did Nick Jackson's. Since the majority of Upton Park Christian College's student body went to Christian schools like that, they abided by similar legalistic, cultish codes.

worldly[Ω] CD during room inspection. Jennie always kept her CD case under the driver's seat of her car or in her underwear drawer in her room. She was very careful, but one day she slipped up and left Creed's *My Own Prison* in her Discman. Her RA found it, confiscated the CD, and wrote her up for fifteen demerits. Sixty more, and she'd be campus'ed.

Larger offenses were things like cheating, lying on off-campus permission slips, skipping church services, or consistently breaking curfew. Those would get you insta-campus'ed.

The greatest offenses would get you suspended for the semester or permanently expelled. It was stuff like smoking, alcohol, drugs, or pre-marital sex.

It was important to the administration at UPCC that the students remained as children, unallowed to make their own decisions, confined to the bubble, protected under the wing of the mother. They could never be treated as young adults. They couldn't be trusted.

Church isn't much different. Sheep must stay as stupid sheep—under the ever-watchful eye of the shepherd.

Becky didn't handle her alcohol very well. Jennie wasn't a pro either, by any means, but she was responsible enough to give them a fighting shot at getting away with it. By mid-September, they were drinking Natural Light and smoking weed Jennie had bought from Bobby. They always made it back for curfew though and went light on the Tuesday nights they had second-floor prayer group.

[Ω] Secular

The last Friday in September, Bobby asked Jennie if they wanted to go to his fraternity party at UT-Chattanooga. He told her to bring a friend, and she brought Becky. They filled out overnight off-campus permission slips that claimed they'd be staying at the Rizzo house.

The frat house was packed, the music was loud, and inhibitions were minimal. Jennie and Becky took shots, smoked weed, and did whippets for the first time. In the morning, Jennie woke up hungover in her underwear in a bed next to Bobby. She didn't remember much that had happened after midnight.

Bobby didn't wake up when Jennie gathered her clothes. When she opened the bedroom door to leave, she looked back. Bobby was passed out on his belly with a wet circle on the bed below the corner of his mouth, which was open so wide she could have put a cucumber in it without the vegetable touching his lips. One of his arms hung off the bed, and one of his legs was wrapped in the sheet while the other was sprawled across the side where she'd slept. He looked like a giant starfish with a hairy ass. She was disgusted. She made for the bathroom and held her hair back with one hand while grabbing the toilet seat with the other.

She searched the rooms of the frat house until she found Becky on the floor sleeping topless beside two guys neither of them had known before that night.

"Becky wake up. We gotta go."

Becky groaned. Jennie looked for Becky's clothes and found what she thought were her jeans. She wasn't sure but didn't care. She helped Becky put them on and gave her a Disturbed T-shirt she found on a desk in the room. They got in Jennie's car and left for the

Rizzo house. Becky slept during the twenty-two-minute drive, only waking up once to open the car door and puke at a stop light.

Becky left her bra and top by the hot tub on the frat house deck. Jennie left her virginity in Bobby's room.

Ω

Jennie and Becky kept their same routine into second semester. They'd come back to the dorms slightly drunk and a little high, but right on time for curfew or prayer groups, and never so fucked up that they'd get busted. The RAs and prayer group leaders had no experience with people who were tipsy and just thought they were silly freshman girls who giggled more when they got tired. They went through droppers of Visine and packs of spearmint gum faster than anyone in the college's fifty-year history.

The parties were their Friday night thing. They looked forward to them all week. Jennie wouldn't let Bobby touch her anymore because he grossed her out, but she tended to get horny when she was drunk and occasionally fucked guys who gave her some attention. She felt immense guilt every time she did it, and told herself she wouldn't do it again, but she did. A guy never got to fuck her more than once though, because she always thought he was gross after the deed was done.

By March, Jennie was re-evaluating her life choices. She despised school and was failing all of her classes. Her major was Elementary Education. After almost two semesters, she'd realized that spending her adult days in a classroom full of dirty-faced little brats was the last thing she wanted. The college party life wasn't all it was cracked up to be either. She was over the highs, sick of the hangovers, tired of using guys, and numb from being used. She was lonely and wanted a change.

The frat party on the last Friday in March was the final nail in the coffin. A phone call around 1:45 p.m. woke Jennie up. She should have been sitting in a desk taking notes during her last class of the day, but she was asleep in her bed. She never went to class anymore. There was no point. Two big naps a day filled in. She'd never slept so much in her life. She blinked her eyes twice to clear out the floaters and flipped her phone open.

Incoming call…

Mom

Her mom was balling on the other line. She asked Jennie to come home and talk to her. When Jennie asked what was wrong, she just said she loved her and needed her to come home. Jennie showered and rushed over.

When Jennie got there, she found her mom weeping on the couch. A quarter-full glass of red wine (which was quite the shock to Jennie), a pyramid of tissues, and scattered documents lay across the coffee table.

Jennie sat beside her and put her arm around her mother. Susan hugged her tightly, burying her face in her daughter's shoulder. Jennie didn't speak. She just held her mother and cried with her. She knew her father wasn't coming back.

When Susan let go, she fumbled with a few papers and said, "Got these in the mail today."

"I guess Dad filed, huh."

"Yep."

Jennie rubbed her Mom's back while Susan pulled another tissue from the box in the corner of the couch and blew her nose.

"I don't know what I'm going to do," Susan said. Her lips pressed tightly against each other and trembled.

Jennie looked into her eyes and, for the first time, saw what a real broken heart looked like. There was a desperation in them, a deep sadness for years of love and loyalty that felt like they'd been thrown away like the carcass of a roadkill deer. Once so alive and vibrant, only to be hit by a Freightliner truck driven by a guy with poor reaction speed on a Red Bull crash. Now twisted with shiny red guts stuck to the concrete and legs stiffened with rigor mortis, hours away from being scooped off the road and wiped from the face of the living earth.

"We'll figure it out, Mom."

"Can you stay with me for a while?"

"Sure."

Knowing she wouldn't be alone, even if only for a few hours, made Susan feel better.

"Thanks sweetie—hang on one second," Susan said as she popped up and walked into the kitchen. Jennie picked up the wine glass, downed what was left and shuffled through the papers. Seconds later, Susan walked back in the room with a full bottle of Pinot Noir and an extra glass.

"Mom!"

"What? You won't have some wine with me?"

"Since when did you start drinking?"

"When do you think? I did always want to try it." Then she whispered, "Don't tell your dad."

They chuckled. Then drank wine, laughed, cried, drank more wine, laughed more, and cried more. Around 8:00 p.m., they ordered Chinese and snuggled under a blanket to watch one of their favorite movies—*My Fair Lady* with Audrey Hepburn.

Even in the worst of circumstances, people can share a moment that may become one of their fondest memories.

By the time the delivery guy from Best China Restaurant rang the doorbell, Susan was fast asleep. Jennie paid for it with money from Susan's purse. She ate General Tso's chicken, hot and sour soup, and an egg roll while her Mom snored. When she was full, she put Susan's food in the refrigerator and sat back down to finish the movie. As the credits rolled, her phone rang. She flipped it open and walked into the kitchen.

Incoming call...

Becky

"Hey."

"What up, girl? It's Becks."

She was Becks now.

"What's goin' on?"

"Are you comin' to the party or what?"

Jennie heard the music in the background. It was 11:00 p.m., and they were already playing Eazy-E. That rarely happened until after one.

"I don't think so tonight," Jennie said.

"Ah, come on. You should really be here. All the guys said they miss ya."

"Yeah whatever. I'm sure there are plenty of girls over there."

"No. There ain't. I'm like... the only girl here."

"What? How'd you get there?"

"Bobby called me... He picked me up at the dorm."

"Becks, seriously. You should probably get back to the dorm before curfew."

"I'm fi-(hiccup)-ine. All these guys are cool. And I filled out perm for us for your house. So you-you gotta come."

"You could've told me."

"It was last minute. Don't be such a square."

Jennie heard someone yell "Shots" in the background. A chant started. Becky screamed, "Shots! Shots! Shots!" Jennie pulled the phone away from her ear and winced.

"Becky, get Bobby to take you back or call a cab. I'm serious."

The noise continued on Becky's end.

"Becky! Becky!"

"See you in a sec babe," Becky finally responded then she hung up.

Jennie sighed and looked at the floor for a few seconds, then went upstairs to change clothes. When she came back down, she tucked her Mom in on the couch, gave her a kiss on the forehead, and grabbed her purse and keys on the way out the door.

When she got to the frat house, she expected things to be wild but never expected what she saw when she walked in that door. Becky was naked and on all fours on the floor getting banged by Bobby and sucking the dick of some guy Jennie had never seen.

Five other guys were standing around them, watching, laughing, high-fiving, and waiting for their turn.

Jennie ran to pull Becky out of the situation.

"Whoa, Whoa, Whoa," Bobby said.

"What are you doing?" Becky said.

"Getting you out of here," Jennie replied.

"No. I w-wanna stay. You should really loosen up," Becky slurred.

"I think you've loosened up enough for the both of us. Get your stuff."

"What a buzzkillin' bitch," said the random guy Jennie didn't know as he put his dick back in his khakis.

"Shut the fuck up before I call the cops and tell them where all your shit is, and how you get underage girls drunk," Jennie said.

He put his hands up as if she was pointing a gun at his chest and said, "Okay, take it easy."

Then Jennie glared at Bobby while one of the voyeurs helped Becky find her clothes.

"What the fuck is wrong with you?" she said to him.

"It all got a little outta control," Bobby said.

"Ya think?"

Jennie helped Becky put on her clothes and stumble toward the door.

"See ya baby," the tool in the khakis said.

"Bye. Call me," Becky said.

"Fuck all you guys. Fucking go to hell," Jennie said.

Two blocks from the UPCC campus, Jennie stopped in the parking lot of the Good Eats Cafe. Walked to Becky's side of the car and made her get out and make herself puke. Jennie held her hair while Becky violently sprayed all over the pavement and both of their shoes. Then Jennie put her back in the passenger's seat and removed Becky's shoes as Becky laid her head back on the head rest.

"You should've come. That was wild," Becky said.

"I did."

"Yeah... Thank you," Becky said as she closed her eyes.

Jennie popped the trunk, threw their shoes inside, and slammed it.

When they got to the dorm Jennie snuck Becky in by the back stairwell door. They only had to make it up one flight of stairs to get to their room by the stairwell. The task wasn't easy and required some luck, but Jennie got Becky into bed without being seen by anyone. She put her on her side in the small twin bed and placed their big, empty popcorn bowl beside it.

"If you need to throw up again, use this."

"Okay," Becky said as she smacked her lips and closed her eyes.

Jennie turned off the lights and laid down in her bed. It was 11:55pm. She rolled around torturing herself. She worried that the whole year had sucked in ways she'd regret for the rest of her life if she stayed at UPCC. She felt like she couldn't help Becky because in some ways, she helped the devil make her.

The street lights shone through the blinds onto Becky's sleeping silhouette. Jennie thought she looked happy as she rested, at least, jollier. If Jennie had to guess, Becky had gained a good twenty-five pounds that year. Alcohol and late-night munchies have a way of doing that to a freshman girl. Jennie had dodged that bullet though, and for that, she was glad. She looked the same as she did in high school.

The clock said 5:25 a.m. Jennie still hadn't slept. All night she thought about leaving between trips to the bathroom to pour out the popcorn bowl and flush Becky's detox. It had been two hours since the last one. She was sure Becky had gotten through it.

At 5:28, she'd come to a decision. She would pack up and move out of the dorm, withdrawal from school, find a job, and move in with her mom, who probably needed her company more than she'd ever admit. Jennie would scrape her time at Upton Park Christian College off the face of the living earth. There would be no fond memories, there would be no reminiscence, and there would definitely be no sadness. She most certainly did not have the time of her life, so good riddance to the Christian college freshman who didn't know who she was. But at least now she was halfway home because she'd learned who she was not. Now she was ready to move on and try to figure it out. It was a glorious mercy killing.

By 6:35, her car was packed, and she carried her last box down the steps. At 7:00 her mom met her on the front porch. Around noon, Becks woke up with a headache and no roommate.

Ω

It was the last Friday of April, and Jennie had completed her first week of training to be a teller at the Bank of America ten minutes from her house. She sat on the couch, took a deep breath, and enjoyed the thought of officially having a job and doing something that wasn't school. The 6:00 local news was on TV, and she was hypnotized by the screen when her mom walked in the living room.

"I thought about cooking tonight, but decided on takeout Olive Garden instead. That okay?"

"Sounds great, want me to go get it?" Jennie said.

"No, I'll get it. I need to get out of the house, and you've been working all day."

"Training."

"Sounds like work to me."

"Yeah, I guess it's the same," Jennie said as she pulled from her bag a folder that contained more forms she needed to fill out before she officially started work the next Monday.

"I'll be right back. You want fettuccini again?"

"Yes ma'am. Thank you."

Jennie looked through the forms as her mom walked out the door. A few minutes later, the news broke a story.

"An unresponsive baby was rushed from Upton Park Christian College to a local hospital yesterday morning. The baby was later ruled dead, and officials said it may have been stillborn in a dorm room. A resident assistant found the infant hidden under a blanket during a random room check."

Jennie looked up immediately, and her heart dropped to her stomach.

"Chattanooga Police homicide detectives are conducting the investigation and said they have identified the mother of the child as freshman Rebekah Miller, who gave birth, hid the baby, and then went to chapel," the anchor said as they showed a short clip of students walking out of chapel followed by a picture of Becky.

"Dr. Donald Germaine, president of Upton Park Christian College, had this to say,"

No matter what the reason, Dr. Germaine loved being on TV His head filled the whole screen.

"It's with deepest sadness that Upton Park Christian College confirms that one of our freshman students gave birth in her dorm room. We're grateful for the timely actions of the dorm's resident assistant and the quick response of the city police and emergency medical personnel to our campus. We're glad to cooperate fully with the local authorities. We offer our sincere prayers and unconditional love to our student and her family."

He kept going like he always did from the pulpit. Like he did when it was 12:30 on a Sunday, and even the most piously devout of his church members started fidgeting and thinking about how long they'd have to wait in the buffet line at Golden Corral.

"While we regret this heartbreaking incident, our faculty, staff, and student body are rallying around the comfort and strength of God's Word and God's people. Romans 8:28 says that all things work together for good to them that love God, to them that are called according to his purpose, and we know that even in the midst of tragedy, God'll use this for His honor and glory. And He's already begun. Becky's repented of her sins and received Christ as her personal savior late last night, and we praise the Lord for that. But please continue to pray with us and for us. Again, our heart goes out to our student and her family; we love them; we ask God to comfort them in this deepest tragedy."

Jennie couldn't believe the Lincoln Logs of shit coming out of his mouth.

"We'll have more on this tragic story tonight at eleven."

"Tragic indeed," the co-anchor added. "In other news, The Tennessee Department of Transportation has begun construction on..."

Jennie turned off the TV, mortified. *How? How did nobody know she was pregnant? How could I not have seen it?*

The more questions she asked herself the more she realized it wasn't that hard to figure out. *How would anybody know if Becky probably didn't even know herself?* Becky was naïve and clueless when she got to UPCC. She wore maxi pads instead of tampons because her mom had told her that girls shouldn't stick anything up there. The church and school Becky went to made the Upton Park Christian high school look like the University of Florida when it came to strict legalistic standards. She most likely didn't even know what missing her period meant. Jennie imagined Becky's horror that morning, the pain, the birth of a baby she didn't know was there, then the panic. It all came together—the weight gain, the stillbirth, the hiding of the baby and going to chapel—Becky was in a state of shock. An unspeakably traumatic experience. Terrified. She'd be kicked out of school, and her parents would probably disown her. She'd might even be forced to apologize in front of her church and wear the scarlet letter forever.

As much as it hurt to do so, Jennie thought about the clean up—the bloody baby, lifeless in Becky's arms. The wrapping of it in a swaddling towel and lying it in a dresser drawer. She saw a blank expression on Becky's face as if she had detached from the gore, unable to process it. Then she imagined Becky sitting in chapel while a preacher railroaded the student body with rhetoric about Christ's blood being on their hands. She saw tears well in Becky's eyes while they welled up in her own.

Jennie understood, but she didn't. Guilt swarmed her, and her heart broke for her friend. But still, she had euthanized the person she was, and she wasn't going back. Even if she wanted to reach out to Becky, she had no idea how to approach the situation. Becky was on her own.

Jennie knew she needed to keep her distance and stay on her new course. But before she made herself forget, she started sobbing.

chapter: 21

The Life and Times of Jesse "Take-All-Comers" Baker
By Jesse Baker
June 10, 2000

LAST YEAR WAS A BIG YEAR for both me and Jamal at our respective new universities. I earned a starting spot midway through my freshman season at Calvin Newman mostly because I shot the ball well all year. I've figured out one thing about college basketball—if you can shoot, I mean really shoot, you'll get minutes. In my first college game, I knocked down five 3's off the bench. Being an outside threat secured my spot in the rotation.

After the fall break homecoming party at Joe's, I decided not to drink during basketball season because I wanted to stay focused. Compartmentalized substance abuse kept me fully engaged with my mission on the court and my school work while keeping me out of the potential trouble that college party life can bring to an athlete. We ended up with a 23-9 record and won our program's first conference tournament championship in 8 years.

Jamal tore it up too. He started for Tennessee State and put up big numbers in the scoring and rebounding departments. He led the conference in boards. Averaging a just under a double-double per game.

Joe's poker game has gone ham. He told me he makes close to $2,500 a month in his home games alone. He's also started playing online on this site called Paradise Poker and has been practically printing money. I gotta get in on some of that.

Deric's been doing Deric shit. Not a care in the world. He works enough to eat and gets drunk every night. He failed all of his classes last semester.

I found myself thinking about Jennie a lot while I was at college. I heard her dad fell off the family grid right after our high school graduation. I still can't believe Jennie ditched our party earlier this year, but I finally got her to answer her phone a few times. She said things were awful at home, and she didn't wanna talk about it. She's been pretty short in our little catch up conversations. Oh, Don—you old dog you. He must be fuckin' around on Mrs. Rizzo. Crazy man. Mrs. Rizzo is so hot. Jennie said they're getting divorced. I'm sure that's been tough for been.

We broke up when I left for college. It was kind of a mutual break up. We agreed that a long-distance relationship at this stage in our lives wouldn't work. And we didn't want to hold each other back—well, she said that part. I secretly hoped she wouldn't look elsewhere for love. But it's college—who am I kidding? I recently heard she started drinking and hanging out with Bobby at UT-Chatt. Fuck man. The thought of her hooking up with that guy pisses me off.

Since I've been back home for the summer, we've been getting rowdy, but Jennie still won't hang out. She said she's been working a lot. Last week, I asked Deric about Jennie, and if he knew why she hasn't been hanging out, why she hasn't been answering her phone, and what the hell she's been up to. He told me she ain't the same girl she was in high school. So I asked him what the fuck that was supposed to mean. He told me to use my imagination.

Fuck me to goddamn tears.

I kept asking questions like an obsessed investigator. If she's been fucking dudes, I'm gonna need a roster. Why am I so pissed about this? We aren't even together and haven't been for almost a year.

Fuck it—I hope she's lost without me. She should be. If she was trying to fuck? Why couldn't it just be me? All that time. No sex. For what? FUCK!

I tried to move on at college, but I missed her like crazy, and I guess I've found myself lost when it comes to love. I swear I didn't fuck any of 'em though. Just the same old—blowjobs. One girl even asked me if I was gay because I wouldn't fuck. I almost fucked her just to prove it, but I couldn't pull the trigger. I've just always wanted Jennie to be my first, and I still can't bring myself to throw that away. Now I feel like a fucking jackoff. I guess I really must love her.

But I don't understand why she's been avoiding me. Maybe she's afraid that spending time with me will magnify the hurt she feels without me when I go back to college. Maybe after all this shit with her dad, she's jaded about men now. Maybe she doesn't want the pain that might come when she hears about my college hookups. Lord knows, I'm being tortured by imagining the shit she's been doing, but I still gotta find out everything.

Maybe, just maybe, she feels somewhere in her heart that she's betraying me even though we aren't together. Maybe I hope she feels this way because I feel this way every time I get my dick sucked. Maybe I think too much of myself, and she's done with me. I hope not.

Anyway, enough whinging. Joe's house looks different now. It's decked to the nines with neon beer signs, a booming sound system, a 50-inch TV, the sickest canvas painting of *The Dude* you can imagine, and a party patio with tiki torches, an outdoor bar, and a huge grill. It's the perfect bachelor pad.

Each night back in town is the same. Like many things in life, the only difference lives in the details.[Ω] A beer to start, shots to speed things up, a bowl to slow things down, a beer to chill, then a run to Taco Bell for a few Grande Combos, throw them down in the parking lot, go back for more shots, more beers, another bowl, someone pukes,[Ω] and everyone passes out one by one.

Last weekend, it was Krystal for a few sackfuls instead of the Grande combos. Everything tastes the same at 2:00 a.m.—FUCKING GREAT. The way each night is different involves where we eat and the ideas that come to us in the parking lots of fast-food joints. Our ideas usually involved some sort of mayhem. We've always considered ourselves the OGs of late-night mischief because we've been at it a long time and have never been caught.

[Ω] Doesn't the Devil live here too?
[Ω] Usually me. They always said I was a pukin' sumbitch.

I can't believe I've never written about this. When we were in high school, our antics made us anonymously famous around the campus of the Upton Park Triple Threat.[Ω] We raised hell on the place. Starting when Jamal got his driver's license, ours has been the greatest run of pranks the Triple Threat has seen in its 50 years of existence. No one suspects us because they assume it's some repressed Christian college students acting out. And we won't tell a soul. Our actions are for our own amusement. Notoriously unknown, we are pseudo celebrities clothed in ambiguity. Anarchists with no faces or names. Legends.

Ω

The soundtrack to our shenanigans is brought to you by Rage Against the Machine.

Back in the fall of 1998, my junior year in high school, Upton Park Christian College was holding student body elections. Campaign signs hung from buildings all over campus. The god of the Triple Threat, Dr. Donald Germaine, walked right under a massive sign made from two king size bedsheets that hung enormous across the front of the Administration building early one Friday morning. There were so many signs that he didn't even notice it. But as he jingled his keys to open the huge double glass doors, he *did* notice the Crown Vic campus security car parked inside the building right in front of his office door.

"Holy Shinder."

[Ω] Church, high school, and college.

Euphemisms.[Ω]

Preachers that use euphemisms aren't aware what they sound like. They love the sound of their own voice and are used to hearing it all the damn time. They think every word they spit is as audibly orgasmic to others as it is to them. Ignorance can be bliss, right?

A few the common euphemisms used to replace cuss words at the Triple Threat included but by no means are limited to:

Shinder, Shiite, Shins, Shiitake—for Shit.
Helen, Hell's Angels, Help Me—for Hell.
Fun, Fundy, Fudge—for Fuck.
Biscuit Eater, Bidder, Bildad the Shuhite[Ω]—for Bitch.
Asinine, Asterisk, Assiter—for Ass.
Bastard—for Bastard.[Ω]

The car blocked the entry into his office. Spray-painted across the car was a campaign slogan that said the same thing as the double king-sized sheet-sign across the front of the building:

ERECT MIKE OCKENBALLS
4
STUDENT BODY PRESIDENT

[Ω] A euphemism is a word you use when you start to swear, catch yourself, and say something that isn't viewed as profane instead. It means the same thing as a swear, but is designed to keep the Christian conscience clear. The only cost is sounding like a total douchebag hyper-fundy.

[Ω] Dude musta been the shortest motherfucker in the Bible. Sorry, that was totally an IFB pastor joke.

[Ω] For some reason, bastard isn't a swear around here.

Back to the Krystal parking lot last weekend...

"Let's go drop some suds in the church fountain," Jamal said.

So we went to Wal-mart and picked up two giant boxes of Tide washing detergent and made our way to the Upton Park baptist Church to soap that bitch up. If we got it good enough, the suds would be overflowing for church the next day.

Jamal slowed the car, turned off the lights, and backed into an alley a block away from the fountain. He's usually our driver because he can hold his drink the best, and he drinks the least. He just likes to kick it and didn't care so much for the binge. And someone has to be the voice of reason so things don't get out of hand.

The Triple Threat had two campus security guards on patrol 24/7. There was no way these guys could defend our urban campus from actual violence, but thanks to these flashlight-wielding snitches, mayhem always required a well laid out plan. Deric has always thought of himself as the man with that plan. For some reason, most of his plans involve people taking off their clothes.

"All right, here's how this is gonna go down—Joe, you stay in the car with Jamal and help him watch for the security guards. Me and Jesse will strip down to our draws because our skin will be better camouflage than our clothes."

"What the fuck?" Jamal said.

"I'm serious, man. See those little trees in front of the fountain? If they roll by, ya'll tell us on the two-way, and we'll just stand behind 'em. Camo'ed up. They won't be able to see us in the dark."

Me and Joe giggled in the backseat.

"That might be the single stupidest motherfuckin' thing I've ever heard. And I've heard you say some stupid ass shit—those trees branch out waist high. They'll see your draws and legs."

"No... Jamal... They won't. The building behind us is brown. We'll blend right in. I swear," Deric said.

"You're so fucking dumb. You guys good with this?" Jamal asked.

Joe couldn't stop laughing. I nodded with a loud hilch.[Ω]

Me and Deric started taking off our clothes.

"Jamal, you watch down the street toward the fountain. Joe, you watch that way," Deric said, pointing down the block.

"Whatever, man," said Jamal.

Deric took off his pants.

"What... The fuck... Are those?" Jamal said, not cracking a smile.

"What?"

"Are those Thundercat underoos, bro?"

Yes. Deric was wearing Thundercat Fruit of the Loom briefs. White with red lines around the dick holster. Liono with his flaming, gravity defying locks held a sword right where Deric's pork and beans rested. He looked at Jamal like it confused him that

---

[Ω] A Hilch is the start of a hiccup and the end of a belch. Perfectly seamed together resulting in a sound that is a product of the bodily functions of someone righteously fucked up.

Jamal thought it was odd that he was wearing Thundercat underoos.

"You can't wear motherfuckin' Thundercat draws, man. You ain't gonna blend in with shit."

"Okay." Deric started to take off his undies. Jamal stopped him.

"Oh, hell naw! I ain't 'bout to be havin' your bare ball sweat on my seat... Out!"

Deric got out and took off his skivvies and threw them right in Jamal's face.

"The fuck? I'ma kill you," Jamal said as he pinched the briefs and tossed them on the passenger floorboard.

Jamal popped the trunk, and Deric stood there stark naked beside me. We each grabbed our box of soap. I clipped my flip phone that would double as a two-way radio to the back of my boxers. We walked toward the fountain—me in black boxer shorts, and Deric naked as a hippie in Woodstock mud. Like a pit bull trotting around at the Westminster Kennel Club dog show—nutsack swinging between its legs for a sleepy national TV audience. Jamal and Joe stayed out of sight in the alley down the block and, no doubt, couldn't stop laughing at the sight of Deric's bare ass streaking down the road.

Upon arrival, I tipped my box into the fountain, grabbed my phone, and said into the two-way,

Chh... "The eagle has landed." Chh...

Chh... "That's a big ten-four." Chh...

Joe replied. I could hear Jamal laughing in the background.

Chh... "Guys, we got company comin' back here." Chh...

Chh... "Security two blocks away. Hurry up." Chh...

"Hurry, Deric. Security's comin'. Just dump it," I said.

Nope. Deric had to spread it perfectly even around the fountain to make sure the suds would become what he'd envisioned. A fluffy water volcano. He just had to have an obese, human-size cluster of bubbles floating down the street to greet the church goers the next morning.

The security car was only a few hundred feet away when Joe said over the two-way, Chh... "He's on you. Hide... NOW!" Chh...

"C'mon!" I said from my spot behind the tree. Deric sprinted beside me. He still held his box.

"Just stand still. He won't see us," Deric said.

The car pulled over, its lights shining directly at our tree beside the fountain. Seconds later, the low beams turned to high beams.

"He sees us," I said.

"No, he doesn't. Just shut up and stay still."

Deric stood like a statue. Holding the box of Tide at his waist with his limp dong hanging underneath it. The security car stayed there for three minutes. I was sure he was calling the cops to bring in some back up.

"I'm gonna make a run for it," I whispered.

"No. Just wait. There's still a chance he don't see us."

Right at that moment, the security car backed out and headed down the street.

"See I knew it. Camo baby."

When security was out of sight, I ran for the car. I wasn't waiting for Jamal to come get us. I let out a big sigh when I sat in the back seat and slammed the car door.

"Jesus H. Christ," Jamal said.

I looked up and saw Deric meticulously dumping the rest of his box in the fountain.

There's a chance the security guard really didn't see us. Or maybe he did but didn't know how to explain the situation to backup.

Maybe the lights and the plants made him think he was seeing some sort of unexplainable apparition. A supernatural phenomenon—a levitating box of Tide with a dangling penis.

Or maybe, just maybe, he decided a naked foot pursuit wouldn't be worth it.

Ω

We didn't always look for mayhem. Usually we just bullshitted and laughed with red eyes and good moods. Like last night at Taco Bell. Joe had bean burrito cheese hanging from his chin. He was sitting shotgun this time.

"You gonna eat that?" Jamal said as he pointed at Joe's face.

"Na, I was savin' it for the birds," Joe said as he wiped his chin. Then he put the stray cheese on the last bite of his burrito and tossed it out the window next to a night bird bouncing around by the car.

I watched the bird pick at it. "Birds piss me off."

"I think I jack off too much," Deric interjected, chewing a mouthful of Mexican pizza.

We looked at him, amused.

"Well, that was random," Jamal said.

"How much y'all jack off?" Deric asked.

"That depends on how much action I'm gettin'—I don't know—once or twice a week," Jamal said.

"What about y'all?"

"Bout the same," I said.

"Probably three times a week," Joe said.

"Damn," Deric said.

"You?" I asked.

"Well... I can't remember a day in my life that I haven't jacked off."

There was a second of silence as we processed the bomb that was just dropped on us.

"What? No fu-hu-cking way." Jamal laughed hysterically.

I couldn't breathe. Deric looked embarrassed and wanted to change the subject, "Fucking those birds man," he said.

"So you jackin' off every day and fuckin' birds? You're a sick fuck."

"No... you know what I mean... fuck 'em."

After we finished off the Grande Combo, we went back to Joe's and sat on the couches and watched some televangelist selling miracle spring water on the *Praise the Lord* channel. I can't look away when evangelists are being assholes. It's like a drug. I love it and hate it. I love to hate it.

"Y'all ever wonder if it's all bullshit?" I asked the guys while we watched the double-breasted used car salesman on TV.

"I'm pretty sure *this* is," Joe said.

"If it ain't, I'm getting' me some of that water. My knees been fuckin' hurtin'," Jamal said.

"I can't believe people actually send money to this guy," I said.

Joe and Deric eventually passed out. Me and Jamal decided to hit the bowl one more time. I walked onto the back patio, pulled *Dark Side of the Moon* by Pink Floyd from Joe's CD case, put it on the outdoor boom box, and lit a fire in the pit on the porch while I waited for Jamal to bring out that real fire.

"This shit's right, B," Jamal said as he lit up the bowl, inhaled, and held his breath. Smoke floated out of Jamal's nose and mouth as he passed me the bowl. He looks like such a pro when he smokes.

I hadn't smoked bud in like a month and am not a habitual smoker.

I brought the bowl to my lips, anticipating the burning in my lungs that triggers violent coughing. The last time I smoked, I coughed into the bowl right away, blowing out all the weed. That was embarrassing. I didn't wanna be that guy again, so I inhaled slowly and held it in for as long as my lungs would let me.

When the alarm clocks started ringing in Pink Floyd's song "Time," I was feelin' right—tingling from head to toe, especially my head. When I smoke marijuana, sometimes that tingling inspires me to wax philosophical.

Me and Jamal started arguing about birds and whether their ability to fly was wasted. Jamal said no because they are free to go wherever they want, so good for them.

I said yes, because they're stupid. Even though they could go wherever they want, they just jump around in dirty puddles and shit. It's a waste.

Jamal asked how I *knew* anything about them, and if I *knew* for sure I'd ever seen one jumping around in same puddle twice. I had no answer for that.

I still wonder though... To be great at one thing, do you have to be shit at something else? Like give and take—balance and all that. Like birds have the ultimate physical advantage, but it's balanced by their stupidity and small ass brains.

I sat there for a second still thinking about the birds, and why I felt compelled to judge them. Then I thought about that televangelist, and how he was feeding heaping tablespoons of shit to stupid, desperate people. And why I felt compelled to judge him.

The spoon I'd been fed from as a kid has been rusty for a long time. I don't even use it anymore, and my feelings about church have turned bitter.

I wonder if men become gods to their congregations and in their own minds because humans can't see God, so we feel the need to make Him tangible, and this leads to the deification of church leaders in denominations like ours. I'm thinking if your faith relies on men, if hope isn't lost, it's soon to be. The food you eat from your tangible god eventually tastes like piss.

I hate church. I might never darken the door again.

We could hear coyotes yipping in the woods as a breeze blew through the leaves on the trees, making a constant swishing sound. We soaked in the music and took another hit from the bowl. The smoke moved like a serpent in an ancient garden, slowly disintegrating in the humid air—the perfect imagery to pair with the aria coming from the boombox. This is my church right here.

chapter: 22

The Life and Times of Jesse "Take-All-Comers" Baker
By Jesse Baker
June 12, 2000

THIS YEAR, I'm gonna own souls. Me and Jamal have been workin' our asses off. He led the conference in rebounding last year, but next year he wants to lead the nation and take TSU to the big dance. I was named to the All-Conference Freshman team this year and plan on being first-team All-Conference next year. Plus, I'm gonna get another league championship.

Being back is nice. Coach Watts gave us the key to the Den again, saying he likes having us back in his gym. He uses us as examples to his current players, showing the young Wolves what real determination looks like and how it can take your game to heights you never imagined.

Joe invested some of his poker winnings in a duplex. He just closed on it and hooked me and Jamal up for a low rent until school starts, as long as we help him get it ready for local college students to live in during the school year. It's only for a little less than two months, but I'm officially out of Chuck's house. Damn that feels good.

$$\Omega$$

Yesterday I went to get the rest of my stuff from Mom and Chuck's...

"Oh, hey baby. Come give your momma a hug. I missed you so much."

"Hi Mom. I missed you too. Hey Dad."

Chuck read the newspaper, sitting in his favorite chair, still wearing his coveralls. Those coveralls are disgusting, and so is that chair. It's older than me and has that scratchy material with buttons that dig in your back if you sit the wrong way. Chuck never sits the wrong way because there's this perma-Chuck silhouette where the inside of the chair has shaped to his body. He can get it to recline in one pull. When I was a little kid, I'd rock back and forth trying to pull it but to no avail. It even smells like his coveralls—metal, oil, and bad breath.

"Hey, boy. Been gettin' in the gym? Ya'll gotta go all the way next year."

I was surprised to hear Chuck sound so encouraging. Maybe he missed me. Maybe he was getting soft in his old age. Or maybe it was his servicing night, so he was in a good mood—fuck me.

"Yeah, we've been gettin' after it."

"Why don't you stay for dinner?" Mom said.

"I can't. Just came by to say hi and get some stuff for the apartment."

"Ah, you don't wanna spend a little time with us? I'm making your favorite... Spaghetti Bolognese," she said as she walked backwards into the kitchen.

"I'm good Mom. I gotta get set up over there."

"Suit yourself. I'll make you some to take with you though. Ya'll have a microwave right?"

"We're two single guys living in an apartment. Of course, we have a microwave."

Chuck snickered but didn't put down his paper. I sat on the couch to try to start a conversation with him. But conversations with my dad feel like work. And they usually lead into some angry Chuck rant about how democrats are trying to lead our country right through the gates of hell or some similar Chuck shit.

Ω

If you think Chuck's crazy, you should meet his brother Frank. I met him only once—when I was 9. It was somewhere in Mississippi and was the only Thanksgiving we've ever spent with Chuck's extended family.

Our ultra-conservative Christian crew sat around an incredible spread. Pot Roast, turkey, mashed potatoes, like 56 casseroles, cranberry sauce, dinner rolls, and Bagel Bites. Frank blessed the food with one of the most heart-felt Republican prayers I've ever heard. Then a web of conversation covered the table. I didn't get to sit at the adult table, but the kids table was close enough for me to eavesdrop.

I didn't know most of these people, yet somehow, we had the same blood. I wanted to listen and learn all

I could about them. Randomly, Frank announced that they were leaving their church and looking for a new one because of their recent missionary conference. Their church was sending a young missionary couple to Africa, and Frank just couldn't get behind that. He said something I didn't understand at the time.

"They lost me at sendin' them missionaries to Africa. How you gonna save a nigger? Such a waste."

My Grammy said, "Mmm." Like she agreed... Wait... Nah... Like she was enjoying her meal. Everyone got quiet—as is customary when conversations get weird around a table. Everyone puts their heads down and clinks their silverware on their plate before they stuff their faces. One person might try to direct the table talk back to the food. It's usually the matriarch of the family. At least that's how it's always been in my house when Chuck makes family dinners awkward. I stared at them because I thought it was weird that they all shut up at the same time.

"This may be the best sweet potato casserole I've ever had, Vanessa."

"Well, thank you, Grammy. I'm glad you like it."

"I just can't get behind that. Guess some things never change," Chuck said.

"So you think they have souls?" Frank shot back.

"Yeah, Frank. I do. And I also think you have issues you need to deal with. This ain't Daddy's Mississippi. And for good reason. And you'd be doing well to keep your bigoted thoughts to yourself so you don't catch a whoopin' in front of your kids one day."

Chuck was stone-faced and stared right into Frank's eyes. A look I knew all too well. It meant an ass beating might be imminent.

Frank laughed sheepishly, looked up from his mountain of food, and caught himself in the cross-hairs of Chuck's death gaze. He gradually stopped smiling and said, "You're serious... How you..."

My Grammy cut him off, "I say this might be the best turkey I've ever had. Did you deep fry it, Frank?"

Whenever I eat with old people, something at the table is the best they've ever had. It never fails. I bet eating in your 80s is quite the experience with continual improvement like that.

"Yeah, Mom. I did," he said, still looking at Chuck and poking at his food.

"So how are the chillens doin' in school?" Grammy asked Mom.

Conflict diversion. Matriarchal Prowess.

We finished eating and left right away. I never saw Uncle Frank again. On the way home, I asked Chuck if he was gonna fight Uncle Frank. He told me not to worry about it. Then he told me to never use that word.

That's how I learned that people classify themselves according to their skin color. I never thought of such a thing. People just looked different. I still don't understand it. Maybe people need to feel like they're better than people who aren't them. And appearance is the most visible difference between us. So the stupidest people on the planet stop at the skin because they lack the intellectual capacity to find a real reason to feel superior. Racism might be a guilty plea—guilty by reason of idiocy. Idiots indict themselves.

It's wild how much conviction closed-minded people speak with. It's like they have to go over the top to prove their point—a point that can't stand on its own merits because it's so logically flawed.

These jackasses are so arrogant too. It's like they can't respect what doesn't look like them because, if they did, they'd be diminishing themselves.

Maybe I'm way off and am a hypocritical idiot myself by assuming that the real problem is simply skin color. There's a chance they're smarter than that, slight as it may be.

It could be the basic need for competition. I mean... isn't this true about countries, church denominations, rival sports teams, business competitors, men vs. men, women vs. women, men vs. women, dogs vs. cats, movies vs. books, and anything else you can imagine.

Whatever *it* is, we do *it* the right way. We're the winners.

Webster's Dictionary says a nigger is black, or has dark skin. Is that really true? Because in the Upton Park Rec Center, I was the nigger. They called me nigga all the time. I called someone a nigga once at the Rec, got punched in the nose, haven't said it since.

Do people just adopt the ideas of their dads? Maybe we've been wearing hand-me-downs for a long time. I wonder if people don't like change because it means they gotta do some philosophical heavy lifting for themselves. When someone challenges an idea that's old guard grounded, it sure seems to piss a lot of people off. The mob forms. The gossip runs rampant. Families stop speaking to each other. Rock stars die strange deaths. People get kicked out of churches.

Sometimes, I wonder if this comparison and competition and superiority complex bullshit is how we progress? I mean, I learned that our country heard Russia was going to outer space. Then, all the sudden, after millenniums of not leaving planet earth's atmosphere, we put someone on the moon. Weird, huh?

Anyway, there's one thing that's clear to me—Chuck's a southern man to the core, but he didn't adopt his dad's ideas about the color of people's skin like Frank did. That's one thing I like about him. If he did, I probably wouldn't be here. Mom's half-Vietnamese. Guess according to Webster, I'm a nigger. Actually, a chink.

Ω

Anyway, back to our living room.

"So what's been goin' on, Dad?"

"Same old... Work, church, more work." He turned a page. "Ya'll hear the Pastor's son is a gay homosexual?"

He still had his face buried in the paper. I was irked that my dad didn't know that you don't have to say both gay and homosexual to get the point across.

"No... I hadn't heard that."

"Queer as a horned dog."

"That's wild, Dad."

"Yep, the deacons are meetin' tonight to decide if preacher's gotta step down."

"Because he has a gay son?"

Chuck lowered the paper to his lap and looked at me. "If you can't handle your own family, how can you handle a church?"

Shit like this is why I gotta get the fuck outta here.

"Welp. Guess I'm gonna go pack up some stuff."

Chuck put his face back in the newspaper. I walked into my room and looked at the posters of my sports heroes. All brothers. All soul. Uncle Frank can eat a dick.

Above my bed, Michael Jordan held a ball beside his head, knees bent and feet back as if he'd bounced off a trampoline. Gold chains suspended in air around his neck. Tongue out. Milliseconds from stuffing the ball through the rim to the delight of awestruck fans. An epic moment—the grace of the greatest captured on a piece of paper that would be rolled up and sold for $2 at the Upton Park flea market down the street. A legend on the wall. Immortal. A human god. One worshipped by young dreamers across the world.

But it's the summer of 2000, and this god of my childhood has retired. He did that once already and tried baseball. He sucked. Maybe he'll come back again. I think Money might have another run left in him. I hope.

But if he comes back, it probably won't be a run since he's getting older and dangerously close to past-prime. If he laces 'em up and steps onto the hardwood again, it'll most likely be more of a jog, like an old fat man trying to burn some calories for his next weigh-in. But I don't care.

I hope he gets bored. I hope the game pulls him back in. I hope he has spotlight withdrawals. I imagine the god and the man might be one. And when the god is laid to rest, only to be remembered on flimsy posters hanging in the caves of disenchanted men about to face their own identity crises, a part of the man dies too. So he has no choice but to prolong the life of the god as long as he can. The comeback could be inevitable.

But that's all conjecture. I don't know about any of that shit. I just stared at the poster and thought of how much I'm gonna miss watching Money play.

On the wall adjacent from Money, stood Evander "The Real Deal" Holyfield. Chiseled. With an angry brow and eyes that stared right through me. Two title belts around each shoulder, and one around his waist. He was the ultimate warrior. Forged in iron, His heart was so magnificent that it couldn't be understood by medical personnel, fans, commentators, or competitors. It could only be admired as unique—one of a kind.

I remember round ten of Holyfield's first fight with Riddick Bowe. I was 12. It had been a full year since Chuck had knocked me out and left me drooling blood on the dirty short grass. I watched Holyfield absorb the most violent punches I'd ever seen a man take in that round. Yet, somehow, he stayed on his feet. I wanted to be him. Unbreakable. I wanted the world to see my heart just like they saw The Real Deal's.

As I stared at his image, I could hear the voices of the ring-side commentators...

"Look at Holyfield. What a warrior!"

"He's got a heart."

"If he weighs 205, his heart weighs about 204."

Sitting at the foot of my bed, I soaked up the nostalgic ambience that I'd leave behind in a matter of minutes. Like a turned page in a book read only one time by one person. Never shared. Never revisited. Locked away in a deep corner of my subconscious.

I realize the child that once lived in this room has been fading away. I don't know what that means yet, but sitting in there took me back to a time when things were just simpler. I miss being that kid. I got up and opened the window that faced the backyard. A warm breeze blew through the screen. I kneeled down so it could blow through my hair and thought about that screen and the faded white spray-painted face smiling back at me.

That faded smile makes me happy before it makes me sad. When I was 8, I put the smile on that screen. I thought the paint vapors would go through the holes, leaving nothing but imaginary happiness that only I knew was there. But Chuck was grilling some hot dogs on the back porch the next day and saw the smiley face painted on my window screen. And he came in and beat my ass.

I got up and packed my clothes, then looked around to see if there was anything I was forgetting. And there it was—my 8-Bit Nintendo hooked up to the 20-inch box TV in the corner. I pulled out my favorite cartridge—*Tecmo Super Bowl.*

Tecmo Super Bowl gave me and Chuck one of our few good moments. It was the only game he ever played with me. One Christmas Holiday, we controlled our own teams and played through an entire season in four days, swapping the controller between our games. He was the Bears and ran Neal Anderson over twenty times a game. I was the Chiefs because I loved the way tacklers bounced off Christian Okoye. One of my fondest memories was hearing Chuck say, "Dammit!" when QB Bills threw a game-winning touchdown to beat his Bears in the Super Bowl. Chuck threw the controller across the room and walked out. It was the only time I ever heard him cuss. I didn't laugh. The Bills were fucking cheaters.

I blew in the cartridge, inserted it, and pushed power. The screen told the story of a tired game system. Gray... Black... Gray... Black...

But this system had a few more runs in it too. It just needed to be handled with the care of a seasoned vet. Like this...

Pull out the cartridge.

Blow in it.

Put it back into the console.

Hold it all the way down with one hand.

Grab *Ninja Gaiden* cartridge with the other hand.

Insert it on top of *Tecmo*.

Press power.

The familiar rabbit appeared on the screen leaning on the word *Tecmo*. Game on. I still had a saved game from the last time I picked up the controller. Barry Sanders and the Detroit Lions were about to win their first Super Bowl. Who woulda thought?

After hoisting the virtual Lombardi Trophy, I loaded all my gear into the car and said goodbye to my parents. Chuck gave me a firm handshake and wished me well. I was a little surprised he stood up from his chair to do it, but it only took him a few seconds to sit back down, pull the lever, and get back to the local news.

"Oh wait. Your spaghetti," Mom said as I was walking out the door.

"Thanks Mom. I'm gonna put the rest of my stuff in the car. I'll come back in and get it."

Mom didn't wait for me to come back in. She already had the spaghetti in a Tupperware bowl on the counter. She ran into the kitchen to grab it and hustled out to my car.

"I'll miss you around here."

"It's not like I'm moving away Mom, and I've been staying at Joe's for weeks now."

"I know, but it won't be the same. You always avoided being at home when you lived here. Not that I blame you. It's just..." She choked up. "... just I miss you. And I love you."

"I love you, too, Mom." I hugged her and she started crying.

"And I'm so sorry," she said as I held her.

"What do you have to be sorry for?"

"I know it hasn't always been easy for you around here."

"It's okay, Mom," I said as I pulled back. Seeing her cry made me sad, but hearing her acknowledge it made me happy.

"Your father does love you. Even if he has a funny way of showing it sometimes."

"I know, Mom. You shouldn't feel bad about a thing. I had a good childhood. It wasn't even hard after Dad came back. And you always made me feel loved. And hey, at least Dad was here and didn't leave us to fend for ourselves, right?"

Fuck, I felt like such a grownup saying that.

"Yeah, I guess. He does work hard to make sure I always have something to cook. I just wanted more for you. I knew today would come, but I tried not to think about it. It just gets lonely without you around here."

I didn't know what to say. I don't know how to make it better. I'm trying to look at life through her eyes as I write these words, maybe that will help me understand her better so I can give her a little more of the love she's given me. I've never been very good at that—being able to feel people's pain and sympathize with their problems. You know—empathy and all. I'm gonna try harder though. Mom deserves it.

It seems like she feels stuck in a lifeless, loveless marriage—the marriage a little princess never envisions and would fully reject as a child, but the experienced woman might not know how to escape.

I understand why a baptist woman might feel like she gets a raw deal. I'll never forget that guy Luke Scott's message where he went off the chain about women. It was the same sermon where he polished his shaft.

Ω

"They'll be serving ice cream in hell before I get my theology from a woman. Ask Adam how that worked out for him. The whole world's damned because a woman told Adam what she thought about things. I don't mind if a momma teaches the kids. It's okay if a gracious, Godly woman follows the instruction of the pastor, but no woman wrote a word in my Bible here. *Men* wrote the Scriptures, got it from God. A *man* named Jesus Christ died on the cross. And *men* are called to lead our churches and families. Hey! I'm glad I'm a man!

"I don't care what's politically correct, and I don't care if it hair lips anybody from the White House to an old man sitting in an outhouse. I'm in charge of what goes on in the church house, and I'm a messenger of God, and what I say is more important than what the world thinks I should say."

Those words didn't sit right. Plus, the guy had just whacked off a medieval weapon, so his credibility was pretty much shot.

I know there has to be a word[Ω] for guys like Scott who told us men how to act and how much more important we are than women.

Maybe because of this kind of "Biblical" teaching, my mom exists as a shell of repressed femininity like other submissive Christian wives who live in a state of comfortable misery. Her society has sentenced her to it for the rest of her life. Forget individuality. Forget personal happiness and freedom. Do your duty. Why? Because the preacher said so. Maybe the pulpit enables the men who took my mom's generation as wives to be self-serving assholes who keep the woman behind the man, rarely beside him.

It's not like divorce is an option, because Mom is devout. Divorce is unscriptural so a woman in her position has to "press on." And if she gets depressed, I'm sure she's told to just read the Bible and pray. After all, that *is* the universal remedy for Christian mental suffering.

Of course, this is all conjecture too, but I can see it in her eyes. Something is missing. I wonder if Mom's all prayed out. Maybe she tries but gets nothing from the man upstairs, just like me. Life happens

---

[Ω] A misogynist is a person who ain't a big fan of women, unless he's fucking one. This type of dude uses them when it's convenient—when they need to bust some spackle. After that, they go right back to their prejudice.

all around her, and the only thing she's learned to do is the only thing she does—she lives with it. But while she's living with it, she might be dying a slow cruel death inside. The saddest part would be that no one would know she's struggling, and would anyone really care?

She is face to face with same ugly truth about human existence that I've been seeing a little more every day—Nobody gives a shit about your shit.

Ω

"I'll be around, Mom. You okay? Dad being good to you?"

"Dad is Dad. You know that. He's fine to me. We just miss you."

What she meant was—he doesn't physically hurt her. Chuck isn't much good to anyone including himself. And by *we* she meant *she* because I don't think Chuck gives two shits. But Mom's loyalty to her man always shows no matter how shitty her marriage may be. I've always respected that.

"I love you Mom. I'll come see you tomorrow, and we can go to lunch or something next week."

"I love you too, Jesse, and I'm so proud of you. My big man."

"Mom, no matter how big this man gets, he'll always be your baby boy."

I squeezed her tight one more time and got in the car. I like to hear her say she's proud of me. I still long to hear those words from Chuck, but such is my life. We crave most what we can't seem to get.

chapter: 23

The Life and Times of Jesse "Take-All-Comers" Baker
By Jesse Baker
June 14, 2000

UNBELIEVABLE. I was at the new apartment setting up my bed and unpacking some of my shit when my phone rang. I flipped it open and saw her name on the screen.

Incoming Call...

Jennie

My heart skipped a beat and my hands immediately started sweating. Stop judging—it's not cliché if it actually happens. I guess that's debatable. Whatever, I hadn't talked to her since spring, so I was excited. I didn't sleep much last night. And I've been re-living it all day. I think I'll re-live it again.

Ω

"Hey stranger."

"Hi, Jesse."

"Whatcha been up to?"

"Not much. Working a lot. You?"

"Workin' on my game and settin' up this new apartment."

"Yeah? Finally moved out, huh?"

"Well... Officially. I haven't been home much since graduation anyway so it felt like my next move."

"Yeah, I saw your Mom at church last Sunday. She seemed well."

"She always seems well, I mean, is well."

"I've always loved your Mom. She's so sweet."

We made small talk and got caught up on each other's stories for about twenty minutes. I had questions burning inside me, but I couldn't fuck this up. She'd finally called me, and I've always had a good feel for time and score.

"Well it was good catching up, Jesse. I'm glad to hear you're well."

"Jennie... You wanna maybe get together soon?"

"I'd like that."

I hoped that was the real goal of her call. But of course, she had to make me say it. It's like she's always playing some long game with me. I kinda like it though.

"How 'bout right now. I'm setting up my new place. Wanna swing by?"

"Umm. Sure. I can be there in about an hour."

"Great. See ya then."

"Okay Jesse. See ya in a bit."

My unorganized unpacking venture turned into a flight of the bumble bee house clean for the next fifteen minutes. After that, I took a 5-minute shower.

Jamal was at his mom's house for the night. So we'd have the place to ourselves. And I already had big plans. Jennie is the only girl in my life that has never been just a hook up, and I miss her—everything about her. The smell of the Davidoff Cool Water perfume. Her long black hair. Her genuine friendly smile. Even her sexy voice. Every word, giggle, sigh, and mannerism is an eargasm to me. I'm intoxicated by her mere presence. So I don't need alcohol, but I wanted to leave no stone unturned to make sure she was as intoxicated by me as I am by her. And maybe I don't think enough of myself to be sure I can do the job alone. So I drove to the liquor store down the block to get a bottle of Patron and some white wine to set the mood.

Knock-Knock-Knock.

The apartment was set up for her arrival. One couch, no TV, and her favorite album playing on the CD player—Dave Matthews and Tim Reynolds Live at Luther College.

"Hi. C'mon in."

I was nervous. She looked more stunning than I'd envisioned. She was a woman now. No Christian school little girl stuff anymore. No long skirts. No flannel shirts. Just dark tight jeans and a Marvelous 3 concert t-shirt. I've always said you can tell a lot about a person by their music taste, and Jennie has the audible palate of God. I also couldn't stop staring at her ass as she walked through the door.

"You remembered," she said pointing at the stereo.

"Been addicted to it since you showed it to me."

"What, two years ago?"

"Yeah. I guess it was. Been on repeat ever since."

"Yeah right. I like your new place."

"Ah. It ain't much."

"Looks just enough to me."

"Yeah. I guess it's all we need."

"Well... something to be said about having all you need."

"Yes. Yes, there is. Wanna drink?"

"Sure."

I walked to the fridge. The kitchen and living room are the same room, so I could keep the conversation going. "Have a seat and make yourself at home. Hope that couch is comfortable enough." Why the fuck did I say that?

"All you need right?" she replied. I was relieved she didn't think my statement sounded as pervy as I did.

"All we need... And sorry there's no TV." *Jesus Christ, what the fuck am I talking about?*

"I came over to see you, not watch TV."

Sweet. Her tone. Oh man. It was so welcoming. I could tell she had missed me too.

We sat on the couch drinking tequila and sipping wine for an hour reminiscing and laughing about good times past. I was hoping she'd make the first move. And of course, that wasn't happening.

"Oh, high school. Things just made more sense in high school," Jennie said as she took a sip from her red plastic cup.

"I heard about your parents. You okay?"

"Yeah. It's been a hard year, but let's not talk about sad stories just yet."

"Okay. I gotcha."

"Thanks."

"Well... if someday you wanna tell me your stories, I'll be there for you?"

"Okay, Bon Jovi." She snickered.

"I forgot how much you hate him."

"It's not that I hate him, it's just, he's too clean to be a rock star. And he's such a douche," she said, shaking her head. "And Bono? Pshh. I want my rock stars to have the songs, the lyrics and the look and all, but they need to have just the right amount of dirty."

"Fuck Bono,"

"Thank you."

"Okay, like Dee Snider?"

"No, he's too dirty. Like dirty old man creepy. I said just the right amount of dirty, not nasty, ya know? Like they're not trying too hard. Butch Walker for example. Not SouthGang Butch. That's trying too hard. Gimme Marvelous 3 Butch—perfection."

"What about Dave? Seems like he'd be a little too tidy for you."

"Dave's not that good looking though. And rules are made to be broken, right?"

"Hell yeah they are. I got one—Jeff Buckley."

"Exactly. If a musician looks good with the perfect amount of dirty *and* sings and plays with soul *and* masters the pen without becoming a walking cliché, he can master me."

"Well... I've been writing a lot. Working on a novel actually."

"Oh yeah... Are you trying to master me now?" She giggled.

"Maybe."

She sipped her wine. I leaned over and kissed her lips when she let down the cup. I think it took her by surprise because she paused for a second. Then her lips pressed back to mine. Passionate as she sat up and straightened her back. Slightly opening her mouth as an invitation into her heart. My hand moved from the back of the couch to the side of her face, and my other hand moved around her belly to caress the inward curve between her hip and her rib cage. Our eyes closed as our mouths opened more to let our tongues dance a slow ballad. Not a *Monsters of Rock* ballad—an Elliott Smith one. My hand slowly moved up the side of her ribs, thumb lightly brushing the side of her clothed breast. I could feel her shiver. Then she moved closer and straddled me as I leaned back on the couch.

Our lips parted for a few seconds as she sat straight up on top of me and took off her shirt with both hands. My eyes followed every newly exposed inch.

I'd seen her body before, but our estrangement brought longing. A newness. And the passion I have for her felt like it had been bottled up too long.

While we kissed, she moved her hips slowly up and down, rubbing herself on me. Jeans on jeans. We rubbed against each other for a few more minutes.

She slowed down, and I reached both hands around her back and unhooked her bra on the first try.

"Looks like you've been getting more experience with that," she said.

"Lucky."

We both chuckled.

"I think we both know better than that, but we'll save that talk for another time," she said as she reached down and unbuttoned my jeans. Taking the queue, I unbuttoned hers. It was tough sitting down, so we stood, facing each other.

"Are you okay with this?" I said like an idiot.

"Don't ask me that. Just let what happens happen. If I wasn't okay you would know, and I wouldn't be here."

She slipped her jeans down her waist and pulled each leg out while I took off my shirt. I've packed on some lean muscle for college basketball and was proud to show her. She kicked her jeans aside and pulled mine down to the floor as she dropped to her knees. My boxers went along for the ride which made my dick upswing inches from her face. I was a little embarrassed at the jarring velocity of this uncontrollable movement—until she wrapped her lips around it.

I had to move away from her. I needed a thirty-second time-out, or this wasn't gonna last as long as I wanted it to. So I led her to her back and kissed her. She laid there with her hair spread upward across the couch and smiled at me.

I took in the sight of her beauty. Her shiny black hair. Perfect dark skin, big brown eyes that could melt me with their sweet glance. And a body that could make even the preacher's son chubby.

"I missed you," she said.

I smiled. And without a thought, I said the dumbest thing I'd said all night, "I think I love you."

She giggled. I was embarrassed again. *Why would I say that now?* My experiences with girls ain't like the movies where the cute dialogue makes everyone stare at the screen with a stupid grin on their face. Boys and girls with perfectly timed romantic cleverness that leads to true love. Real people say unbelievably bland shit like, "I think I love you," or, "You have such beautiful eyes." I bet it takes a while for writers to come up with that shit, and ain't nobody got that kind of time in real life.

"You're crazy. You don't even know what love is. You're just trying to get in my pants."

"I'm already pretty much there so I don't have to say anything."

She laughed again and said, "I don't know much about love. I just know that life takes us wherever it will, but for some reason, I feel bound to you."

"That works for me."

"Does it?" she said with a sincere smile.

"Yeah. It does."

"Good."

She raised her hips and pushed her panties down as she looked right into my eyes and said, "I want you."

She wrapped her legs around my waist as I moved into her. Her eyes closed as she moaned softly. My bottom lip quivered above her forehead. Being inside of her was like nothing I had ever felt. I didn't want her to know I was still a virgin. I lasted around 15 seconds even though I tried to think about baseball, but I kept at it and lasted another two minutes or so. We aren't married, so technically we're impure in the eyes of the religion of our youth. But I could feel God last night, and there is something deeply spiritual about being with her. She is my new church.

chapter: 24

THE LIFE AND TIMES *of Jesse "Take-All-Comers" Baker* will cease to exist as you know it because his life will drastically change in ways that may or may not destroy the boy who was telling you his story.

There also may or may not be infinite worlds with infinite possibilities, and in one of these worlds, there may exist a version of Jesse Baker who tells a fictional account of the exact events that happened here. Which may or may not be real in this world. You could never *know*, but it's interesting to ponder such scenarios.

So who am I to take over his story?

I just am.

And what would it matter who I am? Something that *does* matter is that people learn to figure things out for themselves.

We aren't supposed to be like sheep. Sheep are lazy... and stupid. The dumber the animal, the more rules they need, and the more they rely on external forces for survival. All you need to *know* is that there is a story, and it will be told. The rest you can figure out for yourself.

Some things are better left a mystery.

However, it's not a mystery that life happens and people change. The real mystery lies in a one-word question—why?

Speaking of mysteries—there was a part of the Bible Jesse had been struggling with for years without telling anyone. Since he'd been saved 79 times, he was sure that doubting God was just going to be his cross to bear. He was afraid of what that meant. The verses in question were written by the Apostle Paul.

"For whom he did foreknow, he also did predestinate to be conformed to the image of his Son, that he might be the firstborn among many brethren. Moreover whom he did predestinate, them he also called: and whom he called, them he also justified: and whom he justified, them he also glorified." Romans 8:29-30 KJV

This passage chapped his ass. He always felt like he couldn't believe right, like a cripple can't walk right. He never, *ever*, not once, spoke about this to anyone. He worried that he didn't get picked by God, and his destination was hell.

It's a tough one—this predestination thing. It's worth a good argument for sure. But it's clear that if you believe the Bible literally word for word, the indigenous people of the world, who never had a chance to hear the word *Jesus* much less accept Him as their personal savior, are fucked. And so is Jesse Baker.

Oh, predestination—the biggest thorn in the forehead of the argument for a moral God.

In early August 2000, Jesse asked Jamal something along these same lines while smoking a blunt on a boulder at the top of Lookout Mountain. His blue Accord was parked behind them. The metallic paint job was rusting, and tires were bald, but Jesse loved that car—especially the flip up lights. One of them had wiring issues and wouldn't flip up. It had been that way for two weeks. Jesse didn't take it out much at night because, when the lights were on, it was the flirtiest car on the road—winking at everyone. This sounds cute, but not to cops. Jesse had already been pulled over about the lights and let slide with a warning. But he wasn't worried about getting pulled over that night because, to get to this spot, he only had to drive to the top of the mountain from the party at Joe's at the bottom. It was a little over a mile of twisty road with eight hairpin turns.

They sat with their feet hanging off the edge of mountain boulder. The car's one headlight shot a beam of light through a cloud of smoke above their heads and faded into the backdrop of black sky and distant city lights.

Why were they up there you might ask? Well, Jesse and Jennie were back on. She wasn't off work yet, but she'd be at the party soon. She was always on his mind these days. Jesse and Jamal were almost out of weed and didn't want to share. So they volunteered to make a beer run. Jesse had a joint renting space in his pack of Marlboro Ultra Lights and a case of beer already in the trunk. This wasn't a beer run. It was a premeditated smoke break.

$$\Omega$$

"Do you think crazy people go to hell?" Jesse asked.

"What kinda crazy we talkin' about? Like for real fucked up and can't help it?"

"Sure."

"Naw, I don't think so. I mean, how can you be held accountable for shit you can't control. Ya know?"

"What if some can?" Jesse asked.

"You think crazies wanna be crazy?"

"I don't know. What if there's like... levels of crazy?"

"You think you got some crazy in ya?"

"There's no doubting that. What about retards?"

"What the fuck B?" Jamal laughed. "I don't think that's what you're supposed to call 'em."

"Well, whaddaya want me to call 'em?"

"Shit, not that."

"It's just... I was thinkin' the other day about that kid Ritchie... I mean... He was born crazy. Like God didn't even give him a chance."

"Yeah, Ritchie was a trip, man."

Ritchie was a kid from Jesse's class who was mentally stunted because his mom could drink Shooter$^{\Omega}$ under the table and effectively did the entire time Ritchie lived in her belly. He was—according to Pastor Joel—"very autistic." His alcoholic mother didn't want him, and a church couple adopted him and put him in Upton Park Christian School. He'd rock back and forth in class when he was nervous and couldn't understand stuff. Which meant he rocked back and forth all day, every day. He had bald spots from pinching his hair and pulling it out. He also couldn't control the volume of his voice. And sometimes, he'd randomly

---

$^{\Omega}$ Not McGavin. Shooter from the movie *Hoosiers*.

quote things he'd heard radio DJ's say on the air at the most inopportune times. He was distracting at first, but eventually became invisible. The kids at school got used to him.

The kids in Jesse's church youth group used to go door-to-door soul-winning[Ω] on Monday nights in groups of three with one adult chaperone. One Monday, it was Jesse, Ritchie, Jennie, and Pastor Joel. Ritchie never got to talk. Until this one time...

"So I'm like 14, and we're out door-to-door soul-winning, ya know. It's like me, Jennie, Pastor Joel, and Ritchie."

"Oh shit. Ritchie soul-winning?"

"So I knock on the first door and say—Hello Ma'am, we're from Upton Park Baptist Church—and this bitch slams it in my face."

"Damn dude. Knockin' on doors. Y'all's church was crazy.[Ω] I'm so glad I never had to do that shit," Jamal said.

"I can't tell you how much I hated it man. So we're walking to the next house. I'm fuckin' pissed, Jennie's trying real hard not to laugh, and Pastor Joel's all talkin' like—We'll be persecuted for His name's sake—and shit like that.

"And Ritchie's all rockin' hard like he does and then yells out—And that was 'You Can Call Me Al' by Paul Simon and you're listening to all your favorite hits, past and present on Easy 92.3.

[Ω] Soliciting salvation—like Mormon's in white shirts and ties and on bicycles. Independent fundamental Baptists don't ride bikes, they walk.

[Ω] Jamal went to Upton Park Christian School, but he and his mom went to a different church on Sundays. They usually stayed indoors and got rowdy, and occasionally, someone got knocked the fuck out by the Holy Spirit.

"Pastor Joel's like—Ritchie is something on your mind?

"Ritchie's like—I think I'll witness to this door.

"I was like—Ritchie you witness to people, not doors.

"Pastor Joel's like—I don't know Ritchie, I think you should practice more.

"Ritchie's like—Remember I led you to Christ twice last week."

"Wait—he'd been practicin' on Pastor Joel?" Jamal asked.

"I guess so."

"Classic."

Jesse went on after he hit the jay and passed it back. "So he gives ol' Ritchie a shot at 2314 Union Ave. I still remember the address. Me and Jennie lookin' at each other like—*what the fuck's going on?* He gets to the door and is like—Um, Hi, you tryin' to get saved, sir?

"The dude's like—No son, I think I'm okay today.

"And Ritchie just yells the most Ritchie shit ever—Then you go to hell!"

"No way," Jamal said, laughing.

"Way, dawg. Way."

"Damn B, I bet ya'll were rollin'."

"Yeah, dude at the door was actually pretty cool about it. He just laughed and said, 'Well, okay ya'll good folks have a nice night.' Pastor Joel was pissed though."

"Okay, like, Ritchie ain't goin' to hell," Jamal said.

"Word."

"How 'bout Dahmer?" Jamal asked.

"Na."

"How not?"

"Cannibal, bro. That's next level crazy. He was probably born like that. Can't be right in the head and eat people man."

"Yeah, that is pretty next level," Jamal said as he pinched, sucked, and exhaled slowly.

"I don't know. He might burn. I don't get to decide. Would be cool if I did though. I got a few folks in mind that I'd like to ship south."

"No way. I ain't tryin' to have that responsibility. Ain't nobody'd go to hell." Jamal passed the jay back to Jesse and asked, "How 'bout Ted Bundy?"

"Definitely Hell."

"Yeah, maybe. Hitler?"

"The hottest, bro," Jesse said with a satisfied smirk. He seemed to enjoy playing judge, jury, and eternal executioner. He continued, letting out puffs of smoke with each syllable, "I bet there's a special hell that motherfucker. Like where they cut off your dick and make you wear it on your upper lip over that ugly fucking 'stache."

"Like a tiny mushroom peekin' outta dead grass. I might could ship Hitler," Jamal said.

"Wouldn't he have to be circumcised for it to look like a mushroom?"

"That'd be the best part—in that nigga's hell, motherfucker's Jewish."

They both laughed hard as it started to sprinkle. Jesse stood up and flipped the roach over the edge.

As they caught their breath and walked back to the car, Jamal said, "Lemme make sure we in agreement on one thing, since you prolly know your Bible shit better than me. If Corky[Ω] don't get saved, he aight, right?"

"Bro, He's gotta be golden. It's like the age of accountability[Ω] and shit. Like old enough to understand. I don't know if Corky ever hits that age."

"Word," Jamal said. As they both approached the driver's side door, thunder struck, lightning crashed, and it rained men. Just kidding—it rained rain. Rain that would have pleased Shirley Manson.

"Damn. Guess we'll be hangin' indoors tonight."

"Bitch, Gimme them keys. We know you can't handle shit but the music when you smoke," Jamal said as he snatched the keys out of Jesse's hand.

Jesse didn't argue. He enjoyed being the DJ way more than driving. Some might say his car sucked, but it had a sick stereo. No matter how beat-up the car, a young man in the South was happy as long as his system was on point. In his trunk, a box of tens hung out with that case of beer. The backseats wouldn't stay up all the time, so unless he had multiple passengers, he left them down, opening the trunk to the interior so the music would be louder—so loud they could feel the bass.

These were the days of CD cases and 6-disc changers under the passenger side seat. And his CD case was loaded with the goods. At least he thought so.

[Ω] From the early 90s sitcom *Life Goes On*.

[Ω] The age of accountability is an idea that children will go to heaven if they die before they are able to fully understand the concept of gospel-based salvation. The vagueness of the theory allows for flexibility. And it's always cited when convenient (such as funerals for dead children). In Baptist circles, this age is said to be somewhere between the ages of 4 and 9, depending on who you ask. It could be argued that human beings may never reach this age of full understanding. Jesse would never admit it, but some of the doctrine he'd been fed would never fully escape his brain.

He'd worked on this collection since CDs replaced cassette tapes as the music industry's go-to form of jam distribution.

Once during his freshman year in high school, Chuck found his fairly light CD case of secular albums and threw it away while Jesse was at school. When Jesse got home that day, Chuck was sitting in the living room ready to chew his ass out for listening to that "worldly trash."

But Jesse's resolve would not be broken. He started a new collection—one he'd skillfully hide from his father or anyone else who could pose a threat to his listening pleasure.

On the mountain that night, his rotation was heavy in angry white boys, but Bone Thugs and Harmony got the nod.

Slot 1—Pearl Jam's *Vitology*

Slot 2—Alice in Chains on MTV unplugged

Slot 3—Nirvana's *Nevermind*

Slot 4—*The Downward Spiral* by Nine Inch Nails

Slot 5—Rage Against the Machine's self-titled album

Slot 6—Bone Thugs and Harmony's *E. Eternal 1999*

His recent spiritual angst and perpetual doubt would have been no surprise to Chuck or the people from his home church and school. They always told him "what goes into your head will eventually come out." He never considered that to be a real possibility. But one might wonder.

Maybe it was bitterness toward Chuck, or skepticism of crazy preachers, or something else entirely. Or maybe he was just wired for revolt. Was it a coincidence that many of his pop culture heroes despised all things authoritarian, and he felt the same way?

Maybe these characters articulated how he felt, and his soul was tethered to his taste in entertainment. Different connections for different people. Maybe everyone's like that.

But for whatever reason, a darkness grew in the deepest corners of his psyche that he would never talk about in public because he would become an outcast if he did. He'd have a label—a scorner, a nihilist, an anarchist. The black eye of the modestly dressed, *hold hands and sing Kumbaya*[Ω] society he was raised in. He felt like a lone wolf spiritually. Lost. Wandering unrecognizable terrain in his head. And he still couldn't bring himself to talk about it with anyone.

The rain poured in sheets, and when Jamal took the second hairpin turn, the Accord's bald tires weren't even touching the ground. The car floated right. Surely, a world exists where there is a guard rail on the second hairpin turn down this stretch of road descending Lookout Mountain. This is not that world, and they hydroplaned closer to the edge. Another world may exist where Jamal, the pure hearted star-athlete, never makes a poor decision. This also isn't that world.

Jamal turned the wheel. Nothing. He gripped it with both hands and jerked. Nothing. He'd lost control of the situation when he plopped in the driver's seat a little drunker and higher than he thought he was.

[Ω] Kumbaya means *come by here*. No one ever told Jesse that, and he never figured out why the fuck someone was crying, and then someone was singing. But at church camp, he sang that fucking song anyways. All the kids sang it, and not one of them considered asking what it meant. Wouldn't have mattered if they did, not one person at camp knew the painful origin of that song. They didn't teach the uncomfortable parts of US history in most Christian schools. That would be unamerican.

Jesse's mouth was open, but silent. It's those seconds where time slows down while something is happening so fast, and it's completely out of human hands. You're shooting a pair of square dice down a metaphysical craps table, hoping to hit the lucky point, assuming you even have time to hope.

When the car went off the nearly non existent shoulder, the tires spun on the grass and it tipped broadside off of the mountain and bounced off the trees like a Plinko chip on *The Price Is Right*, rolling and flipping its way down—the scenic route to the same road 50 feet below.

Jesse opened his eyes. The seatbelt still held him in his seat. He saw blinking red lights in the distance. His head was spinning, and his eyes slowly closed again. Then what seemed like seconds later, he could feel rain on his face. His ears rang like someone had shot a pistol too close to his head. It was a familiar sound he'd almost forgotten—the one that followed Chuck's fist across his temple.

"Are you okay?" A distorted voice said as he faded out again.

The next thing he heard was an ambulance, then the cutting of steel, hydraulics, and commotion around the contorted Accord that rested on its driver's side doors. Then he felt his body being pulled. He slowly opened his eyes and looked down at Jamal, whose body crushed in a cluster of metal, seat fabric, blood, and bark. Eyes open, empty and not blinking.

The car smelled like beer. The music still played. And Jesse felt each beat pulsing in his hair.

chapter: 25

BEEP... BEEP... BEEP... BEEP... BEEP...
Everything was dark for a long time, but that damn sound never stopped. He was asleep but awake. It hurt to move. He was terrified.

Beep... Beep... Beep... Beep... Beep...

He wondered if he was dead. He thought of what people used to say in the movies when someone was near death.

"Go toward the light."
"Stay away from the light."

He would have settled for either option, but there was no light. That was his biggest fear. Even scarier than hell. Nothing. Ash to Ash. Dust to Dust. Eternal blackness. Like his old box television when he turned it off. The light flickered and shrunk to a pinpoint before it went dark. He hoped someone would twist the knob and turn him on again. Then he saw the Jamal's blank stare, and the knob was twisted, and his eyes opened. His breaths got shorter and faster as beeps picked up their pace.

"Jesse? Jesse?"

His mom pulled the oxygen mask off his face. "Jamal?"

"He's gone, baby. I'm so sorry."

He choked back a cry and tightened his lips. The contractions in his chest sent pain through his body. His mother held his hand and palmed the side of his face while a tear fell on her thumb. She looked at him with relief. Relief that she wouldn't have to bury her only son.

His right leg was in a cast that went from his toes to hip. His broken right arm was in a cast too, but the broken ribs and collapsed lung were the most painful. Now that he was awake, the doctors and nurses were planning the logistics of his surgery. But it could have been worse. The Bakers could have been planning a funeral.

Jesse's head throbbed, and his watery eyes wanted to close again. A nurse came in and injected something into his I.V. and put the oxygen mask back on his face. Tears ran down the side of it. As coolness coursed through his veins, the beeps slowed. He saw a blurry Chuck standing behind his mom and fell asleep.

Ω

The beeps were relentless, but the blackness subsided for another brief minute. He had no clue how much time had passed since he'd last opened his eyes. Three blurry figures stood by the foot of his bed. The doctor updated his parents.

"It went well. He suffered immense trauma to the right side of his body, but we put a plate on his femur and pins in his arm. Barring any complication, he should make a complete recovery. He's a lucky kid."

Lucky.

"Thank God," his mom said as Chuck held her.

The doctor continued, "He's suffered a severe concussion, but there doesn't appear to be any permanent brain damage. The collapsed lung is a concern. We'll just have to monitor him for another week or so."

Ω

Chuck went to Jamal's funeral by himself because Vanessa wasn't leaving the hospital. The church was full when he walked in, so he stood in a corner like he used to at the basketball games. Everybody knew his history with Jamal and reminded each other at times, but gossip didn't bother Chuck. What did bother him, however, was he never apologized to the kid for that punch.

Come to think of it, Chuck had never apologized to anyone for anything.

He didn't hear a word of the service. He just stared at the casket. Afterward, the pall bearers carried the casket down the center aisle.

Then Chuck saw him—the last pallbearer. He closed his eyes tightly and took a deep breath, wondering what sort of deviltry was at work. When he opened them, Jamal was still there. He rubbed his eyes. Still there.

Jamal wore his Wolves jersey. Number 45. Then he looked at Chuck just like he used to after basketball games. Chuck did everything he could to suppress his tears. His eyes got heavy, and his breath short. So short, in fact, he might have stopped breathing altogether. His face looked painfully apprehensive but happy to see him at the same time. People have this same look when they listen to John Edward tell them what their loved one is saying from beyond the grave—an open-mindedness so desperate that it disregards logic and science.

Chuck thought he might be going crazy, but he looked right back at Jamal and give that patented *Chuck* nod. Jamal cracked a smile and walked out the door.

Chuck jetted out the church side door and made for his car. Then he looked back at the pallbearers loading the casket in the hearse. Jamal wasn't there. Chuck tripped on the yellow parking stop in front of his gold Mercury Cougar. His knee banged against the bumper, but he braced his fall by slapping his open palm on the hood which turned a few heads down the way. He was sweating, pain sliced through his knee, and he felt like he was about to spontaneously combust.

In the car, he squeezed the wheel so tightly that he lost the feeling in his fingers. Then he combusted. He screamed loud as he could, beating his fists on the wheel. Then the dash. Then he punched the radio, which kicked on the song "Achy Breaky Heart" by Billy Ray Cyrus for all of three seconds until he punched it again, turning it to static. Loud static. The chaos continued. The car shook. The longer he screamed with his eyes closed, the worse off he was. He saw them all, his friends that he saw die in the war. They watched him flip out and showed no emotion.

The thought of his only son being that close to death and Jamal heading for the ground took Chuck back to a place he never wanted to go again.

The car eventually stopped shaking, and he opened his eyes, panting. Tears obscured his vision, but he wiped them with the long sleeve of his white button-down shirt. The folks down the way were still staring at him. They always stared.

Ω

The day Jesse got out of the hospital, Jennie came by and brought him his favorite breakfast—McDonald's bacon, egg, and cheese biscuit with two hash browns. His headaches were worse and more frequent.

It was a dreary Wednesday, and rain splattered against the hospital window. When Jennie walked in, Vanessa was sitting in a corner reading a book. Jesse pretended to sleep partly because he liked to hear what everyone said about him when they thought he was out, but mostly because closing his eyes minimized the pain.

"It's a monsoon out there," Jennie said as she took off her raincoat.

Vanessa smiled at her.

"How's he doing today?" Jennie asked.

"I think today's the day."

"Well that's good."

"Yeah, but..." Vanessa sniffled.

Jennie sat beside her and rubbed her back.

"This has all just been a lot. Thanks for being here for him Jennie."

"It's the least I could do."

Jesse opened his eyes.

"I'm going to get some coffee from the cafeteria. You want some?" Vanessa said as she grabbed her bag, walked to the side of the bed, and gave him a kiss on the forehead.

"I'm okay. Thank you though."

Jesse looked at Jennie, who sat at his bedside. She put her hand in his and said, "Hey you."

"Hey."

"Need anything?"

"To get outta here."

"I see your bag over there, that's a good sign."

"Only a few more hours."

Jennie sat beside him for a half hour, and they didn't have much to say. She was a bit uncomfortable and had never been like that around him. He didn't notice because of his own physical discomfort combined with being distraught over the loss of his friend. He thought it was his fault. Then he thought it was God's fault. Then he thought it was both of their faults, so he didn't care much for his Creator or himself at the moment. He'd wrestled with God in that hospital bed, but unlike Jacob's match with the Almighty, Jesse wasn't left with a broken hip. His silver medal was a broken heart.

But Jennie had something to tell him that wasn't the clichés others offered. Many people sent cards or visited Jesse in the hospital and offered him two things he'd always despised—unsolicited advice and soulless Christian feel-good lines. Stuff like...

"God works everything together for good."
"You're alive for a reason. God's not done with you yet."
"This too, shall pass."
"God gave you a second chance, buddy. Don't mess it up."

"Jennie," he said.

"Yeah?"

"I can't believe Jamal's dead."

"I know."

He blinked multiple times. Fighting it. He still felt the need to project his tough-guy image. No one gets to see him cry. Not even Jennie. His mom caught him in a moment of weakness, and he had to make sure that didn't happen again.

While they sat there in silence, holding hands, he thought about the sovereignty of God. He figured if it was true, then God did this on purpose. God murdered Jamal in cold blood. That meant He was also responsible for all the other nasty shit in human history. And for what? To teach people some kind of lesson? Jesse thought there had to be a word for someone who got there rocks off on people's suffering. He made a mental note to look it up later.[Ω]

Jennie still couldn't say what she needed to say. She thought this might not be the time or place. She was probably right. She rubbed her thumb on Jesse's hand and said, "I love you."

"Thanks. I hope you don't change your mind about that," he said.

She snickered. "You're crazy."

Lying there, he couldn't feel anything but anger. Well, that and a substantial amount of self-loathing. He couldn't conceive of a life without bitterness being his dominating emotion. He saw his own dark future—an empty arena and a flat ball on the foul line. A painful image of what could not be.

[Ω] *Sadist.* He never got around to looking that up.

Before the accident, his identity was Jesse Baker—the basketball player. That's who he'd always been and what he'd always known and what he was known for. He was a star on the court and in his own mind which gave him the confidence to act like a star off it. The game was his reason for being. He saw another image—a stellar black hole.

Whether he could physically recover wasn't the issue in question. He wouldn't have it in him anymore, and he knew it, so he didn't go back to college. He didn't die on that road in late June, but the athlete did, never to rock the arena again.

He heard Jamal's words as if he were sitting right next to him.

"Welcome to the end of innocence baby."

"I gonna miss him," he said.

"Me too."

Ω

He checked out of the hospital an hour later. She held her tongue for a week, and when the time seemed right, she finally told him.

"Jesse, I'm pregnant.

chapter: 26

I T TOOK JESSE TWO MONTHS to recover from his injuries. The headaches were still thorns in his crown, but he could finally jog without pain. The news of the baby tempered his angst about Jamal's death. He wondered if God had to take to give. He hated the reaper's choice but gave him a pass for the moment. A pass meant he stopped torturing himself over things he couldn't know. But he was still suspicious, and one day, he wondered if God was a cosmic adolescent playing His favorite video game, and humans were His avatars. And He was way too fast and loose handling the controller.

Deric had a hard time with Jamal's death too and grieved in his own way. He became increasingly angry by the day. Eventually, he took his anger to the Marine Corps. It seemed like a good idea. He had nothing going in life anyway, and he wanted to burn any motherfucker that stood at odds with America.

Joe and Bobby still ran the local poker game. Bobby had also been involved with some less than reputable characters. He invited them to the games, and Joe took them to school on the felt. Jesse played from time to time and made some walking around money.

Jesse and Jennie were peanut butter and jelly. Now they'd both quit school and joined the work force. Mostly because the baby was on the way, but partly because Jesse had started thinking college was a scam. He only went to play basketball in the first place. But he still felt the need to justify breaking from social norms.

"I don't get why we need college. You just pay to end up with some job you hate, working for some prick who makes five times what you do. Eventually, you're stuck. It's pretty much taking on debt to get the shit side of slavery."

Jennie worked for a local bank as a part-time teller, and with a wedding on the horizon, Jesse needed a job sooner rather than later. He could philosophize all he wanted about quitting basketball and school, but it really came down to the baby growing inside Jennie's belly.

Jesse didn't have much luck in his search and ended up taking the most convenient job he could find, a gig Chuck got him working odd jobs at the Triple Threat's maintenance facility. It crossed his mind that becoming Chuck was his fate, and that thought chapped his ass. He hated working in the same building as him, but did what he had to do. And he guessed it was better than the alternative—living with Chuck.

As far as living goes, Joe had tenants scheduled to move into Jesse and Jamal's place on the first of September. So Jesse had to be out, and Joe helped him move his stuff into the Rizzo house.

Jamal's mom never came to get the things he'd left in this world, so Joe packed it all in boxes and put it in a storage unit in case someone wanted it later. He couldn't bring himself to throw it away.

The arrangement to live Rizzo's started by having to drop the bomb on Susan that Jennie was, as an old Schofield KJV would put it, *with child*. The conversation wasn't as awkward as Jesse thought it would be. Susan seemed happy. She insisted that he move in and be around for Jennie and the baby. The house had extra space since Don went M.I.A. Maybe she missed having a man in the house. She did, however, insist they get married as soon as possible.

That didn't seem so bad to Jesse. They spent nearly every non-working hour together anyway, and somehow, still liked each other which had to be a good sign. He asked her to marry him in early October and they decided to have a Thanksgiving wedding.

Most kids raised in fundamental baptist churches seem to get married early. There might be a few reasons this happens...

Starting a family as soon as possible is the "Christian way" and the next normal step in life.

Or...

A couple's parents married young and somehow projected their life timeline onto their kids. In many Christian cultures, if someone waits until their thirties to get married, there has to be something wrong with them.

Or...

If married, a couple finally gets to have guilt-free sex with a person instead of their hand.

Or...

The couple didn't wait, and a baby was on the way. Abortion is murder. Fuck the future. Do what's right and grab that shotgun.

Jesse and Jennie made much love since that beautiful June night in his apartment, so getting married to have sex wasn't the issue. Neither wanted any part of a home like they were raised in. And Jesse didn't care much for the Christian way anymore. Baby incoming. Pump and fire.

There were a few good reasons for the new Baker family to set up shop in the Rizzo house—Susan got fat alimony from Don and would help them get started. Also, both of them could work when the baby arrived because Susan could keep the kid.

They broke the news to Vanessa and Chuck soon after telling Susan. They took the news well too. Vanessa squealed and hugged them and said, "What a blessing!"

Chuck's reaction shocked his son. "Are you-ins gonna get married soon?" he said with a stern look on his face.

"Yes, sir. We're getting married in November," Jesse said.

"Well... Welcome to the family Jennie." Then he turned to Jesse and said, "And welcome to the club, son." Chuck gave him a firm handshake. "Don't mess it up. You got a good'n."

"I won't, Dad."

They got in the car to go back to the Rizzo house, which I guess you could call the Rizzo/Baker house now.

"That went surprisingly well," Jennie said as she pulled her Saturn Vue out of the drive.

"I can't believe it," Jesse said with a satisfied smile.

If only all conversations were this easy.

Ω

Jesse and Jennie only fought about one thing before and after their wedding—the rosters.[Ω] It all started on a night in late September while they were watching one of his favorite movies—*Clerks*. She'd never seen it, and predictably, its content led to a conversation they'd been avoiding since they'd fallen in love. She was reluctant to give up the information, but he was persistent.

"So how far have you ever gone with another guy?" Jesse asked, already thinking he knew the answer.

"Do we really have to do this? I don't care what you've done or who you've done it with," she said. She cared, but was considering her strategy and wanted to procrastinate the inevitable as long as she could.

"I *have* to know."[Ω]

[Ω] A significant other's list of previous sexual partners

[Ω] Certain institutionalized evangelicals feel an irrational need to know the physical scouting report of their partners—especially the males. For many of them, if they come up short of their partners sexual experience, there is an uncomfortable power imbalance. This isn't true of all men who grew up in a purity culture, but was unfortunately the case for Jesse.

"You go first then, But if we're doing this, we can't get mad about it. It's all in the past. We're different people now. Deal?" she said.

His heart melted, and his brain raced. He had to know, so he spilled every horny bean he could recollect. He told her about all the girls from high school, and what base they reached during Jennie and Jesse's breakups. A few of them were Jennie's friends, but not girls in her clique. They weren't people she still spoke to, which was a relief to her.

Then he told her about the time Kelly McGill from Groverton High School sucked his dick in his car after a game at their place. Then about the time Marlene Blackstone went down on him in an empty theater. She got mad because, at times, it sounded like he was bragging. But she tried her best to hide it because the momentum was sure to shift in the second half of this exercise.

She thought about her strategy while she listened to his college stories. She eventually settled on honesty. They were about to get married, and she wanted their marriage to be built on truth no matter how uncomfortable and embarrassing the truth was. She thought there was a slight chance he might bail, but to her, the truth would always be worth the risk.

He went on about the coeds at Calvin Newman. She didn't know any of them. He said the details were hazy because alcohol was always involved. The final count was fellatio with twelve girls, cunnilingus with two, and a fuck-ton of foolin' around. That was his word for it. Fuck-ton.

"Wow, you were busy. Are you honestly telling me you didn't have sex with anyone?"

"Yeah. I don't know... I guess I was programmed to wait for the right time. Or maybe I just couldn't pull the trigger." There was a hint of moral high ground in his voice.

"You're like the girl who sucked thirty-seven dicks then." She giggled and pointed at the screen.

"Whatever, your turn."

"Well..." She paused. "I had sex with a few guys."

"How many's a few?"

"Six."

"Are you kidding? That's not a few. That's a half dozen."

"I was in a bad place last year."

"Who was the first?" He tried really hard not to flip out.

"Well... Remember we promised not to get mad."

"You said that," he shot back.

"Well *try*. I'll be totally honest because that's how our relationship will be."

"I'll do my best, but no promises."

"Bobby."

"Bobby fucking Corban? You fucked Bobby *fucking* Corban?" The screechy wheels were no longer on the rails.

"I told you, I was in a bad place. My dad left. You left. I was depressed. I started drinking and stuff. It was the hardest time of my life."

"Yeah, but Bobby Corban? Why did it have to be him, Jennie? He's such a fucking tool."

"Oh, I know." She swallowed slowly. "I knew this was a terrible idea."

"No, it's fine. It's in the past," he said to himself out loud.

"Who else?"

She ripped off some names he didn't know. Four guys at four different UTC frat parties and one preacher boy at UPCC who fell in love with her during their second semester Biblical World View Class. Two weeks before she quit school he finally got the stones to ask her out. She rode him in his car on that date before he had to be back for curfew. The next day she told him they should just be friends.[Ω]

"Goddammit... Okay... Look... You have to tell me everything. Where? How did it happen? What position?" There was anger in his voice.

"Why? So you can torture yourself about it? And torture me?"

"I just can't believe you fucked six guys."

She started crying.

"I mean..." He paused to think of something he could say that would hurt her bad.

"You want me to say sorry? I'm sorry. I am. You wanna call me a slut right now then just have the balls to say it. I can take it," she shouted, her voice an octave higher from crying. "I've made mistakes. I've done things I'm ashamed of. But I'm NOT the same person as I was a year ago. You hooked up with all those girls that you say meant nothing. How's that any different?"

"My cock... wasn't in Kelly McGill's pussy."

"But it was in her mouth. It's the same thing, Jesse!"

"No. It's not."

"Why? Because Pastor Joel told you sex is special? Fuck you and your technicalities. And your fucking

---

[Ω] The preacher by Jennie had sex with went forward and cried during the altar call the next Sunday morning. When he got married, he never told his virgin wife about their encounter.

high horse. I'm not listening to this. I told you the truth."

"I wish you woulda fucked me first. But you let Bobby Corban fuck you instead. At least you got standards."

"Fuck you, Jesse."

"I shoulda fucked 'em all. Too late now."

The yelling woke Susan. She rolled over in her bed but didn't try to listen. A tear dripped down her high cheekbone and landed on her pillow. She prayed for them.

Jennie stormed upstairs to her room and slammed the door. Jesse sat on the couch fuming. His mind harassed him while he finished *Clerks*. Eventually, he walked up the steps to go to bed. He stopped at her door and opened it. She was curled up on her bed, back to the door. He walked to her, put a knee on the bed, held himself up over her, and leaned down to whisper in her ear. Her eyes were open. They were still wet.

"I'm really sorry Jennie. I was being stupid."

She said nothing.

"I love you."

"Still?"

"Always."

"You're a dick, you know that?"

"Yeah."

They kissed. They made love. They made love really, really hard.

The rhythmic knocking upstairs woke Susan again. She didn't move, didn't open her eyes and had an uncomfortable look on her face, but said aloud, "Thank you, Jesus."

chapter: 27

COACH WATTS SAW JESSE working at the maintenance facility one morning and asked him if he wanted to be a part-time assistant coach for the Wolves. Hesitantly, Jesse said he'd consider it, but Jennie talked him into it later that week. She thought that reconnecting with his passion for basketball would be good for him. And maybe he could become a head coach one day. He took the job and was excited about the new venture. The $800 coaching stipend wasn't bad either. It was a good thing nobody knew Jennie was having his kid yet, or there was no way he would have made it through the Triple Threat hiring process.

Jesse enjoyed working for Coach Watts. He'd been a player/coach on the floor his last few years playing for the Wolves so being Coach's right-hand man was familiar enough.

But duality existed in familiarity for Jesse.

Coaching just wasn't the same as playing the game. He desperately missed the stage, his control over the outcomes, and most of all, the competition. Now he was the guy who sat on the sideline with his grand basketball wisdom, telling people to box out, throw a skip pass, share the ball, hold their follow-through, and even how to think. His seat on the bench felt more like a pulpit. He was always the projected not the projector, and he hated fucking pulpits.[Ω]

Competitors do have to compete though. It's programmed into them. When they can't they might as well be dead because that's how they feel inside. The problem was he didn't see coaching as an alternative form of competition. He was Chuck during the work day and a young preacher at practice—two things he never wanted to be. This might have led to an irrational desire to blow himself up.

Ω

If the baby was a boy, Jennie asked Jesse if he wanted to name him Charles, after Jamal. He said, "Fuck no, we aren't naming him after Chuck." So they settled on James.

At 12:37 a.m. on March 10, 2001, Jennie had a baby girl. They named her Molly. The nurses let Jesse give Molly her first bath with a wet cloth. Then they taught him how to change her diaper. He held her while Jennie slept. Then he put her down and picked up his old journal that he'd found in a box when he moved into the Rizzo house. He brought it just in case. It had been awhile since he'd written anything, but he finally had something to say so he picked up his pen.

[Ω] Adjective fucking. Not verb fucking. Up to this point in his life, Jesse never hit or struck a pulpit. He never stuck his penis in one either.

Ω

The Life and Times of Jesse "Take-All-Comers" Baker
By Jesse Baker
March 10, 2001

Today has been something else. These are new feelings. When I hold her, I'm a different person. It's overwhelming that me and Jennie have brought life into the world. Our blood in my arms. We did this. She did this. Molly is the perfect mix of both of us. I will raise her the best I can and love her my way. Not like Chuck. I won't be him. And I vow to love and protect this baby girl with same sincerity I vowed to Jennie on our wedding day. They make me feel things I've never known were possible.

chapter: 28

DON NOTICED BOBBY'S EYES weren't as red as they had been in previous meetings. He studied Bobby's face while Lucy spoke about life after Cornerstone Baptist and the challenges of raising a child on her own. Bobby sensed it and looked at Don who looked back at Lucy quickly. Bobby smiled. Today was *his* day.

Brian, the preacher's son who knocked up Lucy never told the church he was the baby's father, neither did the preacher. The day Brian graduated from Cornerstone Christian School, Lucy revealed the father's identity to her parents, and they were furious. She opened up and told them everything, and to her surprise, they took her side. Her father called the preacher and asked for a meeting. The preacher obliged.

On a sticky summer afternoon, Lucy and her parents sat in the preacher's office to break the news to him. The newborn infant slept in a mobile car seat by her chair. Her parents expected the preacher to be taken back by the revelation that his son was the father, but he didn't blink. He expressed his gratitude for not outing his son and explained that doing so even now would cause division in the church, but he had a solution. Her father's face turned red as he listened to the preacher's plan.

When he was seconds away from telling the preacher to stick his solution up his ass, the preacher threw out a number—$3,000 a month. A personal check would come on the first Monday of each month. There was one stipulation—no governmental involvement.

Her father yelled at the preacher who took it in stride. Like most fundamental Baptist pastors, he was calculated. And it was obvious the baby was no revelation. He had known for a long time, long enough to start a monthly love offering that spring for families in need called the "Aaron Fund."[Ω]

Lucy stopped going to the church after being shamed at the alter in front of everyone. She couldn't deal with the stares, but she was okay with this compromise. Being a single mother would be hard when she eventually left her parents and went on her own, and $3,000 was a lot of money. She calmed her father, and they accepted the deal. Her parents left the church shortly after that meeting with the preacher, but the checks still came every week.

After giving birth to her daughter, she lived with her parents until she was 26-years-old, when she got

---

[Ω] In the book of Exodus, when Moses was in need—arms shaking over his head and about to drop his staff, Aaron stepped in and held up his arms for him. The pitch was the church would hold up the poor families in their city.

promoted to store manager at Walgreens and transferred to Chattanooga. She did well on her own and hadn't seen Brian in years and wanted to keep it that way.

"Thanks for sharing, Lucy," Nick said.

"Thanks, Lucy," the group said.

"Would one more person like to share tonight?" Nick said.

After a month of sitting in through the meetings and not saying a word, Bobby slowly raised his hand.

"All right. Looks like tonight's your night, Bobby," Nick said.

"Hi. My name is Bobby Corban, and the only thing I know for sure is I don't know shit. Guess that means I don't know myself either."

The group chuckled.

"My life blows, man. I've been to jail. I've been homeless. I don't even know why I'm here..." He looked out the window at the UPBC church building. "I grew up in that church and school over there and saw y'all's sign outside. I walk around here because it helps me remember being a normal kid and not an addict.

"I know y'all probably think I'm in the wrong group, but I tried Narcotics and Alcoholics Anonymous and still ain't got a one-month sobriety token. I hear ya'll talk about how you've been betrayed by these pastors and shit and your struggles with faith and all, and I get it. My dad was a self-righteous dictator... until I was 11, and that asshole walked out the door and never came back. Motherfucker believed birth control was a sin. That's all well and good until daddy bounces. Me, Mom, my 6 brothers and 2 sisters were on our own.

"I don't know if I've believed in anything since that asshole left. But back in the day, man, I had hopes and dreams. I don't know what happened. I just wish I could go back. I got nothin' now."

The circle stayed silent for a few seconds, then Bobby continued.

"Nothin' can't be it man. It just can't. You know what I did yesterday? I was so high I sat in front of a Dollar General with a sign, asking for money to buy blow like a fucking bum. So fuckin' dumb, who begs at the Dollar store? Like that's the crowd that gives handouts. What the hell has happened man?"

There was an awkward silence in the circle until Don spoke up, "Maybe the world just spins."

"Mr. Rizzo, how the fuck does that help?" Bobby asked.

"It doesn't, but I just can't let myself believe in a God that controls it all anymore. I'd hate that sadist bastard and not be able to do a damn thing about it."

"I feel you." Bobby choked up. His eyes filled with tears, then he whispered, "I knew her."

"What?" Don asked.

"Yeah. Your daughter Jennie, and Jesse too. I think about 'em all the time."

"You better stop, kid," Don said.

"You know... No... You're a piece of shit, Don. You know that?" Bobby said leaning forward in his chair, elbow on his knee.

"Whoa. Chill Bobby," Nick said, splaying his fingers.

Nick had only bits and pieces of their stories, and this was the first he'd heard of Don's daughter Jennie, and whoever this Jesse character was. A big part of him wanted to toss his moderator hat in the trash and sit back and watch the action escalate. And that's exactly what he did, and that's exactly what it did.

Don and Bobby had both admitted they were miserable human beings in the circle. At first, Nick figured it was the existential misery that they all bellyached about. This was clearly not the case. For whatever reason, both had forsaken any attempt to live a life with even the faintest hint of morality. Nick wasn't judging, just recognizing the facts they had both admitted to.

Bobby took advantage when it suited him. He burned every bridge with anyone unfortunate enough to come in contact with him. He told Nick at the coffee pot after one of the meetings that he needed a ride to the soup kitchen because his only brother who still talked to him wasn't answering his calls anymore. With no prying, he volunteered details like Nick was the priest in Jeff's confession booth. He'd pawned his brother's 1978 limited edition Gibson Dove guitar, the one their grandpa gave him a month before dying. He used the money to buy crystal meth. His brother found out and told Bobby he was dead to him.

Nick tried to figure out why Bobby was going at Don so hard. There was the obvious reason—Don reminded him of his own father's disappearing act. Then something else dawned on him—people despise certain character flaws they see in others, flaws that they hate are true about themselves.

"What is your damage boy?" Don warned.

Nick let them go. Bobby had a death wish.

"How can you just roll out one day and not think about your kid?"

"You have no idea what you're talkin' about," Don said.

"Yeah, I do. I knew exactly how Jennie felt."

"Don't say her name."

"Why? Does it feel better to pretend she never existed?"

"Fuck you. You don't know anything about me. How dare you? You don't know us. You didn't know her," Don sputtered with a tear streaming from each eye.

"Oh, I knew her all right. She haunts me, man. I coulda loved her. Maybe that woulda saved her from that psycho."

"Shut your fucking mouth!" Don yelled, but Bobby wouldn't stop.

It was getting out of hand, so Nick and the others tried to step in, "Okay, Bobby that's enough," Nick said. But Bobby raised his voice over everyone.

"You should make me pay, Don."

Don looked at Bobby sideways. He was leaning forward with his elbows on his knees, and his hands were shaking in front of him.

"I need to pay because when our golden boy went off to college, his beautiful girl was lonely and heartbroke. Her daddy had left her too. And she came to me. And I did what I do. I got her drunk and got to know her real well. You know, in the Biblical sense."

Don shot toward Bobby so fast that his metal chair clanged against the wall behind him.

chapter: 29

THE WOLVES HAD A GOOD YEAR in 2000-2001. They were a young squad who overachieved and won a District championship but came up one game short of making it to state.

A week after the season ended, the god of the Triple Threat called Jesse into his office. Dr. Germaine had been the senior pastor at UPBC since Jesse was in kindergarten. Jesse couldn't remember ever speaking to him. But that day, he was important enough to have a meeting with the big kahuna. He felt good.

Jesse got there thirty minutes early and wore a shirt and tie. Different scenarios ran through his mind...

Maybe he wants to tell me I did a great job in my first year with Coach Watts.

Maybe he wants to encourage me and make sure I'm okay after the accident and Jamal dying and wants to pray with me.

Maybe he wants to congratulate me about getting married and the baby.

Maybe he wants to thank me for a job well done.

Maybe, just maybe he wants to give me a raise. That'd be sweet.

He forgot to consider the issue that would be held over his head forever at this place, even if it was never explicitly verbalized. The wedding/baby timeline was way off.[Ω] There were other issues that made Jesse a cog that didn't fit into this machine, but none of them held heavier judicial weight than this. Dr. Germaine would have it out for him as long as he signed Jesse's checks.

"Jesse, he'll see you now," said Dr. Germaine's secretary, Linda.

He walked in nervously. He'd never spoken to a demigod before.

"Have a seat, Jesse."

He sat in a plush leather chair across from the preacher who sat tall behind his desk like it was a throne.[Ω]

[Ω] Premarital sex, unwed pregnancy, divorce, and experimenting with homosexuality were life-time employment deal breakers at the Upton Park Triple Threat—unless of course, you were in the senior pastor's immediate family, then you could be redeemed enough to work there. Pastoral Studies majors wanking off to fuck-tons of teen porn in their dorm rooms was fine though. That was between them and God. They were employable. Fuck-tons.

[Ω] Jesse looked up the word throne when he was a little kid. It was a seat for kings and queens. He later defined it as the big white seat God will sit on when he judges our actions and reveals our eternal fate. In high school, he added an alternative definition. A throne is a john. The kind of john that eats shit.

"Jesse, I've been reviewing reports on our employees. It looks like you haven't attended a Sunday school class$^{\Omega}$ in months. Is this true?"

"I've missed a few, but I've been going lately. I just forget to sign in."

Lie. He hadn't been all year. He did everything he could to not darken the door of the Upton Park Baptist Church. Hell, he'd been to two services that year. Christmas and Easter. The only reason he attended those was to watch their plays with the music that made him feel nostalgic. There was a bonus—no preaching during those services.

"Well, you have to sign in."

"Yes, sir."

"I also don't see any record of your tithe.$^{\Omega}$ Do you tithe?"

The church paid the lowest possible wages to all their employees. Everyone except the pastoral staff. The insurance benefits sucked and a retirement plan didn't exist. Everyone was expected to suffer for Jesus and live by faith. Tithe to the church and God would provide. Jesse made about $10,000 that year working full time at the maintenance building. And they wanted him to give at least $1,000 of that back? That didn't really work for him.

"I do tithe."

Another lie Dr. Germaine wasn't buying.

$^{\Omega}$ Every Sunday school class had a sign-in sheet. Crazy as it may sound, the Preacher kept tabs on the grown-ups.

$^{\Omega}$ The concept that a church member is commanded to give 10% of their earnings to the church. It has often been said, that if they obey this command, God will rain "showers of blessings" on them more money than they ever dreamed of.

"Do you put it in one of the envelopes in the pews with your name on it?"

"No sir. I just put cash in the plate."

"Well we need to have tithe records of our employees. Use checks or the envelopes. If you want to work here, you must obey God's commands. And that includes tithing. We need to make sure that we're all obedient to him. We all have to sacrifice our will to God to receive the fullness of His blessings. That includes our money."

Jesse bit his tongue while he thought carefully about what he wanted to say. Tithing seemed like it should be a personal thing—between a man and God. For a second, Jesse stopped thinking so carefully, and started thinking a little more recklessly—he considered this might be his chance to start cussin' the place up.

You need my money that bad? That's a nice new Cadillac you just got. And look at this place. It's massive, and that chandelier in the lobby is probably worth more than my fucking car. We live with my mother-in-law because I can't even afford rent you greedy fucking prick. What's your house look like? How big is your TV? Sacrifice my ass.

Carefully prevailed though.

"Yes, sir. I'll use the envelopes."

"Good. I like you, Jesse, and I always enjoyed watching you play ball, and I'm happy you've recovered from the accident I heard about last summer. Now, if you don't mind, I'll lead us in prayer now. Dear Jesus, I..."[Ω]

[Ω] Jesse knew a thing or two about narcissism, but in the entirety of his time on the earth to this point, he'd never heard someone drop that many *I's* in such a short sequence.

Jesse didn't hear a word of the prayer beside the beginning and the end because he was so fucking pissed. Germaine never mentioned Jennie or Molly or Jamal. There was still a chance recklessness would be the eventual victor of the battle in his mind, and during the prayer he tried to think of the perfect swearing combos he could throw into a magnificent exit.

"... in Jesus' name, Amen."

Goddammit. You were just talking to Him. Why always the third person goodbye?

Eloquently recited public prayers had always been Jesse's pet peeve. He felt they were just for show. When he heard one, it poured gasoline on his already burning agnostic fire. He was convinced that people who prayed like this might as well have been reading poetry because it didn't sound anything like they were talking to a being living in their hearts. The week before, he had an interesting thought about prayer. *If God is really all-knowing, how boring must these prayers be for Him? Some dude gets in front of a microphone and tells Him a bunch of shit He already knows.* Jesse couldn't imagine enduring conversations where he would listen to someone tell him shit he already knew over and over like it was some shocking reveal. *No wonder God's been asleep at the wheel. Dude's fucking checked out.* The last time he went to church—the night of Christmas play—every prayer was an announcement or a thinly veiled spiritual brag.

After the prayer, Dr. Germaine stood to walk him out. Jesse got up and walked beside him. He thought there was still a chance Germaine would mention something about Molly, or how he prayed for him every day since the accident, or how he was doing with the loss of his friend. No such luck. Narcissists struggle with empathy. You have to get outside yourself to consider others.

At the door, Dr. Germaine offered him a handshake as Jesse pulled the clip to lob a vulgarity grenade that would send *fuck* shrapnel to a place it had never been, at least as far as he knew.

"I..."

Germaine cut him off. Much like narcissists, demigods aren't good listeners. And when a man is both, he completely lacks the capacity or desire to hear what simple-minded peasants have to say.

"Son, if you need anything, my office is always open," he said as moved Jesse out the door with a firm handshake, then closed it.

Jesse stood paralyzed, staring at the wall past Linda.

After twenty awkward seconds, Linda, confused, asked, "Are you okay?"

"Yes, ma'am."

He walked to his car feeling like a punk bitch. Seething. He knew now what he'd always expected—Dr. Germaine didn't give a shit about him. He was a pawn on the church chess board. Expendable. Serving only one purpose—to sacrifice for the institution, for the Lord's work. His office experience made him feel like a john. Because he ate shit. It also made him feel like a very specific type of john.[Ω]

When he got to his car, he thought, *Fuck it,* and walked back into the building.

[Ω] One who pays to get fucked by a transvestite hooker. Ten percent for a shot in the ass.

"Hello again. Did you forget something?" Linda asked.

"Yeah."

He pulled a lonely twenty-dollar bill out of his wallet and barged back into Dr. Germaine's office and slammed Andrew Jackson's pompous looking headshot on the desk.

Recklessness prevailed in the comeback win.

"You know what you can do, Donny—here's my last twenty bucks. I'll fast and fucking pray for the rest of the week. Go buy yourself lunch somewhere nice like you do every fucking day with our tithe dollars—you fat piece of enlightened shit. Even better—why don't you shove it, along with your inspired, infallible bullshit, up your authoritative ass."

The preacher was speechless. Nobody had ever talked to him like that before. He took it like an old alpha male who hadn't been challenged in decades and forgot how to fight.

Jesse walked out the door and slammed it behind him. He felt great but found himself out of work. And his cup of coffee in the basketball coaching profession was over too.

Ω

A few weeks later, Jennie put in a good word for him at the bank, and he got a job as a part-time teller making a measly $10 an hour. But it was better than nothing. They worked beside each other and exchanged smiles and jokes all day. He was happiest around her so this didn't feel like work. Until he started getting fed up with men hitting on her, which happened almost every day. Jennie was used to it. It's part of the territory when you're an attractive woman, but this was new to Jesse, and he couldn't get used to it. People had never openly flirted with her in front of him before. Nobody expected she was married to the teller in the next booth until he started getting into verbal altercations with customers.

The first time was mild enough—a simple declaration that she was with him. But the heat of these exchanges rose a few degrees each time during the two months he worked there. The manager finally called him into the office and gave him an ultimatum to stop getting into it with the customers, or he'd be fired.

He was never a big fan of ultimatums and you already know how he felt about authority. He didn't say a word in the meeting except "okay." You didn't have to be the prophet Elijah to predict what would happen next.

It was a breezy day in June, and a regular customer stood in the line. He was a sharp looking guy in his late twenties dressed in a frat guy costume.

Jesse looked up the word *tool* once. He learned it was a piece of equipment that enables someone to put other pieces of equipment together or take them apart.

Much later, he jotted down a new definition for equipment. It resided in the crotch of a man's pants—which could also be called a tool, or a dick—which also happens to be the shortened name of Richard.

He later understood that the word *tool* could also be a man who cares way too much about how he looks and acts as if the earth spins around him. That sounded like a few people he knew—one in particular he knew very, very, *very* well.

The English language can be as ironic as it is confusing. Imagine trying to translate something written in an ancient language that could be just as complicated and subjectively defined as English—no fucking thanks.

Sometimes, words run together. And if you let it run together here,[Ω] you have a guy named Richard Satchel. His friends called him Rick. He wore pastel colored Lacoste shirts, khaki shorts, flip flops, and Prada sunglasses indoors. He was also one of those guys who talked loudly on his phone while standing in lines. He always hit on Jennie, and Jesse had called him on it before, but it was hard for Jesse and Jennie to take him seriously because of his unfortunate name. He became one of their running work jokes, but that day was different. Jesse was in a bad mood because he'd just been bitched out by the boss.

Rick was on the phone and next in line when Jesse said, "I'll take the next customer."

Rick carried on his conversation and acted like he didn't hear him. So Jesse spoke louder.

"I'LL TAKE THE NEXT CUSTOMER."

Rick looked at him and covered the mouthpiece of his phone and said, "I'll wait for her," pointing at Jennie. Then he started talking again.

Jennie processed the transaction for her customer and pretended like she didn't hear, but she did and worried that this situation might not end well. The next person in line walked toward Jesse.

[Ω] Tool=Equipment=Dick=Tool=Douchebag=[insert name]=Tool

"No, you wait right there," Jesse said, stopping the new customer. Then he raised his voice, "Hey, Dick Bag... No... you won't wait for her. You'll get off your damn phone, and I'll take you right here."

Rick whispered, "Lemme call you back," pressed the end button, and approached Jesse "Take All Comers" Baker.

"What the hell is your problem, man? Do you have any idea who I am?"

Jesse leaned forward and laughed obnoxiously loud in his face. This didn't seem like a reasonable reaction to Rick because he wasn't aware that the *don't you know who I am* card is hilarious to a not-so-humble peasant. He stood silently perplexed.

"Oh boy. I'm sorry, I'm sorry. How silly of me." Jesse said through sarcastic laughter.

"Hey Jennie, did you hear that?"

Jennie mouthed the word, "Stop."

A few customers waiting in line started chuckling too. Maybe they knew what a tool looked like—5.75 feet tall in pleated khakis.

Jesse composed himself, leaned forward, and spoke calmly, "If you want me fired, go ahead. They don't pay shit anyways." Then he lunged over the counter and took a swing at Rick, who dodged the punch and scurried out the door, proclaiming that Jesse had just made a "colossal" mistake.

And Jesse found himself out of work, again.

chapter: 30

EVERYONE SAYS LIFE CHANGES when you have a baby. Jesse and Jennie found out quickly how right they were. Molly was all things holy to him, but as a baby, she shared his dualistic nature—she was a holy terror. She didn't sleep much during normal sleeping hours. Susan told them that was normal for an infant, but it felt anything but normal. They were sleep deprived, and every passing minute was another chance for Molly to scream or shit in their faces. She cried so much and so hard that she popped a hernia during a tantrum when she was eight months old and had to have a minor surgery.

Fatigue can make cowards of strong people. It can also make one prone to raging, and Jesse's fuse got shorter and shorter. Not so much with Molly, he figured she was just a baby and couldn't help it. It was shorter with Jennie. They fought a lot during those first 4 months.

Susan was tired too, but she took an average of 17 five-minute power naps a day. Jesse thought she was narcoleptic. Jennie thought she was smart. But they agreed on one thing—she was helpful.

Jesse loved Jennie and Molly, but the fatigue made her wonder sometimes. His brain also seemed to be growing progressively darker every day since the accident. He didn't say anything about it, but she could tell.

She also knew he'd covertly told his old religion and all spirituality for that matter to fuck off. It's not that one becomes darker because they lose religion, but there might be an adjustment period for some.

Back when Jesse was in 11th grade, he had a new English teacher named Mr. Jones who kept assigning books that Jesse thought were lame. He gave the first one a try. It was about a pilgrim carrying a back pack. He thought it sucked huge burdenous sacks. After that chore of a book, he never read anything Mr. Jones assigned again. He just cheated off Cliff's notes.[Ω] Maybe he should have given Mr. Jones's reading list a second chance because there was this one book by a man whose name Jesse couldn't accurately recall. He once said, "I'm sick of him assigning books by this asshole Chad Lewis." Jesse scribbled in his journal during their class discussion on Lewis's book about holes in people's souls—a topic that would probably be beneficial to explore at this point in his life. But he never got around to reading that book.

Sometimes, he wondered what Mr. Haynes[Ω] had been up to.

[Ω] There was a boy named Cliff McBride who sat next to him in 11th grade English. He was an exceptional note taker.

[Ω] Mr. Haynes didn't get fired for assigning a Kurt Vonnegut, Jr. book to the young, impressionable students at Upton Park Christian School, but he did get reprimanded, and the principal told him to only assign literary books with Christian themes. So he assigned *The Last Temptation of Christ* by Nikos Kazantzakis and quit before they could fire him.

That guy who wrote about the God-shaped hole in a person's soul also wrote another book that was assigned to Jesse's 11ᵗʰ grade class—a book about African wildlife, witchcraft, and closets. Jesse passed on that one too. He thought it was a stupid combination, and none of the three interested him individually much less together.

Aerosmith had a song called *Hole in My Soul.* Jesse listened to that song 957 times in one year. He also was one of the few people in the world who thought *Nine Lives* was their best album.

Being out of work wasn't so bad for Jesse during the fall of 2001. He put all his focus into his poker game. Under Joe's tutelage, he relentlessly pursued the mastery of No-Limit Texas Hold'em, shearing the sheep in the home game and learning the tricks of the online trade.

Over the past few years, Joe had become a world class online poker player. He'd made nearly half a million dollars since graduating high school and built a reputation in the online poker community—feared by even the stoutest of competition. He bought a lot of nice things—a boat, jet skis, a Range Rover, and many other man toys. Jesse wanted what he had, but mostly, he wanted to provide for his girls and not have a boss.

When Jesse was in high school, he learned in history class that some old American fat ass named Teddy once said, "Comparison is the thief of all joy," and a part of him believed that was the truth. But the competitive beast in him thought it was bullshit, and comparison was motivation to put his dreams to work just like he did in the Upton Park Rec back in the day. So maybe comparison was the mother of joy, birthing a benchmark of inspiration that could lead to achieving something special.

Since Jesse was a terrible employee, he'd have to become an entrepreneur. Not the entrepreneur of 2018—you know, the ones that flood the Facebook feeds of innocent people who just want to watch an epic fail compilation or a cat spooked by a cucumber, the ones that see email addresses as currency. He became an entrepreneur that played poker for a living, and against all odds, it worked out.

He didn't want to live with Susan forever. He wanted to get Jennie and Molly a place of their own and was determined to make a better life for them than what he had as a kid—a life without Upton Park sounds:

Roaches crackling like Rice Krispies under your feet when you walked into the dark kitchen in the middle of the night for a slug of orange juice from the carton.

The three cranks and pumped gas you gave your car before it started.

Police sirens.

Gunshots instead of fireworks on the 4th of July. Come to think of it—on any given night.

During the summer of 2002, Jesse and Joe took a trip to Vegas for the World Series of Poker. They had big dreams, but they had a plan—a strategy, a bankroll for events and cash games, and a stop-loss. They knew, even at their young age, that if they wanted to gamble for a living, it had to be all business. There was no room for degeneracy. They made their living off the ignorant and the degenerates. Pushing the favorable odds, then pushing the chips in the middle, then more often than not, pulling in monster pots. Always remembering—the bankroll is king. Protect it at all costs and never risk ruin under any circumstances.

That trip turned out to be the turning point of Jesse's career. Lady luck smiled on him, and he finished 2nd in a $1500 buy-in No-Limit Hold'em WSOP preliminary event winning $112,000. This would bankroll him in the mid-stakes online cash games. The artist on the court morphed into an artist on the felt, and the amateur was ready to turn pro.

The timing couldn't have been better because the abrupt loss of Jesse's star status had hit him hard. He'd been depressed and didn't know why. He loved his new life and baby. Maybe it was because he had no competitive outlet during that first year after the accident. Most ultra-competitors can't change. If they can't compete, they may as well be dead.

Joe picked up a big score too. When he got home, he bought a big house on the lake. He planned on keeping his old house at the foot of the mountain as a rental property and was surprised when Jesse asked if he could rent it. Joe thought that would be like Rocky deciding to live in the arena where Ivan Drago put Apollo Creed to sleep, but he agreed to let him live in the old place. They had some good memories there too. After the Baker three moved in, Jesse never drove up that mountain. Not once.

chapter: 31

JESSE AND JENNIE FOUND a nice rhythm in their new house. Every day Jesse kept Molly at home and grinded the virtual felt while Jennie was at work. He tried to teach himself how to cook and made a few disastrous dinners. Jennie choked down these culinary abortions with a smile. To her, it was the thought that mattered.

Susan still babysat whenever they wanted. So they often had friends over or hung out at Joe's. They weren't your normal young couple with a child. They were free, painting their own family portrait. The brush strokes embodied perfection to Jesse. It helped that they had a lot of the same interests, but it was mainly because they shared the same desires—to be together, live it up, and enjoy every moment of their lives. No church, no rules, and no preconceived notions of what a married couple should be.

Jesse was crushing poker. He had a solid system where he played six to eight tables at once across two thirty-inch computer monitors. He played on two sites—Pokerstars.com and UltimateBet.com. His strategy was nearly bulletproof, taking lowest possible risk and keeping 100 buy-ins online for any stake he was playing. As he consistently ran up his accounts, he cashed out only what needed or wanted to spend. That year he made anywhere from $10K-$50K every month like clockwork.

It could be predictable that a newly married couple who had no money growing up, but found themselves in some, would spend without a conscience. The way they saw it, what was the point of having it if you didn't enjoy it. After a year, Jennie quit her job at the bank and decided she wanted to try something she actually *wanted* to do. She enrolled in a local culinary school. The tuition was expensive, and they paid cash.

They traveled the world, saw the rainbows and surfed the pipeline in Hawaii, drank hard liquor out of coconuts in the Bahamas, took a stroll down the Great Wall of China, and took trips to Vegas where they gambled it up, shopped at the finest stores, ate at the finest restaurants and had sexy times in the most luxurious suites on the strip.

Jesse wore Maui Jim sunglasses.[Ω]

Jennie carried a Louis Vuitton bag and walked in Jimmy Choo heels.

He could still grind the felt while they traveled. All he needed was his laptop, a stable internet connection, and a few hours of free time.

When they were at home, the weekend parties were extravagant. They didn't care for going out on the town. Bars had never been their scene. House parties were. Top shelf liquor, skunky weed, and friendly faces both old and new.

On one chilly November Saturday night in 2003, Joe hosted a party at his lake house. It drew some of

---

[Ω] His tool status was up for debate. Maybe it always had been.

their favorite people and a handful of random jack-asses. One jackass in particular was a guy named Tommy who was a former college wrestler at the University of Tennessee in Chattanooga. UTC had a big-time wrestling program, and this guy was an All-American. He was a mountain of a man, 6'3" tall and about 250 pounds. After college, he trained for the Olympics for the chance to compete in Greco-Roman wrestling. He never got that chance. Now he was just a meathead.

The drinks flowed. Joe blended his favorite concoction that night. He called it a "Royal Fuck" because anyone who consumed enough of it became the past tense of its given name. It was nothing more than a slushy, stronger version of a Royal Flush. But Joe had a secret ingredient he wouldn't reveal to anyone. This tasty beverage could sneak up on you. He changed its name because poker was his job. Anyone who's considerate knows not to talk about work at parties because it isolates guests who aren't in the profession.

By 11:00 p.m., and Jesse had already guzzled three Royal Fucks. Wrestling Tommy had pinned four. They were past tense.[Ω] Jesse and Joe and a few other guys were downstairs throwing darts and listening to the Drive-by Truckers while Jennie was upstairs right above them at the kitchen bar, getting the latest gossip from the girls.

"Ha. Bullseye bitch. Choke on that." Jesse still talked shit as much as he did during his basketball days. Then they heard noise down the hall.

Cling... "Ahhh!"... Clank.

[Ω] Royally fucked

"Who the fuck is lifting weights?" Jesse asked as he headed down the hall toward Joe's workout room.

"Oh. That's probably Tommy," Joe answered as he followed. They walked in on Tommy pumping off reps on the bench press with two 45-pound plates on each side.

There were all kinds of different drunks at this party:

The laugh-at-everything drunk—Bobby was that.

The *cry on shoulders of strangers* drunk—also Bobby.

The drunken philosopher—Jesse had become that

The shit-talking drunk—that too.

The quiet, observational drunk—Joe was that.

The hug everyone drunk—everyone but Jesse was that

The angry, macho drunk—Deric was always that, but he was deployed to Afghanistan after 9/11, and nobody knew where the fuck he was that night, so Tommy filled in.

"What the fuck are you doing?" Jesse asked.

Joe snickered.

"Gettin' a lift in... Bitch."

"Oh... Gotta compensate for what's lacking, eh?"

"You got jokes. Why don't you ask her if something's lacking?" Tommy said, looking up at the ceiling.

"What the fuck did you just say?"

"Easy Tiger," Joe said. He knew what Jesse didn't.

"Don't worry about it. You can't throw this up."

"Why would I have to throw up weights to prove my manhood? When I could just throw my hog in your face. That's way less effort." Jesse unzipped his jeans.

"Yeah, well you don't have to throw up weights to get your ass kicked either." Tommy laughed. One of his buddies gave him a high five.

"If you were insinuating what I think you were, somebody's definitely getting their ass kicked."

Tommy took off his Affliction t-shirt and was now in a wife beater.

Jesse laughed, then said, "If you wanna kick my ass, you better kill me."

"You know he's an elite wrestler, right?" Joe told Jesse.

"I don't care if he's Bam-Bam motherfucking Bigelow. I'ma drop his ass."

Mike Cooley shredded a guitar solo through the speakers as Tommy got three-point wrestling stance.

"Dude. All you need is a water polo helmet and a fuckin' una-tard and this would be perfect." Tommy's face turned redder than it was during his mid-bench press attempt to bust a blood vessel in his head.

"Guys! Just relax. Let's just have a good time," Joe said.

"Okay. Okay. I'm just kiddin' man," Jesse said as he extended his right hand. A victorious grin crept across Tommy's face as he rose to accept Jesse's peace offering surrender.

Crack!

Jesse's threw a solid overhand left that sent Tommy toppling over the bench press.

"Don't insinuate shit about her," Jesse said. Then he spit on him.

Jesse, thinking it was over, started walking back toward the dart board. As he stepped into the den, Tommy charged like a mountain ram, spearing Jesse from behind and driving his face into the hardwood floor. Jesse seized. Tommy struggled to pin him in the open room. Finally, he wrapped his thick legs around Jesse's waist and put him in a headlock, cutting off the circulation to his brain. Jesse thought, *"This don't hurt near as bad as it should."*

"Tap out," Tommy said.

"Never. I'ma kill you," Jesse choked back. Bloody spit ran down his lip and onto Tommy's arm. Tommy squeezed his legs around Jesse, who squirmed to get loose. It looked like violent humping.

"This is getting' gay, bro," Tommy's friend said with a chuckle.

"Jesse, tap out," Joe pleaded.

Jesse's face got tomato-red, and his lips turned eggplant-purple, then his eyes slowly closed. Tommy's glazed eyes drifted off into oblivion too, but they were wide open like he was lost in a drunken haze and forgot he was choking a motherfucker out.

"Tommy! That's enough man. You're gonna kill him," Joe said.

Tommy let go.

Jesse laid motionless on the floor.

"Yo, B... Bakes... Jesse..." Joe said, then he turned to Tommy and his friend, "Get the fuck outta my house."

As they stomped up the steps, Tommy's friend said, "Dude, you kicked his ass."

Jesse laid there for another minute, then mumbled, "I'ma kill you motherfucker."

"He's gone. Fuck that guy," Joe said.

Jesse got up. They played another game of darts while he calmed down and then went upstairs to get another drink.

"Jesse, what happened to your face?" Jennie asked.

"Long story. I'll tell you later."

Jennie wanted to pry, but Joe shook his head while he poured a shot and mouthed to her, "It's fine." She rubbed Jesse's back as he downed the shot.

He thought about taking her outside and interrogating her about Tommy. He tried to think of all the names on her roster. The only person he knew was Bobby. *I think there was a Tommy... or was it... Timmy.*

Joe handed him a fresh beer. He twisted off the top and took a sip. She still rubbed his back. *"Maybe it was Tammy... That's hot."*

The conversation in the room was loud, and he had a headache.

"What happened? Are you okay?" she whispered in his ear.

"Me and Tommy got in a fight. I'm fine," he mumbled.

"Why?"

"Don't worry about it."

"Okay?" She looked nervous but didn't push it.

The alcohol buzzed through his veins. He thought more about taking her outside and getting into a knockdown, drag out fight about Tommy. He wanted to call her a slut again. He wanted to verbally abuse her. Then he thought about what it would feel like to hurt her. Like really hurt her. Like she hurt him. He wanted her to cry. He thought about asking her old college friend who flirted with everyone at these parties to accompany him to the bathroom downstairs when no one was looking. Maybe he could fuck her over the bathroom sink. Then he decided to let it go and try to get Jennie in that bathroom. Maybe he could fuck her hard enough to make her cry. That would be way less trouble.

"Another! Who's in?" Jesse shouted. Everyone was in. Joe lined 'em up.

They drank. They got merry.

"I think we should sneak off for about 15 minutes." Jesse said to Jennie.

"15? I'm pretty sure you only need about three."

"Hey... that's not fair."

"Call it like I see it."

"C'mon, no one will even notice."

"You're terrible."

"You have no idea."

She leaned in and whispered in his ear, "Well, I love your terribleness."

Ω

By 2:00 a.m., the party turned into what most of their parties turned into—great conversation over great music chased by tasty beverages in a back porch cloud of smoke. Jesse and Jamal had started this patio tradition years earlier, and as the energy in a party would die down, he always made his way outside with Jennie.

Maybe it was their routine.

Maybe they needed a cigarette.

Maybe it was an unspoken$^{\Omega}$ tribute.

$^{\Omega}$ In Church culture, *unspoken* can also serve as a noun. It is a prayer request that the requester will not mention out loud, but they ask everyone to pray for it anyway. Rarely does anyone ever actually pray for someone's unspoken. It just sounds cool to say and lets people know the requester has a strong prayer life.

Or maybe they just always found their way back to each other.

Joe always made sure the music on his back porch was a change of pace from the upbeat jams played earlier in the night. Party mode became chill mode. The soundtrack to that night's chill mode was composed by an artist from North Carolina who understood full well how hard it could be to grow up. His name was one letter shy of Bryan Adams—a different artist whose level of talent and crazy was substantially lower than the middle-aged child serenading the speakers.

They talked about music, movies, books, sports, life, love, and anything else the night would inspire them to discuss. Occasionally, much to Jesse's chagrin, they'd land on the topics of God and religion, debating tough questions that had no answers. But that didn't keep people from claiming otherwise. Jesse usually remained silent. On the rare occasion he spoke up about such topics, a few people wound up getting offended—not Jennie or Joe, they'd get worried.

They rarely reminisced about high school, but that night they did.

They shared a few stories about the athletic and mischievous exploits of *The 4-Pack*. Only Jesse, Jennie, and Joe knew the stories, but they were solid enough to entertain everyone on the porch. At least he thought so. Especially the way he told them. Like Shakespeare, Jesse never let facts get in the way of a good story.

Jennie smiled and laughed the whole time. Jesse had never spoken a word about Jamal since the accident. It was like he tried his hardest to forget. She just sat back and enjoyed the show. It felt like healing.

Jesse pulled a Marlboro Light out of his pack and lit it. He exhaled. "Y'all remember when Royce and Bryan were beefing over that girl Shana?"

Royce and Bryan were trust fund kids in Jamal's class. They were considered tools by most of the school, and Jamal secretly wanted to see them fight for the girl.

Jesse told the story of how Jamal wrote a letter to each boy—telling them to meet the other behind a local movie theater at a certain time to fight and settle the score once and for all. Each letter was signed by their romantic nemesis and slipped into their lockers.

In a stunning turn of events, both boys proved their mettle as polished tools by going to the dean, letter in hand, to tattle on each other.

Royce was the first to show the dean his letter. Bryan came in an hour later to show his. Since both letters had the same handwriting, the dean assumed that Bryan had penned a letter to himself from Royce when he heard Royce had ratted him out. And so the story goes, Bryan was suspended for three days. The best part—Jamal did it for his own amusement and didn't tell anyone, not even Jesse or Joe until they were both in college. The porch exploded when Jesse told them what Jamal said when he asked him why he wanted to see them fight.

"I just wanted to see if either of them was worth a damn."

Jesse raised his red Solo cup.

"To Jamal—the best of all of us."

Everyone raised their cups and drank. Heads flew back in unison like the congregation on communion Sunday when Dr. Germaine would say, "This is my blood. Drink in remembrance of me."

chapter: 32

CAN SOMEBODY PLEASE roll the fucking credits?

chapter: 33

IT TOOK TWO STEPS AND A LEAP for Don to body block Bobby, who sat in his chair with a smile on his face. Bobby didn't brace himself—not even the slightest flinch—when Don hit him. He welcomed the punishment. They toppled over the chair that slid on its back to the middle of the circle. Don straddled him and threw crushing power punches, one fist after the other, while Jeff and Nick tried to pull him off without much success. Lucy pleaded for them to stop, but Joel stayed in his seat and watched the action.

Smack! Smack! Smack!

Bobby's face was cut and bloody after the first three shots. After five, Don took a break to catch his breath.

"C'mon man. Why are you stopping?" Bobby stammered through the bloody spit.

Don continued the barrage. It sounded like Rocky Balboa in the meat freezer. Don was short of breath when Nick and Jeff finally pulled him off the barely conscious Bobby. He struggled to get back on and deal more pain, but they kept a tight grip and shoved him toward the door.

"I'll kill you!" Don yelled as spun around and ripped free of their grasp. He stormed for the door and slammed it behind him, leaving smeared blood on the handle.

"Please do," Bobby said as he rolled over.

Blood gushed from the cut over his eye and streamed from his mouth. There was a pool of it on the floor, and Bobby, on all fours, laughed at the crimson puddle.

"You need to go to the hospital," Lucy said.

"I'm good," Bobby said, stumbling to retrieve his chair. "I can't die. This ain't the first time I've tried. God's got a sick sense of humor."

"You need real help man," Nick said.

"I'm beyond that buddy. Thanks though,"

Everyone eventually made their way back to their spot in the circle. Lucy went to grab some paper towels from the bathroom to clean up the blood.

"Okay, I'm done now," Bobby joked to lighten the mood. Blood ran down his shirt.

"Thank God," Jeff said.

"Well, we should probably call it a night everyone," Nick said as Lucy handed Bobby a damp stack of paper towels to put on his eye and wiped the on the blood on the floor with dry ones.

"Don't worry about that. I'll get it later." Nick said.

"Can I say something before we go?" Joel asked.

"Sure," Nick said.

"I'm Joel Inglewood, and I'm a God-fearing, Bible-believing Christian."

"Jesus Fucking Christ. I thought that's who you were. I give y'all a great show, and now I gotta listen to this shit all over again from my old youth pastor?" Bobby said.

Nick raised his hand toward Bobby as Joel defended himself, "Hang on, brother. I listened to you all."

Nick moved his open hand toward Joel. "This is a safe place of no judgement."

"Yeah, I've never felt so safe," Jeff said.

Nick rolled his eyes then looked at Joel. "Five minutes."

"Fuck... and I'm not your brother... Joel," Bobby said.

"Let him speak," Nick said.

Joel took a deep breath and began, "Your stories are sad. Your lives have been hard. Those you looked up to have abused you and let you down time and time again. I understand your anger."

"Yeah. This guy gets it," Bobby interrupted.

"Bobby," Nick said. "Can you just chill out? You sat in that chair for weeks without saying a word, and now you can't shut up."

"Well... I'm not high today," Bobby said, putting his palms up.

Lucy and Jeff snickered.

"Go on, Joel," Nick said.

"I'll tell you this. I can't put myself in your shoes because they wouldn't fit. My life isn't like yours. I've always had Christ in my heart and lived for Him. The choices are yours, and they always have been, and there are consequences to every choice you make. If you run from God, he'll chastise you, and things will happen in your life that will hurt. It's His way of bringing you back to his grace."

"I can't take five minutes of this, man. This ain't a fucking Holy Ghost tent revival, *Joel*... It's all so easy to say when you've been charmed, bro." Nick didn't cut off Bobby that time. He just wish he'd made a rule against proselytizing.

"If you want to enlighten me, tell me what's brought you to your knees?" Bobby asked.

"The power of Christ, my friend," Joel said.

"Fucking hell... No... I mean, what in your life has been so fucked up, so wrong that you couldn't move in the morning? What's made you want to go to sleep and never wake up?"

"With Christ in my heart, I've never felt that way."

"Well good for *fucking* you. My uncle had the power of Christ in his heart out on the mission field in Kenya. His wife up and died with no warning one day. Severe heart attack. She was forty-two. Was that some kind of punishment from God? Explain that," Bobby said as he raised his hand in the air. "Serving Christ one minute. The next..." He brought his hand down and slapped his leg. "Dead."

"I can't explain God's ways, but He works everything together for good."

"This shit again," Bobby said.

"Well, let me ask you this: Where is your uncle now? Is he still serving God on the mission field?" Joel asked.

"Yeah," Bobby said, lowering his head.

"Maybe he knows something you don't," Joel said.

"Or maybe he hopes something we can't," Nick interjected.

"Maybe, but everyone needs a little hope. Don't they?"

Silence.

Joel made his way to the door and said, "You're all so bitter. You need to let go. Get saved and get back in church. Or God will continue to do whatever it takes to bring you back."

"Like He did with Jennie and Jesse Baker?" Bobby asked.

Joel stood near the door and searched his soul for the right words to say. He also wanted to be careful with his speech to not incite a violent reaction directed at him. It's a scary prospect to get into a fight with someone who has nothing to lose. Support groups aren't known for physical altercations, but this meeting already had precedent, and everyone was just ready for it to end.

While Joel played Scrabble in his mind, Bobby said, "I'm just trying to figure out how He's the good guy."

Silence.

"Look, I know when I'm not wanted. And we don't have to agree. Y'all just think about it," Joel said.

"Exactly, ain't got a tight little pre-packaged answer for that one, huh," Bobby said.

"I don't, but God might if you took the time to ask Him," Joel said as he pulled his handkerchief out of his suit pocket and used it as a buffer zone between his hand and the bloody knob. Silence. They wanted him gone. He opened it, turned, and said, "My office is right across the street if any of you would like to weigh your options. And we'd love to have you on Halloween at our Judgement House. Goodbye, my friends."

chapter: 34

DESPITE JESSE'S UNCONVENTIONAL JOB, they were as normal as any American family in 2005. Molly grew every day. She had his heart the day she was born, and her newfound sweetness made him love her even more. Her words came together clumsily in the cutest ways. If someone sneezed, she'd shout, "BEE-LO"

"No, Molly. You mean—bless you."

"BEE-LO."

"Like this—bless you."

"BEE-LO."

The highlight of his day was wrapping up the tables he'd spread across the monitors to go downstairs and play with her. He was at her will when it was time to play. They made triangle-shaped pepperoni pizzas from Playdough, played dress-up, colored in books, played hide and seek, painted each other's nails, and did makeovers with funky hair styles. His hair hung to his shoulders which made hairdresser way more fun for her. Jennie was always willing to lend Molly a helping hand to fuck his wig up. They'd take pictures and put them on the fridge. He looked like an idiot in every one but was cool with that.

Their life became a collage of memories with their little girl. Sweet moments like blowing out the three birthday candles that illuminated her chubby little face, building sandcastles on the beach, swimming in those silly water wings, sledding down the hill in a laundry basket in a rare Tennessee snowstorm. Her beautiful big, green eyes wide with amazement every time she saw something she'd never seen, and he wanted to show her everything. When he showed her something new, she usually painted a shitty picture of it with her fingers, but to him, they were up there with the works of Vladimir Kush. He'd hang them on the fridge too.

They took her to Disney World on her fourth birthday. She was awestruck seeing the characters in real life. Before, they only existed on the TV as she fell asleep between her mommy and daddy. Jesse often finished those movies while she dreamed.

Maybe he never really grew up.

Maybe he was making up for parts of his childhood he'd missed in Upton Park.

Maybe he wished he could be a kid again.

Maybe he felt too old, too early.

But it wasn't all fun and games. Happy times with the family soon faded. Somewhere during that year, his brain started playing different sorts of games with him. Some might have been normal coming of age games. Others might have been strange. Others might have been cause and effect. Regardless of the reasons, he was slipping.

As much as he loved his girls, the thing about family life for him was it gradually became a little familiar too. Maybe someone's present can get too familiar if it never changes. A person can get lost in it. They might miss the past, a time when things were more unpredictable, and their life seemed more *in front* of them. Jesse and Jennie were still young, but he didn't feel young. He wasn't the type to live vicariously through his kid, and he forced unfamiliarity by passing Molly off to Susan for all their trips and parties.

They started family life early which may have been why he felt like he was in the middle-age rut that would be his future—a straight line that would never deviate. Maybe people who get married young aren't mature enough to handle the time that's supposed to be middle-age, and they can't handle their present and future becoming one flesh.

This suburban couple had become one flesh so many times that even that had gotten a bit familiar. They didn't make a whole lotta love anymore. They fucked. Not that the sex was bad, it was just a routine—scheduled around Jesse's nuts—every third day like clockwork.

His life became the remix of a song. Different settings. Different instruments. But the same at its core. The soundtrack to life on repeat... forever. He was the domesticated male. The hunter was fed like a lion sitting on a boulder. The center piece of the zoo—too young to sit still, but too old to run away and chase adventure. The duality of Jesse Baker in full force.

Monotony wasn't the only thing playing games with him. Other things lurked below the surface. These games didn't involve chutes or ladders, plastic traps for red or blue mice, or robots that rocked until they get socked.[Ω] He still didn't open up to Jennie about it. He didn't know how. In fact, he may not have even realized they were there.

His lack of spiritual grounding couldn't have helped. He'd turned his back on all religion and neglected things *not of this world* for the sake of his sanity. He believed devout Bible believing Christians were the most insane people on the planet. When he thought about the big questions that used to bug him, it would fuck with his head. And he had enough to deal with up there. His headaches had been getting progressively worse, so he pushed it all away. But the more he sat still, the more bored he'd become, and his boredom brought thinking, and thinking brought existential anguish, and anguish brought more headaches. Everything was so much easier when he could compartmentalize. Deep down he still blamed God for the loss of his friend. He thought maybe if God didn't exist, and the world spun without rhyme or reason, he wouldn't have to be bitter. It was a conundrum.

If God didn't exist, and it all went black at the end, everything was nothing. Meaningless. Hopeless. He'd be dead in a flash of human existence. His life was a vapor after all.[Ω] It would be like he never existed. Bad attention was always better for him than no attention at all, and this star couldn't stomach the magnitude of his own insignificance.

So, he'd circle back to an existing God but couldn't separate that God from the actions the people who claimed Him. And from what he'd learned in church,

---

[Ω] If you're actually of those people who speaks parables and has a metaphorical ear, then it was exactly like these games.
[Ω] The fat asses were right about some things, and charismatically so.

God's deeds didn't seem so humane either. At this point, he figured God and all His people had always been the most hung of dicks—and he'd feel like a fool[Ω] for believing any of it. Nothing made sense.

One night on the back porch at a party at Joe's, he finally mentioned some issues he had with the Bible and religion to a few still-churched acquaintances who'd been invited. It didn't go over well. He asked why a loving, merciful God would condemn people to burn alive for all eternity. Their answers didn't satisfy him, so he asked them why such terrible things happen to good people. One of them said, "Because sometimes God chooses to test our faith, like Job."

To which Jesse replied, "So God's that insecure that needs to kill an innocent person—or people—to test my fucking mettle and see if I'll still love him? That makes no fucking sense. That would be like me cheating on Jennie just to make sure she'd love me no matter what." He laughed after saying this.

Offended, the churched soon-to-be ex-friend said, "It's not like that at all. And no one knows the ways of God."

"Now there we can agree," Jesse said, "but I'll tell you this, that guy they're talking about in the old Schofield KJV, that guy's crazy—not really the type I'd feel comfortable handing off my soul to."

Soon-to-be ex-friend cocked his head and furrowed his brow as if his offense meter was rising with each blasphemous word that proceeded out of the mouth of Jesse.

[Ω] He never called anyone a fool in his entire life though. A Jewish tax collector named Matt, who recorded some of Jesus' conversations (nobody's sure if he got permission to do so) claimed the Son of God said that calling someone a fool was a hell-worthy offense.

Jesse felt this, and it motivated him to continue the blitzkrieg on the old testament God. "And how 'bout them kids who made fun of *God's man* Elisha for being bald? He asked God to take care of them, and what did God do? Sent two fucking bears to eat all 42 of their asses. First, you can't tell me all 42 kids was makin' fun. Second, God sent fucking bears, bro... Bears... To eat some kids pokin' fun of an insecure dude's bald head. Seems like a reasonable reaction to me." Jesse took a drag of his Marlboro light. He spoke the next words like a dragon who'd just blown fire. Smoke surrounded his face. "And don't even get me started on that Abraham and Isaac fiasco."

At this point, now ex-friend told him he needed to get back in church because he couldn't be near God if he wasn't in church.

To which Jesse replied, "No thanks, I'm good."

To which ex-friend made it clear that he thought Jesse had bitterness issues and probably wasn't saved, and that he worried what it would take for God to bring him back.

To which Jesse never spoke to him or anyone like him again.

Bears.[Ω]

But Jesse *did* know he was searching for something, but he was convinced that it wasn't where he used to live. However, he didn't want to feel empty because there was no God, but he still couldn't allow himself to believe in a murderous micromanaging

---

[Ω] Jesse had poked quite a bit of fun at the "man of god" in his time. He didn't know if the story was a parable or literal or if it was even half-true. But he kept his head on a swivel, just in case those bears showed up one day to eat his ass.

god either. He had two choices—hopeless or pissed off.

Conundrum.

His path was dark, and he didn't have a flashlight. He considered the chance that he was a reprobate, and some of what they said was true, but he'd lost the ability to care.

Jennie still had some faith. She could let go and live her life holding on to hope that God cared about her. She didn't have to justify anything or pretend to know His ways.

If you find yourself alone in recovery, it's difficult to keep your sanity. Maybe he didn't *have* to be alone, but he tried really hard to keep it that way. He didn't want to put his spiritual issues on someone else and mess up their head. They used to call that a stumbling block.

Maybe he assumed everyone was as impressionable as he was when he was a child. Maybe he thought too much of himself.

But old beliefs were still buried in his head, and they made war with new thoughts. Sometimes, he wondered—to himself—if predestination was in fact true, and he was doomed to hell because he couldn't make himself believe "beyond the shadow of doubt." He had a hard-enough time believing at all. He didn't want to be the reason someone else got thrown in the lake of fire with him. The hell scenes at the Judgement House[Ω] events all those years ago were still etched on his brain. But he bottled it up.

[Ω] Deric, Joe, Jesse, and Jennie went to Judgement House every Halloween when they were in elementary and middle school. Jesse loved it because it was a great chance for him and Jennie to hold hands, but it scared him every time.

His lot in life was abundant, and he should have been oozing with happiness. Maybe people don't pay the good shit near as much attention as the bad shit. The pain of losing is much greater than the joy of winning. His headaches, depression, and periodical existential meltdowns weren't easy on Jennie. Perhaps the ones who love the depressed are worse off than the depressed themselves.

A few other things lurked below the surface that covertly and patiently crept into the fabric of his psyche—greed and disconnect. He had developed an irrational desire to make more and more money. He played longer hours. Some days, he'd shut himself in his office from morning until night. They'd fight about it, and she'd try to get him to chill out. He'd scale back for a few days, but eventually go back to doing whatever he wanted to do. He had to have more.

During one heads-up match he had to piss so bad, but he thought the fish he was gutting would instantly leave if he sat out for a few seconds. He yelled at Jennie to bring him a bucket. She reluctantly did. He pissed in it and busted the fish.[Ω]

The poker grind gradually took another toll on the way his brain functioned. The online multi-tabling poker professional had to be elite at one thing—emotional disconnect. He played over 4 million hands of online poker from 2001 to 2005, and somewhere along the way, the plug to his feelings had been pulled.

[Ω] Jesse never had to define the word *fish*. He already knew it was an animal that lives in and breathes water. He also knew it was a poker player who fucking sucks at the craft.

A poker pro can't be attached to outcome. You can't lose a $10,000 pot and think—*Shit. I just lost a used car.* That's not how the grind works. Chips aren't money. They're units. Pieces on a game board. And money isn't money, it's long-term investments. Not day to day. Not even month to month. But entire meta game.

After enough time, his losses didn't even affect Jennie anymore. One night in particular, Jesse stepped outside to have a smoke after a grueling session. She joined him.

"How'd it go today?"

"Meh, lost about 16K."

"Whoa. Rough one. It's all right. You'll get it back. Wanna go out to dinner?"

"Sure."

Stoic wives make champs.

It took intentional daily practice. A mindset that he got better and better at with every passing month. You win some. You lose some. But you never let a loss affect your mind. Fish do that, and he was no fish.

Over time, the disconnect couldn't help but seep into his real life, to the point he couldn't feel emotions anymore, and that bothered him. He first noticed it when the family dog Dr. Jack Shepherd was hit by a car and killed. He loved that dog. At least he thought he did. He saw it happen while he was out building a fire for some of their trash. He thought it was funny how Doc freaked out and splooted right in the middle road when the horn honked. The guy who hit him felt terrible and gave Jesse a hundred bucks. He was happy about that and put it one of his overflowing coffee cans.

Jennie and Molly were a mess about the dog, but even their tears couldn't shake him up at their little dog funeral. He didn't throw away ol' Jack's bed on the back porch though. He also kept his nearly full bag of dog food that was crumpled into itself. Jennie never asked why he wouldn't throw that stuff away. She just assumed it was part of his grieving process. He kept the visceral memories of his dog around. Hoping one day, he might look at them with fondness and shed a tear because he missed his dog. That dog was worth a goddamn tear.

He watched old movies he'd heard were supposed to be sad. *Meet Joe Black*, *Old Yeller*, *The Shawshank Redemption*, and *P.S. I Love You.* Nothing. He thought they were all funny. Especially the faces that the actors made when they cried. He was amused by how ugly people were when they cried. He laughed at the screen during *Meet Joe Black* when Brad Pitt got pinballed by two passing cars after one of the most romantic scenes in modern cinema. He played it back three times.

Jennie wasn't stupid. She knew he wasn't himself. He wouldn't make sense sometimes. He was meaner, and she soon realized that he was devoid of emotion. This wasn't the guy she married, and she knew it, but every time she tried to talk to him about it, he'd shut it down and escape to his office. She was afraid of how this new Jesse would be if he got really angry.

She remembered the last time he was seeing red—when he got in that fight with Tommy at Joe's party. That same night, there was a hint of violence in the way he fucked her in the bathroom. She didn't want to test him, so she walked on eggshells and became a master of distraction.

The man had become a machine— a money machine with a high price for functionality. Some days, when he was alone, he understood this about himself, and wanted a little weight on his heart. Not a lot. Just a little. Maybe even one tear or a sniffle.

Jennie longed for it too and wondered if there was a heart pumping in there anymore. She knew there used to be, but didn't understand why he was becoming this shell of a person. The ability to feel pain might just be a bigger part of what makes us human than we realize. It's spiritual. But one should be careful what they wish for.

chapter: 35

IN THE SPRING OF 2006, Jesse got paranoid about the feds trying to take him down and get his money. His tax game wasn't as watertight as Joe's. Joe told him he needed to jump through the IRS hoops, but as long as he paid something and claimed his losses, he probably wouldn't get audited. Jesse didn't want to pay shit. Taxes felt like tithe. He would take huge portions of his bankroll offline through an affiliate player who charged him juice on cash trades. He'd hide the stacks in Folger's Coffee tins. He had a row of them in his closet. Then he'd grind his way back up from $400 games and build his roll healthy enough for $10,000 games. He did this five times that year. He was running with a white-hot deck. He got a VPN to spoof his I.P. address and changed it every time he cashed out. Then things got weird.

He burned his best computer in his fire pit because he thought he was being watched by someone who'd hacked into his system. Then he buried half of his cans of cash in the woods behind the house and used painted sticks to mark the spots and set bear traps near each of them. He figured if they came to get him, they might try to flank him from the woods, and the traps would slow them down enough for him to grab his girls and get away.[Ω] He also paid cash for a new computer and started using this new private internet thing called a Tor browser. He kept all of this from Jennie. He couldn't explain what was going on to her because, by his logic, it would put her and Molly in danger.

The days he succumbed to Jennie's pleas to stop playing so many hours, he mysteriously felt better. The girls became a pleasant distraction, and he could feel at peace for a bit. Almost like he went back in time one year, back to when the synapses in his brain weren't shooting bricks. Then she'd go to work, and he'd drop off Molly at Susan's and go back to his world of obsession and growing paranoia. Then she'd come home, and he would be Dudley-Dad-Right again.

It had been six months since Dr. Jack Shepherd kicked the bucket, half a year since they'd buried him at the tree line of the woods behind the house. A wooden cross stood in plain sight, and his collar hung on it. There was a pile of dead dandelions on the dirt in front of it. Molly collected the weeds and put them on his grave every day for months. She desperately missed her first friend and asked for a new puppy. It was lonely for her at the foot of that mountain when her only living playmates were her grandparents and mom and dad.

On the second Saturday in March, Molly asked Jennie for a puppy again.

"No, Molly. I'm not ready for a new dog," Jennie said as she stirred Molly's Kraft macaroni over the burner.

[Ω]Also—just in case those fucking bears showed up.

"But Mom..."

"I said *no*. Me and your dad talked about it, and we aren't ready yet."

Jesse didn't give a shit. Jennie wasn't ready to house break a new pup.

Molly slid off the chair and stomped away from the table. "You don't want me to have anything," she said.

Jennie stopped stirring and chased after Molly. She caught up to her and grabbed her arm, dragging her to the little girl's room. There were toys everywhere. Molly never had many real-life kid playmates, but she had so many toys. Doll houses stood in a row in front of her bed like a little Hasbro suburbia. There was a toy kitchen in the corner that had everything a real kitchen would have, minus a wine cabinet. Dolls and stuffed animals and books covered the floor so you could barely see the color of the carpet.

"Look at all this! We don't get you anything. You have no idea young lady. You think about what you just said. If you don't get thankful soon, you'll never get a puppy."

Molly plopped herself on the bed as Jennie kicked through toys and slammed the door on her way out. Molly loved playing in her room, but she possessed certain traits of her father, and her life too, had gotten familiar over time.

Maybe most kids are like that, living for the commercials during episodes of *Dora the Explorer*, each one widening their eyes until you can see white circling their pupils, turning them deaf, and triggering intense reactions like, "Mom I want that for Christmas!"

It was spring, and Molly had been making her list for two months. Kid's lists change constantly, and they rarely remember what's on said list when it's time for St. Nick to squeeze his fat ass[Ω] into the chimney, but little kids only consider the present tense. Most toys are bought, played with a few times and forgotten like little plastic whores piled up in round, colorful buckets and stuffed into the closet.

She didn't feel like playing with her old whores that day. She wanted a puppy, and that was the *only* thing on her mind. Her window was open, the sun shone through, and the curtains moved gracefully in the cool breeze. Then she did something she'd never done—she grabbed the little stool by her art desk, put it in front of the window, and climbed out. With her bottom lip pooched out, she walked the backyard, picking new dandelions to put on Dr. Jack Shepherd's grave, pouting about how her mean Mommy wouldn't let her get a puppy.

As she approached the cross on the tree line, she heard a faint whimper.

A puppy? she thought.

She walked through the woods following the whining that called out to her, stepping on twigs and crunchy leaves. Then she climbed over a downed tree, one leg before the other, no more than twenty yards into unknown territory. Her parents had told her she was not allowed to cross the tree line, and as far as they knew, she hadn't. But the call of the puppy and her bitterness toward her Mom made her disregard the

---

[Ω] Nobody can know for sure, but it's unlikely St. Nick was a preacher. His weight problem might just be a coincidence. Wait... how do we even know he's fat?

rules. When people don't understand why a rule exists, even the most innocent of us are destined to break it.

When her feet hit the ground on the other side of the tree, she saw it. Beautiful. Yellow fur with a white belly and pointy ears. Whining and licking blood off its wounded leg. As she stepped toward it, it showed its teeth.

"Molly, we don't pet strange dogs," Jennie once said to her. But her mom was her villain now, not some hurt strange dog. Molly tiptoed toward it.

"Aw. It's okay buddy. Are you hurt?"

chapter: 36

MOLLY! C'MON YOUR MACARONI IS READY," Jennie yelled as she grabbed a plastic Barbie cup and poured tropical punch Kool-Aid into it.

"Molly!"

She sighed, put the cup on the table by the bowl of macaroni that had been cooling, and marched to Molly's room. She opened the door only to find an empty kitchen and a suburb taking an afternoon nap. Plastic whores spread across the floor like the passed-out bodies of the fall break reunion party.

"Molly?"

Weird. She hadn't heard the door open. Then she saw the open window and the stool below it. She walked to it and looked out. Molly walked out of the woods slowly, staggering, stepping on the pile of dandelions on the grave.

"Molly! Get inside right now," Jennie yelled from the window.

Molly didn't look at her. She just kept dawdling. Her right hand looked muddy, and she cupped it on the side of her neck. Then Jennie saw blood shoot between Molly's soaked fingers like the stream of a Super Soaker spraying dark red death.

The blood rushed from Jennie's head in an instant. Her body went cold, and she ran as fast as she could out the door, smashing a plastic whore under her feet.

She screamed for Jesse. He was playing poker with his headphones on in his office upstairs, but she screamed loud enough to get his attention. He took the headphones off and heard her screams continue outside. He scrambled to his feet and glanced out the window. Jennie ran across the backyard toward Molly. The right side of Molly's yellow dress was soaked red as she took one more step and toppled over, landing face down in the grass.

"Molly!" he shouted as he ran for the steps leading downstairs. He stumbled on the first step but made it to the bottom in a flash like his feet never touched a stair. The world muted. No sounds. Only staticky screams. He tore off his shirt while he ran. When he got to Molly, he pulled her from Jennie's arms, and pressed his shirt against the spouting wound.

"Call 9-1-1!"

Seconds later, Jennie was yelling at a dispatcher on her cell phone. Then she stopped abruptly and dropped the phone into the grass. It bounced as the dispatcher tried to calm her and assure that help was on the way, but the dispatcher spoke to the green blades. Molly's blood soaked through Jesse's shirt. Jennie fell to her knees by him, weeping as she helplessly stared at Molly's face. Molly gasped for each breath. Her eyes blinked faster. Her breaths got slower as Jesse's tears and sweat dripped onto her sweet little face. Then she breathed one long slow breath, and whispered, "Daddy... help." Life left the eyes that owned his heart, and she never breathed again.

Jennie howled a primal scream that could part the sea. Jesse shook the baby, desperately begging her to come back. Then he gently laid her on the grass and walked into the woods, crushing dandelions as he stepped on the grave. He reached the log, stepped over it, and saw the coyote. It was afraid, leg mangled and bloody, and stuck in a bear trap. It snarled with blood on its teeth and face.

Jesse looked around and saw a big rock at the foot of the tree by the wounded animal. He got on his knees, grabbed the rock and put it in his lap. The coyote snapped, but it couldn't reach him. He didn't flinch. He looked into its eyes. It growled. He lifted the rock with a hand clutching each side and dealt death. It yelped a sharp shriek on impact. He raised the rock again and smashed the beast. And again. Its skull crunched with another blow. And again. Blood dripped from the rock onto his hair and down his sweaty, red speckled face. And again. And again. And again. And again. And again. When he stopped, he left the carcass with its leg still stuck in the bear trap and with a rock for a head.

chapter: 37

S OBRIETY AND HUMILITY filled the emptiness of the chairs in the circle where Don and Joel sat last week. The four who remained had arrived at a crossroads. This group was formed on principles of non-judgement and acceptance. It served as an outlet to vent anger for people who could empathize and, who also, felt just as alone.

They sat in silence for two minutes. Oddly, Nick felt no pressure to speak, and no one looked at him to kick off their weekly routine of listening and getting it all out. They just sat quietly in their chairs, lonely and bitter, running out of stories, and missing something drastic. And they all knew it, but there's a big difference between knowing something needs to change, and having both the know-how and the courage to bring it about.

Nick's role called for him to open a conversation, but as the silent seconds turned to minutes, he couldn't open his mouth, as if he'd been silenced by sewing his own lips shut like an inmate at the Belgrade Central prison.

After four minutes, Bobby, with a black eye and tiny butterfly bandages on his cheekbone, looked at him and said, "What's your endgame here, Nick?"

Nick couldn't think of anything. There was no endgame, but as he looked at Bobby, his thoughts drifted to his family, and he floated away for a few seconds.

Ω

Reflections
By Nick Jackson

During spring break, I went home for the first time since I left Miles-Franklin and my pastoral studies behind like a mile marker sign that gets smaller in your rearview before disappearing in seconds. Predictably, my dad didn't take my decision well. He told me I was a backslider and to not come home until I stopped running from God and the pulpit.

But here I was, back home without knowing why. I pulled into the driveway. The house looked the same. The American and Christian flags blew proudly on each side of the covered porch. Dad's Buick LeSabre was backed into the carport. The front license plate still preached a one sentence sermon about automobile and religious safety—BUCKLE UP WITH JESUS. Very Hemingway.

I've always walked into my own house, but after three years in Chattanooga and a grand total of seven phone calls home during that time, my break into adulthood felt complete. I no longer lived here and was compelled to stand at the door and knock. Mom's face screamed her surprise. Her tears revealed her longing. And her embrace told me that no matter who or where I was, I would always be her only begotten son.

She invited me inside and scrambled around the house looking for the perfect place to sit and talk. Then she asked if I was hungry, and I told her I could eat. We walked in the kitchen, and I sat in the nook while she made me a peanut butter and jelly sandwich. She grilled me about my college work and asked if I'd met a nice southern belle yet. I laughed that her idea of a girl in the Southern United States mirrored a minor character in *Gone with the Wind*. How was she to know that Southern girls look like any other American girl? She'd never been south of the Mason-Dixon line.

Dad walked in the back door while I had a mouthful of fruit and bread and peanut butter. I would have said hello right away if that was an easy combination to get down the pipe in a hurry, but it's not. I chewed and swashed and choked it down as fast as I could and took a gulp from my pop. Then I stood and extended my hand.

"Hey, Dad. It's been awhile."

"Well, hey. This is a pleasant surprise. I guess you didn't find what you were looking for..."

I chuckled nervously.

"It's good to have you back, son." He wiped the garden soil from his right hand on his jeans and shook mine. Somehow, he still owned powerful space in my head, but I didn't want to leave yet, so I played nice. After finishing my sandwich, we went out to the garden and made small talk while I helped him build a small fence to keep rabbits out. When the job was finished, we sat around the table for dinner. Time seemed to rewind itself as Mom placed her famous shepherd's pie in the center of the table. She took her seat with a beautiful smile on her face, as if this moment put her back in a time when her life had the most purpose. A time when she felt more relevant. When she had a son to raise.

"Let's pray," Dad said as he held Mom's left hand.

Mom placed her right hand palm up toward me, and I put my hand in hers. Her thumb caressed my knuckle. Dad's head was bowed. I stared at Mom's soft face, slightly wrinkled at the corner of her eyes—eyes that smiled at me. She bowed her head. I did not.

"Father, we come before you today thankful. Thankful for this bountiful meal that You have provided. Thankful for the wonderful sermon on the prodigal son that Pastor preached Sunday night... And thankful that our own prodigal son has returned to us." A tear fell onto my father's plate.

Mom whispered, "Amen."

"We thank You for turning Nick's heart away from the world and back to Your grace and service. Be with him as he studies Your Word in preparation to be a light in the darkness. Let the Holy Spirit guide him as he equips himself with the armor of Christ and the sword of the Lord."

I glared at him while he prayed for another two minutes, articulating *his* will for my life as if the hay was already harvested and in the barn.

"Forgive him, Father God, and let him use his time in the world as a testimony of redemption to lead his followers out of the darkness and into the light of your holy..."

"Dad!"

I surprised myself.

He looked up slowly. His face changed with every inch upward, realizing that his wishful assumption was not the case.

"I'm not here because I've changed my mind. I'm here to see you and Mom."

"But I told you not to come back until you got your heart right with Christ. I assumed..."

"You're my fucking parents."

Mom gasped.

"Never use the devil's language in this house, boy."

The tension was tighter than an industrial cable helping a bridge loom over the raging current of a river—a river that would carry away the corpse of anyone who possessed the weakness to stand on the ledge and the courage to jump.

"Or what?" I'd never challenged my father like this before. "Are you going to spank me? I'm a grown man."

"Under this roof and at my table you'll always be my son."

Mom held a cloth napkin over her mouth and nose and started crying into it.

"Then let's go outside so we can talk like adults."

"Are you threatening me?"

"Wha—no! I want you to talk to me like a human fucking being for once. Not some rhetoric spitting pastor trying to convince me that you know what my life's supposed to look like."

"Is that what you think of me?"

"What else am I supposed to think?"

"That's a shame."

"I'm *not* going to be a pastor. I *don't* know what I believe. I just know it's not a bunch of who-shot-john that people made up because the world scares them."

"You are lost, son. You need to get saved."

I scoffed on the verge of tears.

"I knew you'd say something like th—OF COURSE I'M FUCKING LOST." My voice cracked from screaming. Mother wept.

"I'll never stop praying for you, son," Dad's lower lip trembled, and his breaths revealed conflicted emotions. "But you can't be here. I can't fellowship with unbelievers."

"Unbelievers? You're my Dad. You baited my hook when I caught my first bass. You picked me up when I fell in the driveway and knocked out my front tooth," I struggled through every word. "You tucked me in, and took me to the doctor, and pushed me on the swing. You taught me how to work, Dad."

His lips tightened as his bushy mustache and beard became a single thicket of gray-brown hair. After a few moments, he said, "Just go."

Mom pushed out her chair and raced upstairs, weeping bitterly.

"Fine." I walked toward the door behind him, but something made me stop and put my hand on his shoulder while he stared into his glass of Diet Coke. His facial hair trembled. His eyes watery. He wouldn't look away from the tiny liquid tornado forming inside his glass as he twirled it. "I've just missed you guys. I want you to know I've always thought you were a good dad."

I walked out and opened my car door to leave. I looked up to my parent's window. My mom prayed with folded hands. She unfolded them and waved. I put my fist to my heart while I looked into her heart-broken eyes. She blew me a kiss.

I drove away. The mile markers disappeared, one after the other in my rearview.

$$\Omega$$

"I don't know, Bobby," Nick said.

Everyone looked at each other. They were para-lyzed by nihilism. Depression had wrapped its tenta-cles around the group, strangling them, suffocating them. Nick tried to think of something to say that wouldn't violate the unwritten motif of the cir-cle—which was now a square. This group existed be-cause they wanted no advice, no well laid out plan, no rules. They wanted nothing but a platform for their pain, and after all the stories and anger and hurt they had shared, nothing was what they were left with. Meaninglessness. They would die and go to the dirt like every other living thing that had spent fifteen sec-onds under the sun and vanished into eternity like it never existed.

It was only now—since they had poured out the contents of their glasses, every drop of intoxicating bitterness, on the floor of this room during the last eight Tuesday nights—that they realized there was nothing left. They felt better during the venting pro-cesses, sure, but with nothing more to fill the cup, they were dry—emptier than ever before. Before, at least they had their pain to love and cling to. It made them feel alive.

Then the door opened, and an old man in blue coveralls walked in. He had a thick beard and hard miles on his face. All the eyes in the room followed his steps, hoping this new blood might have something to give that could put meaning into the meaningless.

"Is this some silent Buddhist thing?" Chuck Baker said.

Everyone laughed.

"No. Nothing like that," Nick answered. "We've been sharing our stories over the last few months. Have a seat."

"I saw an old friend of mine the other day. He told me I should come over here and talk with ya'll."

chapter: 38

EVERY DAY WAS HARDER for her. If your splitting hairs, she wasn't technically alone. Jesse was physically there, but he'd effectively given up the ghost, and what remained was terrifying. She had felt him slipping before their mid-March nightmare. But after the funeral, she could see that he was officially gone.

She waited for him to speak. The long game used to work so well. It didn't anymore. She tried to forget the last thing he said to her. It was right before they left the house to bury Molly.

Jennie sat at the kitchen bar. The tears never stopped. She had been staring into a cup of coffee in her favorite mug, the one Molly painted at a pottery place where kids could make ceramic treasures. Tears dripped and swirled in the brown beverage. The smeared paint on the mug wasn't much to look at, but the childish statement that wrapped around it meant the world to Jennie. She would never use another cup. There were plenty of clean ones in the cabinet. But she'd wash that one every day.

She didn't hear him coming. He just breezed by, opened the liquor cabinet, and poured Jack Daniel's whiskey into a glass. Neat. He guzzled it in his black suit. Then he said the words that echoed in her head from that day forward,

"You could've just let her get a fucking puppy."

And that was it. It had been three months, and he hadn't uttered a word to her since. Maybe he couldn't look at Jennie without seeing the baby. She felt that way about him. They didn't sleep in the same room, and she'd given up on trying to talk to him.

Susan came by sometimes, but she was a wreck too. About once a week, Jesse's mom, Vanessa, would come to check on them. She didn't say much either. Maybe nobody could think of anything to say because they knew nothing could help. They just drank coffee and danced around elephants. Sometimes, Vanessa tried to come up with a game plan to snap Jesse out of his funk, but he would ignore anyone's attempts and just sit in a trance on the back porch staring at the woods. Occasionally, he'd lock himself in his office and play his old game consoles. He usually slept in there, if he slept at all. Jennie stopped checking. She didn't even know if he showered anymore. Nobody knew how to help him. They all hoped he'd come back to them. They hoped time would heal some of their pain, but there are some scars that never heal. And there are some people, once they start down that slip-and-slide into the pool of madness, you best fucking run.

Jennie was sure everyone who stopped by the house meant well, but she wished they'd all leave her alone.

How could she talk him off the same ledge she was trying to talk herself off? She could still hear the anger in his voice from that day in the kitchen. The blame. It was the same tone she used on herself.

She didn't think she could deal anymore. Maybe she didn't want to. Maybe she couldn't do it alone. A month after the funeral, she tried to watch a video Jesse made for her when Molly was two. It was a slideshow set to the beautiful music of Sigur Ros. She made it through about twenty seconds before she couldn't see the screen for the tears in eyes. She just wanted to forget. She needed the *real him* to come back. And quick.

Then one night, she was in the shower when she heard their bedroom door squeak open. He walked in. She anticipated a loving reunion. Maybe an apology. Definitely some shared tears that were a long time coming.

She pretended not to hear him and let the water run onto her face and moved her fingers through her hair as the stream ran through it. Then he opened the shower door and stepped inside. She could smell his body odor and alcohol as he breathed heat on her neck. She turned around, and he looked down her body. She looked into his eyes. They were black and empty. She grabbed the bar of soap and lathered it in her hands. She thought this was the way it had to be. This was her chance to bring him back. He grabbed her by the shoulders and turned her around. She didn't want it to be like that, but she was desperate. She hadn't existed to him for so long that any attention felt better than nothing.

Until it didn't.

Her hands palmed the wall of the shower. She let him enter her from behind. She moaned. His thrusts started fast, but his erection wasn't strong and kept slipping out, so he went faster.

"Slow down," she said.

He didn't. He put his right hand on her shoulder pushing her down further, and her feet started to slip. Then he pushed her head against the tile on the wall and a cut opened above her eye.

She screamed, "Stop it, Jesse!"

A line of her blood dripped down the tile, and he slipped out again. He saw the blood and turned her around to face him. She teared up, but he couldn't notice because the water from the shower head was streaming down her face. He thumbed the wound gently, and she flinched. He looked at her like he used to. Then he kissed her. She kissed him back even though his beard smelled like a distillery. For a few seconds, she felt the softness in the touch of his lips that she'd longed for.

The feeling didn't last long enough. He grabbed her by the arm and led her out of the shower to their bed. She laid on her back, and he entered her again. As he moved, his gaze never left his penis until it fell out again. He looked at her, and she saw the darkness back in his eyes. Then he flipped her over, and he kneeled on the bed behind her.

She was crushed and afraid as he violently thrust into her over and over. She didn't moan, she cried. He didn't know the difference anymore. Before he slipped out again, he leaned over her and pushed the back of her head down. As the cut above her eye bled into the bedspread, he pressed his open palm over her ear. Her ears rang, and she could hear the muffled slaps of his pelvis against her ass. She felt his rage. It crossed her mind he wanted to kill her.

She saw glimpse of her past. This was a position she'd been in before, but had tried her hardest to forget—a drunk and high Bobby Corban pounded away at her virginity at her first frat party, getting softer with each stroke. After telling him no twenty-six times on that drug-fueled night, he eventually got her high enough to concede. It was all fuzzy to her, and not in any way what she wanted. She couldn't even remember how it happened or how it ended.

Jesse kept going. She yelled for him to stop. He finally did when he fell out again and wasn't hard enough to get back in. He left her face down on the bed and went back to the shower. It was still running. She laid there crying for a while before she peeked in. The water ran down his back as he masturbated.

All she wanted was comfort from the only person on the planet who could give it to her. All she got was rape.

She laid on her side in bed and prayed. When he was done showerjacking, he walked into the closet, put on some clothes, started digging around, and walked out the door with his old leather journal that he'd only picked up once since high school. She took a bath to wash away how she felt. Then got in bed and cried until she fell asleep.

Ω

The next morning, she sat at the kitchen bar over her coffee mug and wrote this note:

This is my last will and testament for anyone who cares. Whoever wants to claim anything I own can have it. Nothing amounts to anything anyway. My heart can't recover. They're all gone. This can't be fixed. If hell is real, it can't be worse than this.

Jesse, I miss the old you. Maybe we'll meet again and things will be different.

Molly, I love you baby. And miss you so much. I will hold you soon.

Yours always,
Jennie

Ω

Vanessa found her body on the dining room floor. Her cheek stuck to an outline of dried vomit. The note and an empty bottle of pills was on the table. She didn't look beautiful dead.

chapter: 39

The Life and Times of Jesse "Take-All-Comers" Baker
By Jesse Baker
Maybe... September 2006?

I'M SITTING IN MY FAVORITE CHAIR on the back porch. It fits my posture perfectly so I don't move much. I smoke Marlboro Reds now. I'm reading the box just like I used to do with my Captain Crunch. The warning says these things are gonna kill me. Funny.

I've been out here awhile. There are about ten empty bottles of Jack on the ground by my chair, and the bottle at my feet is almost tapped. At some point, one of us is gonna have to go to the store. Jennie hasn't bought whiskey for me in over a month. I don't see her much these days and couldn't even tell you if she ever leaves the house. We don't talk anymore. At first that wasn't her choice. Now it probably is. I can't look at her.

She used to bring me sandwiches. Now, I think she just stays in our room. I have to get my own food these days. Most of time it's a big bowl of cereal. I've been emptying the boxes one by one. I always put them back in the pantry. I put empty milk jugs in the fridge too. Subtle reminders.

Last night I thought maybe I'd talk to her. Maybe I'd walk upstairs and apologize for checking out. What if we could recover together like addicts that met in rehab. Maybe we could plant a tree and keep it alive. Maybe we could relapse together. Maybe we could fuck. Maybe we could die together. Maybe she'd go get some fucking groceries.

It was a haze. That's my life now. When I got up there, she was in the shower. She looked real good. I'm pretty sure we fucked. I don't really remember, but I woke up in this chair.

I gotta get another coffee can. I know they're watching. They're always watching. I'll get it all out, eventually. Then they'll have no evidence when they raid the house. I found the perfect spot to bury one yesterday—fuck them.

Remember that game *Alladin* on Sega Genesis? I thought it was gonna suck, but it was so good. That Indian kid was good at runnin' from the cops. I wonder what happened to my old Sega. Was he Indian?

I bet I could find two sticks and learn more about fire by acting like an Indian. Fuck the Feds. Maybe we're supposed to go back to being like Indians.

Why do we need electronics anyway? That's how they watch us. I bet they can see us through the lights. I gotta burn it all. I'll miss my Nintendo though. It's gotta be too old for them to use it against me. I bet it's alright.

$$\Omega$$

Jesse walked inside. He burped and threw up a little in his mouth and spit in the sink. Then he turned on the cold water, cupped his hands, and slurped it. Water splashed his face, and he dried off with a towel that reeked of mildew when it hit his skin. He normally didn't notice foul smells, but he was feeling fresher that morning. He walked to the dining room headed for the stairs to gather more electronics from his office for the pit.

And there it was on the table. Jennie's note and the hollow uncapped pill bottle on its side. As he moved closer, he saw her feet, and with each slow step, her contorted body was made known to him.

It was finished. Her dead body triggered the final stage of metamorphosis. Like an emergency protocol. His old life washed away. He had become new—born again—a cicada who'd stepped out of his old skin and left a crunchy shell clinging to the bark of a white oak. His new skin was scaly, ashy, hairy.

He stepped over her and went upstairs. He didn't read the note.

The plastic burned, sparks snapped, and the flames rose higher than house. He burned everything but his Nintendo, the old twenty-inch T.V., and his old flip phone. The smoke filled the sky above him. He worried that it might draw attention from the feds, so he hustled inside and stuffed some clothes in a backpack. He filled his biggest gym bag with his hunting rifle and a handgun and an axe, a sleeping bag, and three cash-stuffed coffee cans. Then he went to the garage and packed his camping supplies and made for the woods.

Chh... Jesse Baker. Over and out. Chh...

chapter: 40

MOST PEOPLE JUST WANT TO BE SEEN. It validates their existence. Maybe that's why rock stars tour into their 70s. It isn't the money—most are loaded. It's the stage. When the stage evaporates, the withdrawals might be paralyzing. There's no medication, no rehab, and the sickness doesn't go away. The star just searches for their next fix. Jesse used to feel that way. Now he'd rather disappear.

Ω

The Life and Times of Jesse "Take-All-Comers" Baker
By Jesse Baker
I have no idea.

I used to feel a lot of shit. I'm depressed. I'm hopeless. I used to be a star. I gotta compete. Fuck... all... that. What a whingy ass bitch. Things are way better now. I'm different. Jesse 2.0. That don't scare me either. We all change. That's just the way the world goes 'round. Prine... so boss.[Ω]

I'm just takin' a trip. There's road construction, and I'll take the back way. I'm gonna hunt and fish these woods on this mountain now.

I can't remember how I got here.

I feel like it's got something to do with the samurai. They've all been on my mind today—warrior cultures and glorious deaths.

Elliot Smith stabbed himself in the heart twice, and his autopsy showed no hesitation wounds. That's hard as fuck.

Occasionally I pop out on a road. I walk 'til I see a gas station, stop in, and grab some supplies. It's the usual stuff. Beef Jerky, Marb Reds, and PBR. And Fun Dip.

Last week, I saw my senior picture taped to the glass entrance of one of my pit stops. It said *MISSING* in big letters at the top. Chuck's number was the point of contact for anyone who had info on my whereabouts. I hoped the clerk wouldn't recognize me when I bought my stash. He didn't. I ripped the sign off the door when I walked out.

I think God's a monster. They never told me that, but some days, I feel like He may be. Maybe He's like Bruce Banner and only becomes a monster when he needs to fuck shit up for the greater good.

I'm a God. But they ain't gonna nail me to no cross. I could get them first. I could turn into Hulk to

---

[Ω] ***Editor's note—John Prine wrote a song called *That's the Way the World Goes 'Round*. Jesse liked that song but was in quite a bit more than a half-inch of water.

get this shit done. I bet if I tapped into more brain power, I could be a superhero.

There was this cool arcade game called X-Men. I used to be Wolverine. Magneto was the bad guy. He could move metal and use it as a weapon. It mighta been realer than I thought because he'd suck all the metal outta my pocket while I tried to slice and dice his ass. And I'd leave the mall broke as fuck.

Why do most villains have the same story? They pull you close, try to get you to join them, threaten you if you don't, ask for more than you bargained for if you do, hunt you down if you don't. I guess they just wanna burn you.

You know what—I wanna burn shit.

Maybe I'm no superhero. I'm all the villains in one. The supervillain.

Or I could be Robin Hood. The anti-hero. I could rob for the people. Cartoon Robin Hood with the animals is the best. I could be a sly fox and make Prince John suck that thumb and call for his mommy. Or maybe I need to become a monster to do God's work. Nobody knows His ways right, but maybe I'm getting warmer. They think they know. Fuck them in their stupid asses.

The other day, I saw a hitchhiker waitin' for a ride to come along the mountain road. A young kid. Younger than me. Shit. I wonder how old I am? I also wondered how old the kid on the road was and if he was a villain or hero or civilian. I figured everybody needs money. And who am I to judge? I reached in my pocket and put a hundo in his hand. He dropped his duffle bag and gave me a hug. He smelled like shit, but maybe I do too. I'ma have to jump in that spring.

Maybe I could walk to California and start making video games. That has to be where they do it. I could make a game about a hitchhiker. A reality game you get sucked into until you don't know where your real life ends and where the game begins. You'll have to figure out whether the person who picked you up wants to help or wants to kill you. Or wants to make you their slave... yeah.

If you killed someone who tried to help, you'd become a serial killing hitchhiker in real life. Then your goal would be to keep killing without getting arrested or killed yourself. To beat the game, you'd have to do the job you were put on the world to do until you die of natural causes.

If you let yourself get killed, it would be game over.

If you become someone's slave you have to play the game fourteen hours a day as a slave until you die.

You couldn't quit. That be a sick game.

Yesterday, I walked by a scruffy looking dude playing guitar by an open case with some money in it. He wore a fedora. What kind of rock star wears a fucking fedora? Maybe he needed some motivation. I wondered if his stage was smaller than the venues he used to play. Or maybe he was just getting started. Nah. He was too old, and his chops were too slick to be a noob.

I admired the guy. His eyes were closed, and he played with soul for whoever walked by. I didn't see anyone coming or going. Maybe he just played for himself.

I've always liked the song "Mr. Bojangles", so I pulled out another hundo and put it in his case. Fuck what anyone says—Jerry Jeff's original version is the best. The guy played on and didn't acknowledge me. Maybe my super power is invisibility now. I bet that's why the feds haven't found me. The hitchhiker saw me though. I gotta figure out how to use this shit at will.

I move around all the time and set up different camps. I'll stay for a few days, then move on to the next one. My favorite place is under a boulder the size of my goddamn house. The mountain goes straight up, and the rock hangs overhead. I've been here for a few weeks now. I can't leave. Sometimes, I hope it falls on me—not so I die... I can't die right now. To test my powers, see if I can hold that shit up like fuckin' Atlas man or some shit. Maybe throw it down the mountain and watch it roll. I buried the last coffee can here.

I know my way around pretty well now. Sometimes, I go back to the old place and look around. Nobody's ever there, but the grass is always cut.

I like being lost, but if I ever need to get somewhere, my phone's got this compass on it.

Look, I know what you're thinking, but don't worry. I thought about that too. I'm always a step ahead. I took the SIM card out so they wouldn't track me. But I don't think I need this compass anymore. And maybe they'll figure out a way to hack it and find me. I wouldn't be able to do God's work from prison. So I nailed it to a tree by my camp for target practice.

The first few rounds I fired missed and whizzed through the brush behind it. I wondered where the bullets landed. Then I fired a shot at the sky and wondered where bullets shot in the air on July 4ths in Upton Park ended up. Then I saw a cloud that looked like a flaccid cock so I pulled the trigger again. I imagine gravity might pull the bullet back to earth and split someone's head open in some shitty place. Like Idaho.

I've never been there, but I bet it sucks.

Maybe my bullet leaves the earth and picks up steam as it travels through space and eventually approaches some other planet and splits some alien's head open. The alien detectives won't close the case because they can't conceive of a bullet traveling millions of years across the galaxy for a kill shot. Maybe it kills an alien serial pedophile. Could that be my destiny? To exact justice on another planet millions of years after I'm dead because I took one random shot through a fluffy white dick and balls.

Balls.

You know two other arcade games that were awesome. The Simpson's and NBA Jam. I wonder if there's a button we could push that would trigger real-life big head mode. Or if I could trigger big hog mode and everyone had to walk around with couch pillow size bulges in their pants. They'd have to rethink how to size pants. 32W 58CB 32L. Cock bulge gets an extra letter because it's my fucking idea, and I want it that way.

Imagine a salesperson on a ladder reaching for the size you want to try on.

"What did you say your cock bulge size was, sir?"

Ω

Jesse fell asleep in his camping chair with his journal in his lap and awoke when the sun's warmth hit him in the face.

He opened his eyes and looked around. His mouth was dry because most of his saliva had dribbled down his beard and onto his shirt. He smacked his lips. A string of drool dangled like it would off a St. Bernard. His phone was still nailed to the tree, and he remembered he still needed to destroy it. He cracked open a PBR and lit a Red.[Ω] Then he picked up his handgun, walked to the tree, aimed, and fired. His hands were steadier than they'd been the night before. He held a deep breath. The phone exploded on the first shot sending plastic shrapnel in every direction.

"Jesus Hank Williams Christ!" It was a familiar voice. *"I think a piece flew into my eye. Fuck!"*

"Who's there?" Jesse barked.

Deric Harris walked out from behind the tree with his chin tucked into his right collarbone, holding his hand over his left eye.

"Holy dogshit. Deric?"

"In the flesh, bitch."

"What the fuck are you doing out here? I thought you were in Afghanistan."

"I was. Now I'm not. The better question is, what the fuck are you doing out here?"

"I pretty much live out here now."

"Shit, man."

"It ain't so bad. Wanna fish? I got a sick spot."

Jesse grabbed his empty plastic two-liter Cheerwine bottle that had fishing line and a hook tied to it, and they walked. Deric looked like he hadn't had a shave or haircut in years just like Jesse.

"Wow, bruh. You look like shit," Deric said.

"Who are you to talk?"

[Ω] Breakfast of champions

298

"Well, I been in BFE for the last three years. I got a reason."

Jesse said nothing.

They got to the spring—Jesse's new favorite place. The trees opened a circle to the sky allowing the sun's rays to make transparent sparkles on the water. It was so clear they could see the fish wriggling on the bottom. On the mountain side, A small waterfall splashed on the rocks below. Another perfect boulder sat across from the waterfall like it was itching for someone to jump off it. There were a lot of boulders out there, but none as magnificently placed as this one. It was as if God himself fancied nature swimming and made the perfect place for it.

One time, Jesse wondered if God swam in trunks or a Speedo. Then he wondered how big His shlong was. Then he wondered if rain was actually Jehovah's bukkake on the face of the earth. Then he thought about how he used to look up and open his mouth and try to drink rain when he was young. Gross.

Jesse showed Deric his fishing strategy.

"Make sure the bottle is baited and hooked right and tight. Then throw it in and sit and watch. If it bounces, they're snacking. But when it starts skiing, dive in and get you one."

"Does this really work?"

"Sometimes."

They perched on the rock and waited. The company was a nice change of pace for Jesse. He hadn't spoken a real word to anyone for a while, and Deric was the perfect company because he didn't insist on talking or attempting to heal him.

"This a sick spot Bakes."

"It's nice."

"Ya know, we had our share of shit storms out there. You know what Marines do in a shit storm?"

"What's that?"

"Don't talk about it."

Jesse chuckled. "Word."

"Yeah. But we fuck a lotta shit up. And lemme tell you somethin' Bakes. It feels pretty fuckin' good."

They watched closely as one bottles bounced, then it skied.

"I got this one," Deric said as he stood and took his clothes off in what seemed like one fluid motion. Imagine what it would look like inside Superman's phone booth, except Deric wasn't wearing underwear outside his pants. No Thundercat underoos either. He got buck naked again.

A few hours later, they were both buck naked on that rock, and Jesse's dirty clothes were plastered across the rocks under the waterfall. The bottle scheme scored some fish that day, and they took their catch back to camp. Jesse tied his clothes to his backpack and put on his boots. Deric was bare-assed and barefoot.

At the camp, Jesse put his damp clothes back on. Deric did not. Jesse cleaned the fish with his Ka-Bar USN Mark 2 utility knife he'd bought from an Army Surplus store down the road from his house three years before.

"That's the same knife we use in the Corps," Deric said.

Jesse tossed the headless brim into the pan over the fire.

"Lemme get one of those," Deric said.

"Hold on man. It takes a few minutes to cook."

"Just gimme one of the cold ones."

"What? Okay?" Jesse said as he tossed one over.

"That's good shit."

"Better if you cook it."

"Na man, sushi's good for me."

"To each his own I guess," Jesse said as he threw a fish in the pan.

"I'll tell you one thing I'm thankful for. My place in the gotdam food chain," Deric said.

"I feel that."

"Animals ain't got no soul, ya know."

"Meh, ya think?"

"Yep... and I think there's some people that ain't got no soul either."

Jesse wondered who he might be referring to. Then he thought of a dude he was sure had no soul—Dracula. Then he thought of another guy.

"Like Coach Henson."

"Ah yeah. Fuck that guy... Why didn't you write about him in your little diary?"

"It's a journal."

"Whatever helps ya feel better 'bout your little pecker, buddy."

Jesse sucked in his gut, pulled his waistband out, and looked at his penis. Then he sat in the chair, leaving the fish charring in the pan. He pulled his journal and pen out of his backpack. Time stopped like it did back in the day when he carried on conversations with himself. It was like the world around him went black and he was sitting, cramped, in his middle school desk as it floated in total darkness. But he was illuminated, as was the desk, like there was a spotlight in space. He remembered a night he'd long forgotten. It was a terrible night.

Ω

The Life and Times of Jesse "Take-All-Comers" Baker
By Jesse Baker
When the fuckever

I might have been ten. We had an all-night youth group lock-in, and it was really, really late. The wooden bleachers in the church gym were pushed back against the wall, ten feet straight up and steep behind where I sat on the only available row. I think I musta got sick, maybe that's why I wasn't playing in the pickup basketball game. Someone had carved a love story into the long wooden plank beside me. Initials in a heart. I felt worse.

Deric walked out of the locker room with his head down staring at each step. He plopped down right on the romantic art. We sat there in silence. Then Coach Henson walked out of the locker room. He was tucking in his shirt, and his fly was open.

Ω

"Fucking Henson," Jesse said.

"They're everywhere, ya know. In the Middle East, you see some really fucked up shit. Them Taliban goat fuckers ran in groups of four or five. And they always had some little boy runnin' around with 'em. Swear, no more than 8 or 9-years-old. I always wondered about them little kids, so I did some recon. I asked some villagers why they always had a

little boy with 'em. They told me they was "chai" boys. They got tea for them Tally fuck holes. But that ain't all, man. They fucked those poor kids all the time. They carried 'em around like fuckin' sex toys, Bakes."

"Fuck me."

"Yeah. Well we got one of those bastards. We tortured him for days, maybe a week. I couldn't look at him. Every time I did, I saw that motherfucker Henson. Fucking animal. We fucked him up so bad, man. He gave us all the intel he was givin' up, so I put a hole in his face."

"Damn."

"My team was good with it. They knew what he was. We let him off easy. But you know, I used to hunt with my dad before he died. And when we killed an animal, we skinned it and ate it. This seemed like the same shit, so I cut off that motherfucker's forearm and skinned it and had myself a nice drumstick. Most of my crew grabbed some too. We ain't had shit but beans and spam for months. Shit actually tasted good."

"Jesus Christ man."

"What, you think eatin' a deer is fucked up? Same shit—animals, bruh. Animals."

"I guess."

"People are the worst kind of animals, Bakes."

Deric ranted for what seemed like hours and Jesse listened. A few times Jesse's mind wandered while he watched Deric's mouth move.

"Fuckers get away with so much. I think our species would be way better off if the consequences made people shit their pants."

"I don't know, bro."

"Yeah, you do. I mean look. We got courts and juries. But there ain't no real justice. Shit man, look at OJ. Look at

Henson—that bitch just had to get registered and go to a minimum-security hotel for a couple months."

"He should die," Jesse said.

"Ahh. Now we're getting somewhere. Motherfucker got you too, didn't he?"

Deric didn't insist on an answer. Jesse's pen trembled in his hand. The world around him went black again. The spotlight came on, and he wrote...

Ω

The Life and Times of Jesse "Take-All-Comers" Baker
By Jesse Baker
How the fuck should I know.

I'm sad, I think. Actually, this feels different. Numb. The hallway of the locker room is dark. Really dark. Lines of light shine through the square grate on the bottom of the door. I hold the handle for a minute. It's hard to take another step, but I open it.

It's loud and bright and all the kids are playing ball. I don't wanna play. I just wanna go home and play Nintendo. The game doesn't stop when I walk onto the court. They play around me. I'm in the way. I walk to Deric, and he looks at me. A pass hits him in the side of the head. He slumps over holding his ear. The game stops, and I lean down to him.

"Coach Henson needs you in the locker room."

"Why?" he asks with the left side of his face red. I shrug my shoulders.

I walk away and sit on the bleacher. He asks for a sub and jogs to the locker room. He swings the door open and disappears. I watch my classmates play. It's all my fault.

chapter: 41

IT WAS 3:00 a.m. The world slept. Jesse Baker didn't. He threw his gear in the trunk, slammed it, and got in the driver's seat. His palms sweat alcohol. He wore black, and Deric, once again, had a good plan.

It was all under control. He'd been busy. Hours before, Jesse dug up one of his Folger's coffee cans and stuffed envelopes with enough cash to get both underpaid campus security guards to walk away from their cars and take a few hours off. He also broke into Upton Park Baptist Church's 2,000 seat auditorium and prepped the place for impending hell, disabling the smoke detectors, fire alarms, security systems, and filling 20 cans of gasoline that he put in a row across the front of the stage—just like the man-eating offering plates.

After a twenty-minute drive, Jesse pulled up to a small old house that sat back about a hundred yards off a country road. He turned off the lights and slowly pulled into the gravel driveway. The yard was toothpicked with signs. Outrageous signs...

WARNING: DOG BITES, OWNER SHOOTS.

GO TO CHURCH OR THE DEVIL WILL GET YOU!

THIS HOME IS A MUSLIM FREE ZONE

BUSH/CHENEY

As they approached the house, Jesse understood why so many signs were planted in the yard—to divert attention from the one closest to the house.

REGISTERED SEX OFFENDER LIVES HERE

He pulled close to the house. Deric cocked his pistol and said, *"Wait here. This'll only take a second."*

Alcohol seeped from all of Jesse's pores now.

Within two minutes, Deric emerged from the house, dragging Bill Henson, who wore nothing but tighty whiteys. Henson's hands were cuffed behind his back with duct tape. Strips of the shining silver covered his mouth and eyes, and he was bleeding from the right corner of his receding hairline.

Deric threw him in the trunk and slammed the driver's side door.

"Let's go."

Jesse parked the car in the old alley by the church. The same spot where Jamal parked when they sudded that bitch up.

"I got him," Jesse said.

"Roger that."

Jesse grabbed his pack out of the backseat, strapped it on his back, and opened the trunk. Deric stood by him and lit a Marb Red. Henson whined be-hind the tape as Jesse pulled him out. Deric took a smiling drag, looked at the moon, blew a few smoke rings at it and said, *"What a fucking bitch. Full moon, though. Cool."*

While holding Henson by the arm, Jesse grabbed his axe—a big one like firemen use. "Shut up, or I'll kill you right here." He led Henson down the alley toward the auditorium. Deric followed about five feet behind.

When they got to the doors, Deric said, *"Now what?"*

"Behold I stand at the door and knock," Jesse said.

Deric gave him side eye.

"Just fuckin' with ya. I still got the key from when I worked maintenance with Chuck." He pulled the crowded key ring out of his pocket and jiggled it. "I got all them keys, bro." He unlocked it and went in like an angel bringing a sinner to the Great White Throne Judgement.

In the auditorium, Deric doused the pews with the gasoline cans while Jesse duct taped Coach Henson to Dr. Germaine's throne on the stage. After he finished binding him, he grabbed a can and poured with Deric. Row after row.

Henson blindly tried to hop loose. The legs of the chair banged and scratched on the hardwood stage. Jesse speed-walked back toward him—head tilted down, firing a lunatic death glare through his angry brow that was somewhat wasted on Henson's duct taped eyes. But maybe Henson felt the glare. Because he whimpered and shook like he was ass naked in the Arctic. "Stop moving." Jesse said as his fist broke Henson's nose.

He went back to pouring, and when they finished, he started working on the stage. He chopped away at the pulpit, cutting it down to small pieces and throwing each one into the fire pit that he'd carved out of the center of the wooden stage hours earlier. The hole was already filled with leaves, sticks, and few other flammable items from Jesse's old house. Jesse then grabbed a stack of hymnals from the choir loft, ripped them apart page after page, and dropped them in the pit. All while singing, "There is pow'r, pow'r, wonder working pow'r... in the blood..."

"In the blood," Deric bellowed from the pews.

"Of the lamb."

"Of the lamb."

They sang the great hymns of the faith for twenty minutes while they worked, surprisingly tuneful renderings of...

"Leaning on the Everlasting Arms"
"In the Sweet By and By"
"Are You Washed in the Blood of the Lamb"
"It is Well with My Soul"
"Standing on the Promises"
"When the Roll is Called Up Yonder"
"How Great Thou Art"
And they finished with "I Surrender All."

They knew every word by heart. Henson wept the whole time like an old lady stricken by the Holy Ghost—or like a guy who knew he was about to die. After the last note, Jesse walked to the throne and hit him across the head with a hymnal. Henson yelped like a malnourished mutt in a dog-fighting ring. Jesse looked down at him and said, "How embarrassing. You're not gonna die well, are you?"

Henson made a series of grunts through the tape.

"What's that? You got something to say?" Jesse asked while pouring fuel into the pit. He shook out the last drop and said, "Tough shit."

Deric dumped the last can on the pews and walked up the platform steps. Jesse pulled out a Red and lit it.

"Smoke?"

"Of course."

Jesse flipped Deric a cigarette. It fell on the floor.

Deric pulled a flip phone from his back pocket and pushed some buttons.

"You bastard. Is that my old phone? Where'd you find that?"

"We needed a burner for this job. I took the initiative."

"That's not a burner man. They'll track it to me. Who are you texting anyway?"

"Don't worry about it."

"Dude, they track me through my devices."

"You're insane man. Why would I have your phone?"

Jesse took a slow drag and relaxed a little. He thought he remembered burning it in a box with his old electronics before he went to the woods. He wasn't 100% sure but let it go.

Henson grunted again.

Jesse turned around and yelled, "Shut the fuck up!"

"Let him talk. Everyone's entitled to a few last words," Deric said as he stepped toward Henson.

"He ain't entitled to shit,"

"Well... maybe I'm curious. Or maybe I just wanna see him beg." Deric's tall frame loomed over Henson from behind the throne.

Jesse kneeled before it and said, "You like this, don't you?"

The tape over Henson's mouth was slimy from snotty blood that ran from his nose. Jesse ripped it off in one fast pull. Then he took the tape off his eyes. Tears immediately ran down Henson's cheeks.

"Please! Please! I'll do anything!" Henson begged.

Deric chuckled and looked at Jesse. *"See. I told you this was a good idea."*

"Will you suck my fucking cock?" Jesse whispered in his ear.

"Anything! Please, and I won't tell anybody about any of this. Just let me go."

Jesse circled him slowly until he stood in front of him again.

"Why... Why are you doing this?" Henson sputtered.

"Oh, I think you know," Jesse said.

"Honestly. I-I-I don't."

Jesse put a hand on each of Henson's lower thighs, squatted in front of him, and leaned forward until their noses were only a few inches apart. Each eye stared unflinchingly into the eye across it for a few seconds of stone silence. Then Jesse spoke softly while his eyes broke their stillness with sharp microscopic twitches like a drunk driver trying to focus on the moving index finger of a cop.

"Let me rephrase... You can suck *my* fucking cock... *this time.*" Jesse never blinked. Henson looked away.

"Cmon man. Just pretend he's still in 5th grade," Deric said.

Henson wept and said, "I'm sorry... I'm so sorry."

"Sorry? That's it? You're sorry?" Jesse said.

Jesse pulled his Ka-Bar from its sheath around his hip and meticulously moved it inches from Henson's face.

"Please, Please, don't," Henson said.

"Shhh... Shhh..." Jesse said as he pressed his index finger over Henson's lips. "I want you to look at me now. Look into my eyes,"

Henson obeyed.

"Do you know who I am?"

Henson leaned his head back a few inches. Jesse moved closer.

"I said... do you know... who I am?"

Henson shook his head.

"I am the lamb. Innocent and abused by man."

"The Lord will forgive every iniquity," Henson said.

Jesse laughed. "You see that's the problem with redemption. You fuck with some kids, and you think you can just repent and get a free pass."

"The Lord has forgiven me. I know it," Henson said.

Jesse mocked him in a whiny voice, "Oh, lord, I'm a depraved, wicked sinner. I repent, I'll change... Wait... Weren't you just trying to suck my cock a second ago? Repentant my ass. The Lord won't do shit for you now."

Henson glanced at the death rate calculator in the back of the auditorium as it crept closer to his number.

"Go ahead. Ask him," Jesse said.

"Lord, please forgive this young man and help him find it in his heart to forgive me as you have," Henson cried out.

"Deric, you feel that?"

"I got nothing over here, Bakes."

Henson looked around, puzzled. Then he looked at Jesse's eyes, which, for a split-second, seemed to move independently of each other. Staccato.

Jesse pulled his silenced gun from its holster and shot him twice in the upper arm. Henson screamed as blood streamed out of the small holes in his skin. Jesse dragged the chair forward onto the large metal grate he'd put over their makeshift fire pit in the stage. Henson faced the gasoline-soaked pews. Then he grabbed a small end-table from the edge of the stage and put it next to where Henson sat. Then he cut Henson's wounded arm loose and stretched it across the table.

"Move that arm and I'll shoot you in the face?" Jesse said.

Henson nodded while he sobbed. He really didn't know who Jesse was. It could have been any of them. He felt them. Their faces teased him as he tried to narrow it down. There was genuine remorse in his cries as he gathered himself for one last attempt to save his own life.

"My whole life has been backwards. The things I've done... There's nothing I can do to make it okay. I may have done terrible things, but I *am* a person."

"That's debatable," Jesse said as he put down layers of tape over Henson's loose wrist.

"Please. I'm God's child. We aren't that different. The same thing happened to me when I was a kid. It messed me up. Messed up my head, but I've put away my evil. Jesus cleansed me. God has forgiven me. I'm not the same person. You must believe me," Henson said, tears streaming down his face.

"Well that's just fine. I haven't."

"Please. There's no going back from this. It'll haunt you forever."

"There's alotta of things that'll haunt me, Bill. This... will *not* be one of them."

Henson *knew* the moment Jesse said his first name. When Jesse was in high school, he only called him Bill on the rare occasion their paths crossed. Bill always let the not-so-subtle disrespect slide. He had to.

Henson figured it was over, but he still held onto a glimmer of hope. Enough hope to keep it to himself that he recognized his executioner.

"Before you die, I want you to see what you have waiting for you," Jesse said.

"You get to see this motherfucker burn!" Deric shouted from where he stood now—halfway down the center aisle. His voice echoed in the auditorium. It was the aisle where a repentant man once tripped and fell right before he reached the alter, but he played it off to perfection by rolling into a Tim Tebow prayer stance. Amazing Grace.

Jesse remembered that moment and chuckled while the irises of his eyes twitched again. He inhaled his Marb Red, closed his eyes, and slowly blew out the smoke through his nose. Then he tossed it into the puddle of gasoline below the front of the stage. Fire branched out to the pews like it was a glowing Nile Delta, setting them ablaze one by one. The colors of the rising flames blessed his soul, oh, did they bless him. His projector itself was now a fiery furnace of its own making.

He walked to the back of the platform, picked up the axe off one of the pastoral staff chairs, and circled Henson's chair again, dragging the axe behind him as he quoted scripture that rose from the forgotten wasteland of his brain, the place where dogmatic thoughts had gone to die. He preached. It was the kind of fire and brimstone preaching the boys at the IFB conference would have loved. They might've even beat off their Bibles.

He started quiet.

"For the wrath of God is revealed from heaven against all ungodliness and unrighteousness of men, who by their unrighteousness suppress the truth."

His voice crescendoed with every sentence, employing the oratory tactics he'd learned from listening to the best in the business.

"The Lord is a jealous and avenging God; the Lord is avenging and wrathful; the Lord takes vengeance on his adversaries and keeps wrath for his enemies. The Lord is slow to anger and great in power, and the Lord will by no means clear the guilty. His way is in whirlwind and storm, and the clouds are the dust of his feet."

"Hayman, brother. Preach," Deric yelled as he beat the shit out of the Gideon Bible he'd pulled from a pew.

The fire rose around them. It was Jesse's turn to be deified. He was the projector now. The flames were his congregation. And he was eager to pour out his wrath on the unrighteous.

"The mountains quake before him; the hills melt; the earth heaves before him, the world and all who dwell in it. WHO CAN STAND BEFORE HIS INDIGNATION? WHO CAN ENDURE THE HEAT OF HIS ANGER? HIS WRATH IS POURED OUT LIKE FIRE, AND THE ROCKS ARE BROKEN INTO PIECES BY HIM."

As he shouted his last word at the top of his breath, he wielded the axe and hacked off Henson's arm below the elbow. Blood poured from the severed limb and rolled off the table and through the grate above the fire pit. The fingers on the detached forearm twitched. Henson's screams fell weaker by the second.

Deric walked up the steps of the stage and picked up the severed arm, pulled out his Ka-Bar, and started skinning it. *"This is gonna be good."*

Jesse looked at his own hands. They were soaked in blood.

Deric pulled back the skin and cut it at the wrist. The fingers dangled below the grip of his fist. Then he pointed the knife at the arm. *"You know, He got this right. My last meal is exactly like I hoped it would be."* Then he looked at Henson who was slouching in his chair with his chin on his chest. Unconscious. *"Eh. I think he fucking shit himself?"*

Deric put the arm back on the table and grabbed the gas can that was sitting by the pastoral staff chairs and handed it to Jesse.

"Sweet spices to anoint him," Jesse said, showering Henson with gasoline. Henson groaned and squirmed in his chair. Jesse emptied the can and flung it into the congregation pews and stepped away.

Then Jesse's world glitched like a video game error.

It unglitched.

"Where's you're loving God now?" Deric yelled from the center aisle. Then he pressed a button on the flip phone. A distant boom shook the doors of the auditorium. *"Just texted God to go ahead and send us a little atmosphere. He's good, bro. He's good."*

Henson's eyes were wide as Jesse stood before him and raised the silenced gun. In a quiet voice barely audible over the flames and thunder, he said, "Give the devil my best, will ya, Bill?"

"Wait, I—"

Bang. Bang.

Two quick ones in Henson's forehead. Dripping holes less than an inch apart. Then he put the arm on the table, pulled another Red out of the pack and lit it with a match. Then he lit the matchbook and flipped it through the grate into the fire pit under Henson's chair.

It glitched again.

Unglitched.

Jesse was in the center aisle now. Deric stood on stage, cooking the arm over the rising inferno that charred Henson's body. He pulled it out of the fire and took a beastly bite. The fingers on the hand wiggled as he chewed off the bloody meat. Then he pulled it away from his face and closed his eyes.

"MMMMMM..." He opened his eyes and looked at Jesse. Blood covered his entire face below his nose

Sopping wet red. Shining and running off his beard. He flashed a red-stained smile and said, *"Want some?"* Glitch.

Unglitch.

Jesse chewed a mouthful on the platform and looked at the human drumstick in his hand. Then he looked at his arms. Smoke rose from second-degree burns. It didn't even hurt. He basked in the glory of his transcendence of pain.

"That's good eatin' there, hoss," Deric yelled from center aisle. Glitch.

Unglitch.

The fire raged to his right and left and behind him. His life soundtrack jammed. Despite the scorching heat, Jesse strutted to the beat toward the double doors directly under the death rate calculator. Each step in perfect rhythm. He looked like a star, but forgot that badasses don't turn around to look at the mayhem they left in their wake.

Deric took selfies with his last meal and a blackened, crispy Bill Henson.

Jesse heard the sirens. He was sure Deric had fucked up. That phone was all the Feds needed to get him. He panicked and ran. Glitch.

chapter: 42

CHUCK TOOK A DEEP BREATH and hissed through his teeth as he exhaled.

"My son burnt down that church ten years ago today. A decade..." He paused. "Y'all know what it's like to watch the person you care about more than anything in the world lose their mind?"

Ω

The square—now a pentagon—listened intently as they ever had while Chuck told the story of his only son, Jesse, through his eyes. It was clear, if insanity is hell, then watching a loved one lose their mind has to be the purgatory in closest proximity to the fire.

Regret hit Chuck hard when he went inside after the last Saturday Fight Day. The way he saw it, he was the worst dad a boy could have, but he didn't know how he would change when he got out. The only thing he knew was he wouldn't hurt Jesse or Vanessa again. They say domestic abusers don't change. If that's the rule, Chuck was the exception, but he was a man of few words, and apologies weren't happening in the Baker house.

When Chuck saw his boy in that hospital bed after the accident that claimed Jamal's life, he knew he'd messed up and wished he could start over, but there are no do-overs. He told no one he did the best he could as a father because he knew he didn't.

He thanked God over Jesse's hospital bed and prayed for a second chance with his son. And then Molly came along.

Molly was his second chance in more ways than one. She did something to him. He was her Paw-Paw, and she loved him, and he loved the cute way she said Paw-Paw. He taught her how to play kick the can like they used to when he was a kid on his dad's farm. Jesse always looked at him like he was crazy when they'd come in for family dinner all hot and sweaty, but he saw Jesse hiding a smile, and he liked that. She was the perfect reminder—the purity, the hope that no matter what he had done as a father, he could be anything he wanted to be to her. Every fleeting moment with her was another chance to be the father he never was. He hoped Jesse would see it and open the door for him.

If only he would have talked to him before it was too late. If only he was more eloquent and able to articulate his feelings. Maybe things could've been different.

When Molly died, it crushed everyone in the family. Psychologists talk about the stages and types of grief, and sure, there are many examples in modern clinical studies, and you could have witnessed these stages play out in the family. But in real life, stages of grief for the surviving bereaved don't seem as neat and tidy as they do in theory. And what about the person who was already showing signs of mental illness and goes through an event that catastrophic? And how can the people surrounding this mentally ill person help him in any way when their own hearts have been run through a wood chipper and spewed out in the form of saw dust with no shape or purpose?

Chuck went through his own cycle of grief, but skipped out on denial. He had dealt with enough death in his life to understand the reality of Murphy's Law when it decides to become prophetic.

He cursed God while he worked on cars and painted walls and fixed air conditioners and tested sprinkler systems on the Triple Threat campus. He spent two days destroying the engine of a campus security car, then told the chief of the maintenance department that it was beyond repair. When he left the office, he went back to the car and spent three hours fucking it up more. For no other reason than he felt like it.

Chuck tried to connect with his son on Jesse's patio a few times. Jesse just stared into the woods out back. Chuck thought maybe he was punishing him or something, like it was all *his* fault. He figured maybe it *was* his fault because he couldn't quite shake the feeling that he *too* had played a role in his granddaughter's death and the visceral demise of his only son. No matter how small the role. It was a domino all the same.

They would sit on that patio for hours. Chuck tried to think of something profound to say that would help Jesse deal with the grief over losing Molly

Eventually, Chuck stopped trying to talk. They just stared at the trees, and Chuck's mind raced.

Chuck did bad things in the war that he would never tell a soul about. While sitting on that patio, it crossed his mind that he deserved any badness that came his way during the rest of his life, but why Molly, Jennie, and Jesse. Yeah, yeah, the sins of the father and all that. But if that was the case, the collateral damage seemed extreme. He dealt with it by persecuting himself. Most people have a hard time not making everything about themselves—Chuck was no different.

At Molly's funeral, Chuck knew something was wrong with his son—something more than the obvious. Jesse didn't cry, he sat up straight and spaced out. He didn't touch or so much as look at Jennie, and she was, understandably, an emotional mess. They all were. Except Jesse—he didn't shed one tear.

Jesse was a blank chalkboard that had been lazily erased. Like the one in his high school choir classroom that he once quickly swiped with the eraser when the teacher walked in. Swear words peeked through a wall of green and chalk dust.

When they lowered the baby's casket into the ground, everyone gave their condolences to the family and hugged their necks. Chuck shook Jesse's hand after it was all over, and it was limp. It certainly wasn't the handshake he taught him when Jesse was a little boy. Jesse looked past him at the hole in the ground. Even though Chuck probably could have counted on two hands how many hugs he'd given out in his life, he wrapped his arms around his son and gave him the best one he had. Jesse never moved his arms from his side. It felt like embracing a corpse, a feeling Chuck knew a little something about.

Then, when Jennie died, Chuck thought the worst. He worried that his boy might have snapped and ran off. The cut over her eye was a little concerning to the authorities, but she could have gotten it any number of ways. Jesse's disappearance raised questions too. Everyone looked for him for weeks with no success. The toxicology report confirmed Jennie overdosed on sleeping pills, and there was the note. Everything pointed to suicide, so they eventually closed the case and stopped searching for Jesse.

That left Chuck and Vanessa on their own with their search. Joe helped a little at first, but he knew they wouldn't find him if he didn't want to be found. They all assumed he just took off because he couldn't deal with it. First Jamal. Then Molly. Then Jennie. Jesse was a 21st century Job, but the version of Job that might have been if he took his wife's advice to curse God and die. Chuck always thought there was no way Job could've kept all his marbles together with all that pain and death on him. A verse in his Old Schofield KJV was a thorn in his side as he helplessly witnessed his son's mental decline.

"... but God is faithful, who will not suffer you to be tempted above that which ye are able; but will with the temptation also make a way to escape, that ye may be able to bear it."

Chuck had started to think the Apostle Paul might have been full of shit. Paul wrote random letters to churches that became the stone tablets of Chuck's church. The preachers preached his words more than

Christ's. Maybe Paul was their hero because he was more relatable than Christ. He was more human. Maybe not more human. Maybe less god. He was them.

Jesse's spiral tortured Chuck to the point he couldn't go an hour without thinking about the possible causes for the wretched effects.

Maybe a man can only take so much before he breaks, and everyone could be one epic tragedy away from madness.

Maybe some are just predisposed to it.

Maybe a life without hope is madness.

Or maybe I caused this...

Jesse had no god, and he buried what was left of his hope with his girls. Shortly after Jesse and Jennie got married, Vanessa tried to talk to him about his budding agnostic beliefs, and some days, she would cry when she was alone because of the things he told her. Chuck could never talk to him about it because he had a difficult time with belief himself. But he did always hold on to hope, and he tried to keep his head down and walk straight because he hated the person he was before he found Jesus. Of course, he didn't care much for himself after, but at least he was sufferable for most part, and most importantly, he could feel. He could even feel pain again. It wasn't always that way for him.

When Jesse disappeared, Chuck looked for him everywhere. He asked half the city if they'd seen him.

He printed out missing person flyers with Jesse's senior portrait on them. It was the best one he had. Every gas station and grocery store had his flyer on their wall. A guy at a store down the road from Jesse's house told him he was hunting one day and saw a naked man walking around the woods and talking to himself. He told Chuck he just left because the naked guy scared the "bejeezus" out of him. Chuck knew it was Jesse. He walked the mountain woods where the hunter had seen him for weeks. He worried he'd find him dead somewhere, strewn on the rocks at the foot of a cliff or worse—hanging from a tree. That thought slowed his search efforts. He covered less ground and called it a night earlier every day.

He found a few camp sites and sat at them on Saturdays from sun up to sun down. After searching for months, he figured Joe was right, "you ain't gonna find someone that don't wanna be found."

Vanessa and Chuck still kept up with Jesse's old house. Jesse had paid Joe cash for it, so there was no payment. They just paid the water bill and the taxes and kept the heat on. Vanessa would go over and clean from time to time, and Chuck mowed the yard. They wanted it to look nice if he came home, but they had other reasons too. They couldn't quite let go.

An explosion woke Chuck in the middle of a stormy night in June 2006. Then Vanessa's phone rang. It was Jesse.

"Mom."

"Jesse, baby, where are you?"

"Mom, I... I..."

"What is it, honey?"

"I wanna come home."

"You can always come home, Jesse," she said, in ears.

"But I can't. They finally got me."

"Who has you?"

Then she heard faint yelling on the other line, "Get your hands behind your head..."

CLICK.

She started balling as Chuck grilled her about the call while he scrambled for his clothes and put on his boots. He went outside and followed the illuminated sky like a wise man chasing the star of David. He ran toward the burning church building. Upon arrival, he asked a neighborhood onlooker what happened.

"I think some loon lit it up."

Chuck looked around. No more than fifteen minutes before, he was asleep. As the flames raged, and smoke filled his nostrils, it crossed his mind that he was in a nightmare. Red, blue, and strobe lights bounced off everything. Chuck thought he saw that loon sitting in a squad car, and ran toward it, shouting Jesse's name. But before he reached it, an officer wrapped him up.

"Jesse," Chuck shouted.

Jesse looked at him through the glass. "Dad?" he said. Inaudible to ears outside the car. Another officer came to assist with Chuck's removal from the area.

"You can't be here," one of them said.

"That's my son. Let me go."

"Dad," Jesse yelled. This time, faintly audible. Suppressed by the glass. "Where's Deric? Deric's still in there."

Chuck spun and escaped their grasp and ran toward the car. One of officers shot volts into his body with a taser. Chuck stiffened, convulsed, and fell to the ground. Six feet from the car.

Jesse kept yelling, "Dad. Dad. We gotta get Deric outta there."

But Deric was still in the Middle East.

The police booked Jesse and questioned Chuck. Then they questioned Jesse, which was an exercise in futility. Then they questioned Chuck again. It was obvious to them that Chuck wasn't involved. He was just a father afraid for his son. They kept asking about Deric. "Who's this Deric he keeps raving about?"

Chuck told them the only Deric he knew was Jesse's high school friend, but to his knowledge, he was still serving his country overseas. They told him his son was in a heap of trouble. They also said he was crazy. Chuck left pissed, but had held his tongue. They didn't understand what his boy had been through.

When he left the police station, he walked UPBC ground zero. The church was a shell of pillars and a pile of ash surrounded by a perimeter of police tape. Firetrucks and squad cars were everywhere. It was pandemonium. He couldn't believe what his son had done, but part of him was happy he was still alive.

Chuck felt a heaviness in his chest when he learned later that his son had killed someone in that auditorium, and he suffered a mild heart attack when the details were revealed. It left him hospitalized for a week, but he made a full recovery.

Jesse's case was open and shut. His lawyer pled not guilty by reason of insanity to the murder charge and the felony arson. The lawyer was good—worth every penny Chuck emptied from his savings account

Chuck was never as poor as people assumed. He was just the most frugal man in Tennessee.

They put Jesse in an institution. Vanessa brought him spaghetti and snacks sometimes. Chuck would go see him too. It was a painful habit, but he thought it better than if his son were dead. He held out hope that Jesse would make a comeback and get on the right meds. Reality chipped away at hope with each visit.

They diagnosed Jesse with paranoid schizophrenia. They told Chuck and Vanessa he wasn't suicidal, but he just "regresses to childhood as a defense mechanism." Chuck couldn't make much sense of all the scientific jargon, but he got the basic ideas and thought the doctors sounded smart and figured they knew what they were doing.

Like most mental patients, Jesse had good days and bad days. On the good days, he wrote in his journals at night, filling at least one black and white composition book a month with drawings and musings in handwriting that mirrored his old 3rd grade assignments. On the bad days, he screamed, cried, tried to fight guards, cursed during therapy, and occasionally wrote or drew something terrifying. On his worst day, he claimed he was Satan. That day lasted almost a week. They strapped him to a bed, and a staffer fed him with a spoon.

But as the months went by, his bad days came less often. And after nearly three years, institutionalized life became more manageable. The therapy sessions were tough at times, but he didn't curse or threaten anymore. He'd cry and tell his doctor that he just wanted to go home and play Nintendo.

After four years of institutionalized life, the dark one rarely peeked out, and if he did, he only stayed a few minutes, and it usually happened in a corner when he was alone. Child-like Jesse seemed there to stay. He was the oldest 9-year-old in the world, and the only one with a 5-inch beard. He had a good routine and had become a staff favorite with his innocent demeanor. Eventually, the stuff let Chuck hook up Jesse's old Nintendo in the common area. He even got to hang Jesse's old posters in his room. A happy lunatic was better for everyone than a deranged lunatic.

When Chuck visited, he'd pilfer one of Jesse's recently filled-up journals from his room. On his next visit, he'd return it and check out another. Jesse never noticed. Chuck even got one of his friends on the police force to loan him literature from their evidence locker—the original leather-bound book that contained *The Life and Times of Jesse "Take-All-Comers" Baker*.

Chuck never went to another basketball game. Instead, on Friday nights, he sat on his old porch in Upton Park where he used to bark instructions at his amateur prize fighter, reading the journals and sipping scotch neat. He'd laugh and cry and, some nights, make eye contact with the faint spray-painted smiley face on Jesse's old window screen. When he stared into the white splotch eyes of the cruelly happy reminder of his failure, he'd wish more than anything that he'd done better.

Ω

After ten years..." Chuck's voice cracked. His breaths got heavier as if there was an anvil chained to his lungs. Each inhale shook with fatigue.

"I still mow the yard. My wife still kneels at the ol' dog's grave and puts new dandelions on it while she prays. It just don't get any easier."

Lucy sniffled and lifted her hand to wipe her nose with the long sleeve around her wrist. Nick's eyes were filled with tears. Jeff held his face in his hands with his elbows on his knees. Bobby sobbed. None of them were in any condition to speak. None of them wanted to. Confronted with this level of pain, they felt only empathy. It was the most human they'd ever felt in their entire lives. No waiting for their turn. No thoughts of their own problems.

"You know..." A tear streamed down Chuck's face. "... It's the craziest thing. God answered my prayer. I got my second chance. My son is so nuts that he's like a little guy again. I go play Nintendo with him at Moccasin Bend... We think we know what we want... I never wanted this." Chuck removed the governor from his emotions and let his pain run full throttle.

Nick had never seen someone cry like *that*. It was a different level. A line of sweat ran from Chuck's hairline and down the side of his face. It glistened pink in the light as it trickled into his beard. He wept in a way only read about in a Book—a conflict so painful it could be the most spiritual moment in recorded human history—a shared pain between a Father and Son—the agony of the garden called Gethsemane.

When Chuck gathered himself, he said, "I don't know what it all means, but I ain't angry no more. I hated God for long enough about all this, and anyways, I'm just a stupid old man. I still don't know what I want. How the hell am I supposed to know what God's doing out there. And what makes me think I deserve to?"

Chuck wiped his face with a handkerchief he pulled out of his coveralls when Bobby spoke up. "You're okay with that? You're okay with what He's done to them."

"Who am I to say it's His fault? How am I supposed to know that?" Chuck shot back.

"But you believe God's in control right?"

"What do you think?"

"I don't know."

"Exactly. We don't know diddley squat. That's the problem. We pretend we do. I'll tell ya'll somethin' feel now though—my pain ain't all bad. Some people go their entire lives without having anything that means enough to them to hurt this bad. If it weren't for the bad, the good wouldn't mean a thing, would it And if it weren't for the good, the bad wouldn't hurt You can't have one without the other. That's the gift ya see—it was the source of my anger for so long, but I think now it might be why we're different from monkeys. We're the ones special enough to get a glimpse of the happy and the hurt that love brings."

"But..." His breaths got short and choppy again. "I miss that baby... and I miss Jennie... and I miss my boy."

A few seconds passed, and Bobby spoke again. "How do you come out of pain like that?"

"You don't." Chuck's laughed like he was still trying to convince himself with a smile that meshed ope, sadness, guilt, and desperation. "Why you think still mow the grass?"

"There ain't nothing I can do about it, son. A tattoo ain't comin' off. But I ain't dead yet. I'm gonna go home and kiss my wife and hold her tight. And tomorrow night, I'm gonna go to that asylum again and play with my kid. And every day I'm still breathin', I'm gonna fight. It hurts, but I gotta do everything I can to not make it worse because I know I sure as hell could."

Silence. All eyes were locked on him.

"Y'all try not to get too stuck in all this... *what's it all mean* stuff. You'll get lost in it. And if y'all got anybody, give 'em a hug will ya. Cause them's good minutes you got with 'em. And they ain't gonna last forever, so I'd recommend you don't miss 'em."

αlpha

AFTER BEATING THE HELL out of Bobby at the meeting, Don wandered like a lost sheep for five days. He was scheduled to be a head liner for his company's annual conference, but he missed his flight. Banksy's Auto Parts was in a mad scramble. He had 23 missed calls and 79 unread texts, but these attempts to contact him were a futile endeavor because his phone rested at the bottom of the Tennessee river.

It took him eight years to visit the place where his daughter took her own life and his granddaughter gave up the ghost. When he pulled up to the house at the foot of the mountain, he saw Chuck riding a red lawn mower and Vanessa kneeling at the tree line. He hadn't spoken to Chuck since Jennie's funeral, in fact he hadn't spoken to any of his old Upton Park Baptist acquaintances until the night he walked into his first Agnostics Anonymous meeting.

He walked toward the riding lawn mower, and Chuck slowed to a stop. They sat on a fallen log near the woods for two hours. They are the only ones who will ever know what they said to each other, but as the sun was setting behind the trees, Don got in his car to eave, and Chuck raised his hand as he drove away, and they were one day closer to forgiving themselves.

At 10:07 that night, Don pulled into his old driveway. He stood on the porch, sober as the day he was named head deacon at Upton Park Baptist. He stared at the door, then lifted his shaky index finger an inch from the doorbell. His confidence wavered, and he dropped his hand back to his side and took a step to his car.

Then, without thinking, a split-second of divine courage coursed through him, and before he knew it, there was no going back. And he was glad for that, no matter what the outcome.

Susan answered the door in a Tennessee Vols sweatshirt that she'd owned since college. She gasped. Tears welled in her eyes. It took years for her heart to break, but after such a long time of loneliness and hurt, it only took her a few seconds to wrap her arms around Don, who looked at the ground in shame.

He had come home and would never leave her again. He saw Jennie in her face, smelled her in the sweatshirt, and felt her spirit in Susan's embrace. And for the first time in a long time, he wasn't afraid—he was thankful. They would have many things to work through, but it was this moment that mattered, and the next days would have to take care of themselves. It was the perfect pain with the perfect person. The only person who knew him.

Don broke down in her embrace.

Ω

Lucy Hartwell and Jeff Wright went on their first date the next Saturday. They shared a bottle of wine and laughed at each other's jokes. Instead of listening to their friends in the circle at the old warehouse, they went on about living their lives, and quickly realized they were fond of each other.

Ω

Bobby sat on the small, square concrete porch of the duplex where he'd been crashing. He flipped through a brochure for the New Life Recovery Center. He'd never been to rehab and was afraid it might not work for him, but he decided earlier that week he needed something—hope. He wanted to try to live each day better than the last. He put the brochure in the front pocket of his backpack. This would be the hardest thing he'd ever done, so he prayed for the first time since he was a child—not for salvation, or money, or health, or forgiveness, or any of the other things he was told to pray for in his Christian school days. He prayed for the strength to change. And for the courage to do whatever it took. He wasn't sure if anyone was listening, but that didn't matter because hope lived in his heart.

A black Audi pulled up to the curb. He took a deep drag on his Camel and flicked the butt into the dead brush by the porch. He opened the passenger door and plopped into the seat, placing his back pack between his feet.

"You ready for this?"

"Can't be worse than you beating my ass in my last attempt at healing."

"Yeah. Sorry about that," Don said as they pulled away.

Ω

Recovery
By Nick Jackson

On Saturday, September 27th, I sat in our circle waiting for someone to show up. By 7:32 p.m., every chair was still empty. I was alone. A pasty white dot on a dark page. I breathed deep and quieted my mind. Before I knew it, my heart was filled with something I least expected—an overwhelming sense of gratitude.

I'll never be the same after meeting these people and listening to their stories, but it's time for us to move on—to live our lives unshackled from our bitterness and pain, to take back our stories and search for our truth. For so long, we nurtured our misery and bathed in our anger—NO MORE.

Of all the things I've heard in my short life, I'd never heard anything like the story Chuck told in our meeting, and I doubt I ever will again. After the meeting, I asked Chuck if we could meet for lunch that week. He obliged. I told him I wanted to know more about Jesse's story.

He told me his son wasn't a monster, and he wasn't always crazy. He became. That weekend we shared a drink on his back porch in Upton Park, and he showed me the journals.

I realized that there could be more to Jesse Baker than just an adult with a serious mental illness. I can't tell you one specific reason for his psychotic break because there could be so many, but it also could have been an unavoidable outcome.

I still have so many questions and so few answers, but I've started reading the Bible again—actually, just the words of Christ, the words in red. I've stumbled across an idea that I'd never pondered—something never discussed in my old church. At twelve, Christ baffled the experts with His understanding of scripture. To the preachers of Christ's time, the pharisees, His knowledge was supernatural, unfathomable. Then—whoosh—He disappeared from recorded history. For eighteen years, nobody *knows* what He did or where He went.

There's never been a man so studied, so revered, so placed under the microscope as Jesus Christ. Which begs the question, how could we know nothing about the time in His life between twelve and thirty?

When He came back from wherever He went and whatever He was doing, He inspired people with very humanitarian, albeit unpopular, speeches. As He traveled, crowds grew larger, and people from all walks of life wanted to hear what He had to say. But the leaders of the "church" didn't care much for Him.

Judging by the tone of the texts I'm reading, Jesus didn't care for the methods of the "holy" men of His day either. He wasn't a big fan of virtue signaling prayers or public displays of piety. It angered Him when he witnessed the "church" acting as a place of greedy commerce. He even wrecked shop and whipped ass in the tabernacle one time.

I'm not sure He ever changed His mind about this. Sometimes, I like to imagine Jesus visiting a modern day Baptist church—the look on His face when he sees he coffee shop in the lobby. I often wonder what He would think about the multi-million-dollar auditoriums, the Cadillac-driving preacher men, the money and time spent on entertainment, and the worship of the greatest show on earth.

We get hints from the stories in the Bible and parables from Christ himself. But because men think they need a map—that true north on paper, an articulated life plan—our churches may have missed one of the most important hints in the Bible: There is no road map telling a man how to go from educated to enlightened. It's up to us to figure that out for ourselves. Christ went dark when He took His journey because it was His and His alone, and any record of it might have kept us from beginning our own.

I imagine my journey will never end.

This morning, I *am* thankful for the baseline of understanding that the old stories in the Bible have given me, but I need to grow. I wonder what my life would look like if Luke Scott had kept the facade alive and never revealed himself as a stunted pervert. Would I have stayed on the path of arrogant complacency? In losing my religion, I now feel I have a chance to find my faith.

But this path... honestly... It's so lonely. I fear everyone I've ever known wouldn't understand me anymore. Pain stabs me through the screen when scroll my Facebook timeline. So many posts project that old-time confidence and unshakeable faith.

I want to accept them for who they are. Most people choose to believe in the narrative that gives them the most hope. And I think that should be okay.

But what about me? The friends I grew up with the mentors who have invested in me, even my own family—would they accept me for who I am now Could they associate with me?

My dad made it clear he can't, and I know he care about me more than anyone.

The deconstruction of my faith has felt like death. I'm actually grieving. Grieving the loss of peo ple I love who will never see me the same way again Worse, I grieve the death of the person I've been my entire life. And buried with him, every story he once believed. Part of me is ashamed. Part of me is sad. Par of me is angry. But all of me feels alone.

But despite my solitude, I like myself now. And now that I don't have the comfort and shelter of an unquestioning belief structure, I am truly free to pur sue God. The God of nature. The God of the reject and the outsiders. The God of Love. I've walked away from my religion to follow Jesus.

I will replace the constructs that divide and labe us with the God who connects all things. And hope fully, I'll find community one day.

Sometimes, it saddens me to think of all the peo ple who have been robbed of their personal spiritual ity because they adopted the ideas of their father without ever thinking for themselves. Then it sadden me to think about my own arrogance in assuming know anything about them, and even more, that think I *know* anything.

I recognize my frailty and have often asked God to forgive my arrogance in claiming to know things have neither the capacity nor the experience to know He has never, not once, said anything back, and I don' oresee him talking to me anytime soon. I don't even get dreams. But some days, I have peace when I embrace the idea that there are certain things I just can't know. And I feel connected to something or someone I can't see. I hope that's God. It sure feels like it.

I doubt I'll ever write that novel. I'm tired of looking back. I want to move forward. I want to love the gift that is my life, and the Giver. And I'll try my damnedest to love others.

And I won't be going to church, unless we're talking about church with friends over a few beers on the back porch. Maybe one day my dad will visit. Wouldn't that be something?

I had a surprising text conversation with my mom last night. She asked me to come home. I told her I wasn't sure if Dad would be okay with that. She told me he'd been telling her that he missed me and felt bad about last time. She told me he was changing.

I miss them too. So much. It's not being around them or talking to them that I miss. I miss their acceptance and, most of all, Dad's approval. I know that seems silly, but he *is* my dad, and maybe me and Jesse are alike in a lot of ways. Maybe we're all alike, and the only difference between me and a raving madman is a tragic sequence of events.

So today, I'll drive home. I don't know what to expect when I get there, but it can't go any worse than my last visit.

Ω

It was Halloween night when Nick pulled into his parent's driveway as the sun was setting through the trees. The Jackson porch looked like the front of a Cracker

Barrel—four rocking chairs and a big checkers board. His dad waited for him in the chair closest to the door. A big bowl of candy sat at his feet.

"Come here, son," he said as he got out of his chair and hugged Nick tighter than he had in years.

"Hey, Dad."

"Have a seat right quick. Your Mom's cooking supper. How was your trip?"

"It wasn't bad. I'm starving, though. Figured Mom would have a spread tonight so I haven't eaten since breakfast," Nick said as he sat in the rocking chair next to his dad. "Since when do you do Halloween?"

"Ah, since I stopped getting all worked up about stuff that don't matter."

"When did that happen?"

"I don't know. A couple months ago."

"Is everything okay?" Nick asked, worried that something drastic would've had to happen for his father—John Jackson, the most stubborn, *stuck in his ways* man in Ohio—to re-evaluate his life.

"It is for now. We can catch up on all that later."

"Okay?"

"I've been thinking a lot about the last time you were here, and I wanted to tell you I'm sorry, son."

"It's fine, Dad."

"No. It isn't... Me and your mom left the church."

"Really? Wow. Why?"

"I haven't felt right about how we left things last time. I even talked with preacher about it. That didn't go so great. We got into a heated argument."

"You argued with preacher about me?"

"Yeah, he prayed with me and asked God to do whatever it took to bring you back to his will."

"You've said that to me, Dad."

"I know. But when I heard someone else say that bout you, it sounded different."

"What did you say?" Nick asked.

"I told him not to pray for pain to come to my oy. He said a few things. I said a few things—It doesn't natter."

"Where do you go to church now?"

"We're still looking for the right one," Nick's dad aid as two little kids around the age of ten walked nto the porch. One wore a bloody hockey mask and arried a plastic machete, and the other was a Jedi. ohn picked up the bucket of candy and put it between is knees. It was the good stuff—Sour Patch Kids, wizzlers, Skittles, and Fun Dip. He knew what kids ked from his years of working in the church bus ninistry.

"Grab two," John said as the children reached in. Vhen they got back to their mother on the sidewalk, he whispered something to them.

"Thank you!" the kids yelled out simultaneously vhile they walked toward the next house. John and Jick waved.

"This is fun," John said as he flipped Nick a Fun)ip. "I'm sorry I never let you do this."

"It's okay, Dad. I had a great childhood."

"Yeah, I still feel bad though. It's weird. I've been eading more lately. Some really thought-provoking tuff I should've read a long time ago. And I've also een going back to what Jesus said in the Bible. It oesn't seem like He cared too much for us church- ype folks."

"That's crazy. I've been doing the same thing," Nick answered with a smirk of satisfaction on his face.

"Yeah, and you know what else is interesting?" John said as he handed a Sour Patch and a Skittles to a Hobbit who immediately said thank you. "Thinking about what he'd be doing if he was here today. I doubt he'd be hanging around church."

"Yeah, doesn't seem like His MO, does it?" Nick answered.

"Not really. I bet He'd be with the normal old sinners, just like He was in the Bible."

"Yeah, his church would probably be some damaged people around a campfire in the woods," Nick said as his thoughts drifted to a lost, desperate, and dying Jesse Baker stumbling across Christ in the woods. Then Nick thought a story from the Gospel of Luke—a madman whose path crossed the Messiah. Hope dwells in the possibility that what is lost can be found. "I'd love to visit that church," Nick said.

"Me too, son."

"Doesn't make a very good case for our old church, does it?"

"Now I didn't say that. You can't begrudge someone their traditions. I know for a fact that the church has helped me keep my life straight at times. Some people need tradition and good folks around them to stay out of the ditch."

"But that doesn't mean I have to buy in," Nick said.

"That's what I wanted to tell you. I think that's where I went wrong, son. I think it's where we all went wrong. I believed in the way of our church my whole life, and I tried to force it on you. Follow your heart, ake your own road to God, and I'll stand by you, no matter what."

"Just so you know… I'm not an atheist, Dad."

"I know that, but even if you were, you'd still be my son, and I'd love you and pray for you to find the peace that God can bring."

"It's just—I guess—I don't want a distributor. I need the Manufacturer."

John Jackson pondered his son's words while a 4-year-old Count Dracula reached into the bucket for a Fun Dip then skipped back to his Mom, who was pushing a stroller. She said, "Jesse, did you say thank you?"

"Thank you, Mr. Jackson!" the little vampire said.

John waved. Nick's heart was heavy.

"Dad… How sick are you?"

"I'll be all right. I'm a fighter. That Manufacturer you're looking for… He deals good hope."

Ω

That same Halloween night, Chuck visited Jesse at the Moccasin Bend Mental Health Institution. The visits to the asylum were his favorite part of his weekly routine. They would eat dinner in the cafeteria and play Nintendo in the common area. Some nights, they played *Castlevania*. Some nights, they played *Contra*. Others, they played *Double Dribble* or *Mike Tyson's Punch-Out!* That night, they played *Tecmo Super Bowl* for hours just like they used to. In a way, Chuck was getting his chance to start over with his son. It wasn't the way he wanted, but desperate people take whatever they can get. And when it was time for Chuck to leave, he gave his long-haired, bearded son a kiss on the temple and walked to the door.

"Dad."

"Yeah?"

"Can I stay up and play one more game? It's not a school night."

"Sure, son. I love you."

Jesse smiled. "Thanks, Dad."

Acknowledgements

I want to express my sincerest gratitude to all the wonderful, talented writers who have helped make this book possible: Sherry DenBoer, C Rose, Leonardo Maniscalco, ST McClellan, and Marina Davidson. You're the best of the best. Thank you.

And to all the preachers who placed man-made, self-righteous belief constructs above the words of Jesus Christ, and made all of us feel like shit all the goddamn time, thanks for the inspiration. But fuck you.

And to God, wherever and whoever you are, I needed to get this off my chest for sake of my sanity. I hope you understand. And I love you. Talk to ya later.

About the Author

J.T. Langhorne is an author from Tennessee who loves his wife and kids, dogs over 30 pounds, and 90s nostalgia. He builds incredible sandcastles, relaxes with video games, and sucks at golf.

Institutionalized is his first novel. Hope you enjoyed it. A review on Amazon would be clutch. Thanks for reading.

Connect with J.T. Langhorne on social media

Twitter — @jtlanghorne1
Facebook — @jtlanghorneauthor
Instagram — @jtlanghorne

Made in the USA
Columbia, SC
30 July 2020

15016326R00212